Poisoned Kisses

STEPHANIE
DRAVEN

First published in Great Britain 2011
by Mills & Boon, an imprint of Harlequin (UK) Limited,
Large Print edition 2011
Eton House, 18-24 Paradise Road,
Richmond, Surrey TW9 1SR

© Stephanie Dray 2010

ISBN: 978 0 263 22374 3

Pr   d in Great Britain
by   owe, Chippenham, Wiltshire

STEPHANIE DRAVEN

is currently a denizen of Baltimore, that city of ravens and purple night skies. She lives there with her favourite nocturnal creatures—three scheming cats and a deliciously wicked husband. And when she is not busy with dark domestic rituals, she writes her books.

A longtime lover of ancient lore, Stephanie enjoys re-imagining myths for the modern age. She doesn't believe that true love is ever simple or without struggle, so her work tends to explore the sacred within the profane, the light under the loss and the virtue hidden in vice. She counts it amongst her greatest pleasures when, from her books, her readers learn something new about the world or about themselves.

To my husband, who is my light in every dark storm and the man who carries me over all life's thresholds.

Prologue

Ares climbed over the rubble of his burned-out armory, his mood black as the soot-covered remains. *So much waste,* he thought, kicking aside scorched artillery crates. All harmless shrapnel now. So many mortars reduced to ash…so many bullets warped from the heat, deprived of their savage destiny on the battle-field. Magnificent guns destroyed without ever finding their way into the hands of even one ferocious warrior. *It was a travesty.* And the broad-shouldered god decided that someone should have to pay.

"Who did this?" he roared, discovering one of his vultures hovering over a dead body. At his approach, she left off tearing at the corpse's gory innards and flapped her wings. With a rush of wind that spiraled the dust and autumn leaves around her, she rose into the form of a willowy redhead and licked the blood from her scarlet lips.

"The guards say it was a woman who blew up the armory," his vulture explained, shoving the gutted corpse onto its back. The dead man's belt was *unfastened,* his pants unzipped, as if he'd died while taking a piss. "This one caught her and decided to have a little fun…"

"It doesn't look as if he had a chance to enjoy himself." Ares noted the dead man's face, stiffened in shock, as if he couldn't fathom what had happened to him. But Ares knew what had happened.

Kyra had happened.

His daughter was lethal with a blade and knew how to defend herself. She was also a rebellious child with a knack for finding new and unique ways to annoy him. "What about the file on the hydra?"

His minion twitched. "It's gone. Kyra must have taken it."

Ares liked the look of fear in his vulture's expression and was hungry to take out his frustrations on her. There could be pleasure in it—for him, at least. He reached for that fiery hair, yanking his vulture's head to the side so that her throat was exposed. "And where is my daughter now?"

"I—I don't know," the vulture stammered. "They shot her, but she escaped."

Bullets wouldn't stop Kyra. As a nymph of the underworld, she crossed the thresholds of life and death at will. What's more, she was immortal. He'd seen to that. There wasn't a wound she could suffer that wouldn't heal. She could appear to mortals in her own guise, or fade into the mists like an apparition. The fact that she'd let his guards *see* her meant that she'd *wanted* him to know she was responsible for this.

The unmitigated gall of the thing! For Kyra to destroy *his* weapons was almost too much to bear. And to add to that insult, she'd taken the file on the newest hydra—a man whom Ares intended to add to his monstrous menagerie. Admittedly, the war god admired Kyra's audacity. After all these years, most of the forgotten ancient immortals slunk away like beaten dogs to live mundane modern lives, but *his* daughter was still certain she was fated to do something glorious. And he couldn't fault her for it, even if it drove her to test him like this.

Ares was an indulgent patriarch, after all. Unlike his own wine-soaked lecher of a father, Ares encouraged the fierce nature of his descendants. He'd even made war with them at his side. Oh, how mortals had trembled when Ares rode into battle with his twin sons, Phobos and Deimos, at the reins of his chariot! How the mortals had screamed in terror when he unleashed his monsters. Fire-breathing horses, hydras, chimeras and minotaurs... *Oh, how he missed those days.*

And he intended to relive them with Kyra at his side. If only she'd accept her true destiny. Instead, she was in open rebellion against him. Did she think he could be stopped by blowing up his munitions? If so, she was wrong. Lesser gods might fade away, but the forces of war remained eternal. No one sacrificed at Zeus's temples anymore. The science of spindly weather-men had reduced the once fearsome sky god into an old man who spent his days in a taverna complaining about the loss of Greek culture to the European Union. Exhaustion, science and some of the newer gods of peace and goodwill had crowded the old gods off the world's stage. Even crafty Hecate had been relegated to being a fortune-telling gypsy!

But Ares was different. It had been a long time since anyone had seen him as the Greek god of bloodlust, glowering from beneath his plumed helmet, but men still worshipped him, whether they knew it or not, because *war* was different, too.

The new gods didn't glorify it, and science only made it more deadly; it bankrupted the victors as well as the vanquished. War was a senselessness mankind couldn't explain. Warriors no longer called for Ares by name, but they still made bloody sacrifices. And whereas Zeus once ruled the gods of Olympus, Ares meant to rule now.

So how was he to deal with Kyra's rebellion? Perhaps it was a phase that would pass. After all, his daughter was born to viciousness. Kyra claimed to abhor war, but the wreck she'd made of this armory only proved that she was bred for destruction.

The sooner he forced her to accept it, the better.

Chapter 1

Kyra was dressed to kill. Literally.

Just beneath her short red skirt and only inches above her high-heeled boots, a small but deadly hunting knife was strapped to her thigh. A gun might have been more useful, but Kyra preferred the weapons of an older, less complicated time.

A knock came at the nightclub's bathroom door—probably another gaggle of drunken Italian socialites—but Kyra wouldn't be rushed. She stared at her reflection in the mirror to steel her courage. She might not be able to thwart Daddy and his bloodthirsty minions, but she could do this *one heroic thing* for humanity. This was her destiny.

But the mirror reflected a distorted image. It was cracked, as if the thumping club music burst through the wall from the other side. Still, she could see that

her plunging pearlescent halter top complemented neither her black tresses nor her ghostly pallor. No matter.
Kyra never let mortals see her true form, anyway.
Tonight, her prey would see her as she wished him
to see her: with blue eyes and cropped platinum hair;
after all, she'd studied Marco Kaisaris long enough to
know his type. And she was ready. Hydras like Marco
were dangerous, but surely not to someone like her.
She just had to kill him. Like Theseus and Perseus of
old, she had a monster to slay.

With that thought, Kyra gave the bathroom door a
shove and it swung open like a gate to the underworld.
She stepped into the nightclub's press of bodies and
people made way for her, as if they sensed her power.
As the dance beat drummed at her pulse points, she
brushed against the crowd, and it excited her because
she had a nymph's nature; she found the vitality of
humans to be infectious and distracting. This was, of
course, one of the many dangers of getting too close to
mortals.

The club was dark but for the strobe lights that
shined spots on the walls, purple as evening shade,
purple as wine. The grape kaleidoscope illuminated
the writhing bodies on the dance floor, flashes alter-
nating with pitch-black. But the darkness posed no obstacle for Kyra. Like all nymphs of the underworld,
she carried an internal torch. Her eyes could penetrate

the darkness. She could see through a crowd, through clothes, through flesh. Her eyes could even breach the barriers around men's souls.

And from the bar, her quarry's soul lit up like a flare.

She knew Marco Kaisaris even though the face he wore was not his own. He was dark, brooding and slightly unkempt. He wore an expensive dress shirt open at the collar, the glimmer of a gold chain at his throat. He didn't look like an arms dealer, but then he was almost as good at disguises as she was. He wasn't *just* a mortal man, after all. He was also a hydra.

Kyra slipped into the standing-room-only space next to him at the bar, pretending to dig for money in her purse. She felt his eyes on her—an intense, wary stare. Fortuitously, a group of revelers pushed her a little closer to him. She pretended it was his fault.

"Do you mind?" she asked in Italian, grateful that the club was quieter here.

Marco shrugged, taking a swallow from his glass, which was filled with amber liquid and ice. "I was just sitting here."

Oh. His voice. It was baritone and beguiling, with a hint of a New World accent. American or Canadian— she couldn't be sure. Either way, it was the kind of voice that'd make a normal woman swoon and it weakened even Kyra's immortal knees. *Gods above and below,* Kyra thought. What justice was there in the world that such a voice could belong to a monster?

Recovering herself, she brushed his leg, but his expression betrayed nothing. Everything about his posture was guarded. Sexy, but guarded. That's when Kyra noticed he held a picture of an older man and was tracing the edge of it with his thumb. Naples was known for its criminal element, so the photo was probably of some contact Marco was meeting tonight. A supplier of munitions or a thug looking to buy an arsenal. Someone in Marco's violent business. "Friend of yours?" she asked in English, motioning with her chin toward the picture.

"My father." A look of melancholy passed over his face as he slipped the photo into his shirt pocket, but that's all he said. He didn't want to talk. And that was a problem because she'd planned to lure him somewhere private with the promise of a steamy encounter; she couldn't kill him in the middle of the club with everyone watching. To make matters worse, her cell phone was vibrating. It was probably *her* father calling to rage at her for destroying his arsenal. Daddy thought it was Kyra's destiny to join him, but she had no intention of being a part of her family's legacy of war. If anything, she wanted to make up for it.

Renewing her resolve, Kyra turned the phone off

and flashed Marco Kaisaris her most charming smile. "Mind if I sit here?"

Marco motioned toward the distinct lack of empty bar stools. "Sit where?"

Okay, she'd have to be a little more aggressive. "How about if I sit right here?" Before he could do a thing to stop it, Kyra slid into his lap. It was a crucial moment. There was a good chance he'd thrust her away, alarmed at her forwardness. But as the backs of her bare thighs pressed against the weave of his linen slacks, his breath caught, and it wasn't just with surprise. He liked it.

This shouldn't be too difficult, she thought. Her nymph's charm made it easy to seduce mortals—even special ones like him—and she felt him respond, his breath warming her neck. Encouraged, she shifted wantonly with her hips, precisely timed with the music, careful not to let him feel the sheathed knife on her leg. He liked that, too.

She could tell because he wrapped one arm around her waist and inhaled the cheap perfume she wore. It smelled like overripe passion fruit and candy and he reacted as if she were just a confection—one little taste wouldn't hurt. His teeth grazed her neck beneath her choker where a glowing peridot stone hung like a tiny lantern in the dead of night. She tilted her head for him and felt him go hot all over.

"You're shameless," he finally whispered, the scent of expensive alcohol on his breath.

But I'm not shameless, she thought. There were many shameful things in this modern world, but her sexuality wasn't one of them. How was it her fault that men were so easy to arouse? "*I'm* shameless? What about *you?* You look guilty of something."

He let the cool glass in his hand slide wetly over her shoulder. "And what do you think I'm guilty of, *Angel?* Give it a shot."

Angel? Oh, she was going to enjoy killing him. "Are you telling me to guess?"

"No," he said, his mouth finding the soft spot behind her ear. Then his voice lowered. "Unless you *want* me to tell you what to do."

Her stomach fell away with arousal. *Yes.* Absurdly, she did want that. Just for a few minutes. It wasn't sex with mortals that was dangerous for nymphs, after all. Just all the emotions that came after. Still, best not to let him get the upper hand. "If you tried to tell me what to do, we'd only end up engaged in a fierce battle of wills."

She felt him smirk against her neck. "Mine is hard as iron."

His *will.* He meant his *will* was hard as iron. Trying to steady herself, Kyra fanned her fingers over the bar. They came to rest on an unopened pack of cigarettes.

Marlboro Reds. Old school. "Yours?" she asked, and when he nodded, her lips curled in mock disapproval. "Bad addiction to have."

"I'm not addicted," he countered, one hand stroking her arm. She loved the callused feel of his fingertips on her smooth skin. "I only smoke when I'm trying to come to terms with something." Kyra almost asked him what he was struggling with. But she didn't dare. She shouldn't care. *Couldn't* care. It'd only make it harder for her to kill him. "I can quit anytime," he said.

"How about now?"

He paused, then crushed the whole pack in his fist, tossing it behind the bar like so much trash. He looked smug at her openmouthed stare of astonishment. "Like I said. Iron will."

He might think so, but he couldn't resist *her*. She was sure of it.

Marco called to the bartender. "A drink for the lady."

"And what if I'm not a lady?" Kyra asked, with a provocative smile.

"That's okay," Marco murmured, grasping the nape of her neck. "I don't plan to be a gentleman tonight."

She let him bring her back to his penthouse; even from the marbled foyer she glimpsed just how well the monster was living off his ill-gotten fortune. If he'd chosen any of the artwork here, he had exquisite taste. But this probably wasn't his penthouse, just like the face he wore wasn't his own. He was a hydra of a thousand faces—an impostor—which made it all the more remarkable that he didn't seem suspicious of her; he apparently brought women home with him all the time.

No, Kyra thought. Killing him wasn't going to be difficult at all.

The only problem was that he was an astonishingly good kisser. His mouth was on hers, dizzyingly warm. It surprised her how much she actually liked the way his stubble scratched her cheeks and the animal way he bit her lower lip every time she pulled away for breath. He wasn't shy about touching her, and he wasn't taking his time.

He pushed her back against the door, a rapid strike, all strength and speed. Caged in by his strong arms, she saw that his eyes were stormy with challenge. She felt her insides quicken in response. Oh, he *so* didn't know who he was dealing with.

Kyra gripped a thick handful of his dark hair and when his hands snaked up under her top, thumbs brushing over her nipples, she thought he was rather daring for a creature that could be killed; he'd been wary in the bar, but now that he'd committed himself to having her, there was no hesitation in him at all.

The heat of him delighted her. The roughness of his touch. The bestial sounds he made, as if he meant to devour her. Kyra's heartbeat crashed in her ears, as if the thumping roar of the club music had followed them here. She told herself it was just the allure of his mortal energy, the dangerous deception of a man's desire. But had it felt this good the last time she'd taken a mortal lover?

Maybe Marco was different. The clues in the file she'd stolen led her to believe that in addition to being an arms trafficker, Marco Kaisaris was a war-forged hydra, a mortal man, a monster that could be killed. Now she wondered if he was actually some shape-shifting trickster god, which would excuse her attraction to him and relieve her of guilt for what she was about to do. Stabbing an immortal, after all, wouldn't cause any lasting harm.

His scent—somewhere between man and musk— drove her crazy. Meanwhile, his kisses had become frenzied as if pleasure was such a fleeting thing in his world he had to consume it before anyone took it away from him. As Marco nipped at her neck, his mouth moving over the luminous gemstone she wore, her own gasps cut through the stillness of the penthouse apartment. Whoever he was, *whatever* he was, he was rocking her world.

But Kyra prided herself on not being one of those silly nymphs who dallied with mortal men and fell helplessly under their spell. She'd taken plenty of lovers and cast them aside when she was done. After all, she was built for carnal passions, for stolen pleasures in the dark. So, it wasn't Marco's all-consuming sexual prowess that was giving her second thoughts about killing him. It was what she saw inside him, beyond the surface. A looming shape of almost unfathomable grief. Beyond the veils of darkness in which he wrapped himself, she glimpsed a forlorn desperation to know and be known, to understand and be understood.

This, she hadn't expected. Sincerity, pain, need. His vulnerability was subtle but potent sex magic. It made her curious; there was a longing in her to let her eyes open wide and illuminate everything inside him. Unfortunately, that would drive him mad, and that was one thing Kyra would never do to a mortal again. Besides, there'd been a reason she'd tracked him down for months, a reason she'd slipped into his lap tonight, and it wasn't to satisfy her curiosity or to enjoy herself with a sexy stranger.

Like her father, Marco Kaisaris made a profit selling weapons. He was a merchant of death. The underworld was filled with victims of the bullets Marco sold. No matter what her lust-soaked mind wanted to see inside him, he *was* an evil man and if she wanted to make up for all the pain and chaos her father had caused in the world, Kyra had no choice but to kill him.

The hydra *had* to be the reason Kyra still had her powers while so many of the old immortals had lost theirs. This was her destiny. Still, it was with true regret that she realized Marco's groping fingers would soon discover her hidden knife. With a long-suffering sigh, Kyra stopped him. Marco pulled back, a slow and frustrated tilt to his lips. "Am I going too fast?"

Gods above and below, his voice just wrecked her. The heat of it seared a path from her belly down to the quivering place between her legs. Oh, how she wanted him to touch her. But when he tried to put his hand under her skirt again, she didn't let him. "Wait. I've got something for you."

She turned slightly and, with one hand, secretly unsheathed the knife beneath her skirt. The motion between her legs must have looked particularly obscene, because Marco's eyes narrowed with desire. "Don't be a tease, *Angel*."

"Oh, I'm no angel and I never tease." With that, Kyra thrust the sharpened blade at his chest, aiming directly for the heart. But something went horribly wrong. She'd prepared herself for the blood, the resistance of blade against bone and the death grimace. What she hadn't counted on was Marco being nearly as fast as she was. Kyra knew that Marco had military training. Still, she could hardly believe how deftly he blocked the blow with his hand. The knife slashed open his palm from fingers to wrist and red blood sprayed the carpeted floor.

His expression twisted in surprise at her betrayal, and he used his uninjured hand to grab her wrist. He slammed it against the wall so hard she thought the bones in her hand might have shattered. "Drop the knife," Marco growled, all sincerity and need now replaced with the hard features of a furious and injured man.

There was nothing for Kyra to do but struggle. He couldn't kill her with that knife, but he *could* hurt her. Even for an immortal, pain was pain. Suffering was suffering. And Kyra was afraid of it even though she didn't have to fear for her life. So she brought her knee up hard into his stomach.

He grunted with the impact, but didn't let go of her wrist. Instead, he used his leverage to flip her to the ground. She thudded to the carpet, her body splaying awkwardly. And before she could scramble to her feet, he threw himself on her, forcing the air from her lungs. He had her wrist in his grasp, twisting it to the breaking point.

"Drop your weapon!" Marco shouted like the soldier

he'd once been. But Kyra bucked under him, clenching her free hand into a fist and punching him in the jaw.

Marco rocked back from the blow. "Bitch!"

Then he backhanded her in retaliation. Kyra tasted blood in her mouth—her own, she hoped. The sting of his slap had made the entire right side of her cheek red-hot. In thousands of years, few mortals had ever dared to strike her, and those who *had* tried paid for it with their lives. All the forces of the underworld bubbled up inside her. She was the daughter of Ares and rage was overtaking her, boiling out of control. She remembered the armory she'd blown up, where her father's guard had confused her with a human and tried to rape her; she'd shown him with fatal accuracy how mistaken he was. Now she'd show Marco Kaisaris!

As she pulled herself up like a specter from a grave, Marco recoiled. "What—what the hell are you?" he stammered, staring, his tone more loathing than fear. In their struggle, she'd become so enraged that she'd stopped projecting the shape she wanted him to see. He saw her *real* face now, the depthless blackness of her nymph's eyes, and he seemed as horrified as if he'd glimpsed three-headed Cerberus.

Taking advantage of his surprise, Kyra rolled to her feet with the grace of a cat and crouched on tiptoe behind a desk for cover, realizing that her high-heeled boots may not have been the ideal choice for an assassination. "The real question, Marco Kaisaris, is, what are *you?*"

At hearing his real name, Marco's expression turned murderous. Later, she'd have to admit that he frightened her. He was stronger and faster than she'd anticipated and now this entire mission had gone awry. She could try to fade—try to disappear before his very eyes—but her concentration was broken. Perhaps she ought to escape and try again another day. As these thoughts raced through Kyra's mind, Marco rushed toward her. She lifted the knife—this time in self-defense—and he flipped the elegant desk behind which she'd sought refuge as easily as if it were dollhouse furniture. Papers and knickknacks exploded through the air and the desktop slammed her, knocking her back where she smashed her head on the wall and slumped to the floor.

Kyra lay there for a moment, stunned. Had she blacked out? Scrambling out of the wreckage of the desk, she realized that the penthouse was quiet.

Damn it to Hades! The door was open and Marco Kaisaris was gone.

She wondered why he hadn't tried to kill her when he'd had the chance, but then she felt the sickening burn. She was smeared with Marco's blood and it stung like fire. It was ever-deepening agony. Rushing to the bathroom, she hurriedly scrubbed her arms clean. Too little, too late. The hydra's blood wasn't just burning her, it was also seeping into her skin and making her sick. Waves of nausea flowed over her; she sank to her knees and tried not to retch.

If she'd been a mortal, the poison of his blood might have been enough to kill her. As it was, her world started to spin. Marco Kaisaris was no trickster god. His blood wasn't divine ichor. His wounds hadn't closed up on their own. And even from the bathroom she could see that where his blood had pooled on the penthouse floor was now a sizzling mess, as if someone had poured acid on the carpet. His blood was poison. Deadly poison. There could be no doubt now that he was a hydra and needed to be stopped.

If only she could get up from the floor.

She'd cut him deep. Crouched in an alleyway, Marco tore his shirt off and wrapped it around the wound like a makeshift bandage. With his uninjured hand, he fumbled in his pocket for his cell phone to call an ambulance. The woman in his penthouse would need one. Yeah, she'd tried to kill him, but she had *no* idea who she was dealing with. By now, his blood would be soaking into her skin and eating her alive. He wasn't sure what the hospital could do for her, but he wasn't eager for another dead body on his conscience.

"Si prega di identificare se stessi," the dispatcher squawked into the phone.

Identify himself? Under other circumstances, the question might have made Marco laugh. Who exactly was he? He wasn't the guy who rented the penthouse. He wasn't the guy he looked like now. He wasn't a soldier anymore and he wasn't even the do-gooder son of a Greek immigrant—not according to his father or his sister. "I'm nobody," Marco said, then hung up.

The blood coursing from the cut on his hand had soaked through his wrapped shirt and dripped down his battle-hardened stomach in a deadly scarlet rivulet. Every time a drop of it spattered on the ground, it hissed and sizzled where it fell. Marco hated to leave his blood anywhere, but he couldn't do anything about it now. His breathing was still erratic—partly from the pain of his wound and partly from the shock of what he'd just seen. What the hell *had* he just seen? An angel, a demon or some creature with powers like his own?

One thing was clear: his enemies had obviously tracked him here and sent the woman to assassinate him. This identity—this borrowed face he wore—was thoroughly compromised now. He'd have to change his appearance and there was no time to wait for a more private moment. Pulling himself deeper into the shadows, Marco braced against the brick wall and steeled himself for the transformation. He closed his eyes and remembered the face of a blond haired, blue-eyed Russian smuggler who'd once tried to steal a shipment of shoulder-mounted rockets from him. Marco had long since dispatched the Russian to hell, but he'd been wounded in the struggle—which meant that now Marco had a useful but grisly souvenir; he could assume the face and identity of his old enemy. It was his curse; he could take on the form of anyone who wounded him. A power he could neither explain nor fully comprehend. Perhaps it was a madness—inherited from his mother. Whatever it was, he couldn't stop himself from quivering with disgust at the slow creep of flesh as his face began to transform. Marco didn't have to look in the mirror to know that his eyes were now blue, and his hair like yellow straw. Except for the wound on his hand, his enemies wouldn't know him.

No one would.

Chapter 2

Kyra found herself in an ambulance, squinting into the peculiar light. Her arm was caught in the grip of a blood-pressure cuff and she realized that her heart must have stopped because a stunned paramedic loomed over her with paddles.

For one moment, she understood mortal fright. It used to be that the dying would take comfort to see her by their bedside with her torch in hand. Now, if they opened their eyes to see a dark nymph like Kyra standing beside the men with the paddles, they feared her as an evil harbinger. Sometimes they screamed in terror.

These days, dying mortals only wanted to see angels. Some of her fellow nymphs of the underworld played along, pretending to flap ridiculous feathered wings, singing, "Follow the light!" But Kyra refused. She was a *lampade,* a guide, a warrior for men's souls. If mortals didn't want her to attend them at death, she still had a heroic destiny to fill. Which is why she'd gone after the hydra, and how she ended up on this gurney in the first place.

She was shocked at how wretched she felt; her skin was clammy, yet she felt as if she were being boiled alive. Under normal circumstances, she'd have already recovered, but the hydra's poisonous blood had weakened her somehow. With difficulty, she tried to sit up. It was then that the emergency medical technician reached for her peridot choker, perhaps with some foolish notion that removing it would help her to breath. His mistake. Kyra's choker was the only keepsake she had of her mother's. Anger that this stranger should try to take the precious stone gave her a surge of strength. Kyra stared into his eyes, trying to see if he was an enemy, or perhaps one of her father's minions. But when she couldn't illuminate his soul, her insides flailed in fear. Had the hydra poison extinguished her powers altogether?

It took her more than three attempts before she was able to pull the needles from her arm. All the while, the paramedic tried to restrain her. Again, his mistake. Self-preservation gave her the power to pin him against the vehicle wall. "Don't make me hurt you," she growled.

The paramedic shrank away, the whites of his eyes showing like a horse about to rear up. He seemed to have realized all at once that she was no ordinary mortal woman. There was a chain at his throat upon which dangled a little golden cross, and he held it up as if to ward against evil. Just what did he take her for? Angel or devil? The mortals could never decide! Muttering a curse at him under her breath, Kyra leaped out of the back of the ambulance before he could stop her.

The rising sun knifed through the lavender cloak over Lake Avernus, its light cutting a thin golden gash across the dark waters. Kyra didn't like mornings. It was *night* that protected her—it always had. Luckily, it was still dark enough that she didn't have to obscure her true form. Escaping from the ambulance had seemed like a good idea, but as Kyra staggered toward the little villa apartment that was her lair, she feared she'd collapse before she could make it home.

Marco Kaisaris's blood had done this to her.

Things that killed humans rarely affected immortals this way. Then again, the poison in Marco's blood was no ordinary kind of poison. It was the poison of a hydra. Achilles, the great warrior of the *Iliad,* died when he was shot in the heel with an arrow dipped in hydra poison. And he wasn't the only demigod to die this way. Hydra blood had also killed mighty Hercules. The thought sobered her. Hercules was the son of a god, but his mother was mortal. Just like Kyra's.

Surely she was nothing like those legendary heroes. They had died young, whereas Kyra had lived for thousands of years. They had walked among the living, whereas Kyra drew breath with shades in the underworld. She'd never thought of herself as vulnerable. She'd lived so long, and so recklessly, that death was nothing she'd ever contemplated for herself. Was it possible that Marco Kaisaris's blood could actually kill her?

She needed to get to Hecate. Perhaps her old mistress had just enough magic left to brew a curative potion. Even if she didn't, who else could guide Kyra over the threshold from this life into the next but the goddess of the crossroads? Yes, Kyra had to get to Hecate. Nothing else was as important. She kept going on pure adrenaline, feeling vulnerable, naked without her powers. It was disorienting to rely on normal human sight—luckily, she found the street where Hecate's shop was illuminated by a swinging lantern at the end of a rusty hook. The worn and faded sign over the door read *Notte Incantesimi: Tè e Chiromanzia*.

The Night Enchantments Tea and Palm Reading shop was the last refuge of the once-powerful goddess who had—for centuries now—been reduced to fortune-telling and serving herbal infusions. Hecate's black hounds bayed in greeting and the goddess appeared in the parlor doorway wearing an absurd embroidered gypsy robe, a sprig of yew berries in her luxurious silver hair. "My best little nymph has come to call on her old mistress," the once-mighty goddess crowed.

Then Kyra collapsed at her feet.

Chapter 3

There was no point in disguising himself here in the Democratic Republic of the Congo, a place Marco still thought of as Zaire. The militias knew him. Some even feared him. And though the corrupt government called Marco the Merchant of Death, many of the locals said he was their salvation. And that's why he kept coming back. Why he would keep coming back as long as they needed him.

Marco's driver—a dark West African named Benji— was waiting for him at the jungle airstrip. "That's quite a bruise on your jaw, Chief," the kid said, glancing at him from beneath the sweaty bandanna on his brow. "And your hand doesn't look good, either. Trouble at the border?"

Marco didn't answer; after all, he didn't want to tell anyone about the she-devil that attacked him in Naples.

Instead, he put his sunglasses on, retreating behind the shades as they rattled along the dirt road.

Their vehicle was a patchwork of rust, duct tape and white paint. It made a fat, slow-moving target. With all the money he made selling weapons he should be able to afford a better ride. He should be less vulnerable to his enemies…enemies like the siren who had tried to stab him.

Reminded of her, Marco flexed his hand around the disintegrating bandage. It was a deep cut that would scar, but meanwhile his blood was eating through the cloth. He couldn't risk going to a hospital, so he'd stitched it himself in the back of the cargo plane and now it hurt like hell. It was no consolation to him that his attacker was, no doubt, hurting worse—if she was even still alive.

Who was she? No, more importantly, *what* was she? In the club, he'd taken her for just a rich party girl looking for a quick hookup. But in his penthouse, she'd literally transformed into another woman—one with ethereal skin, raven hair and unnerving black eyes. She'd been like an angel of death, knife at the ready. Until that moment, he'd always thought he was the only person in the world with this…affliction. But now he knew he wasn't the only one who could change faces. The woman had the same power, and she'd used it to hunt him down like prey.

They stopped at a jungle checkpoint. These government soldiers should have tried to halt the spread of weapons throughout the Congo, but that wasn't how things worked here. Benji simply paid the customary bribe to the guard who waved them through. Then they veered away from the city, heading into rebel territory, winding up steep roads into the mist-soaked mountains.

Africa was a furnace, even at this higher altitude. A little bit of hell on earth. A cluster of gun-wielding boys dressed in camouflage marked the entrance to the stronghold on the road up ahead. They were playing some kind of game with rum and matches and Marco growled. "How many times do I have to tell him that they're just little kids?"

"They're little *killers*," Benji muttered under his breath. "And the general doesn't listen to anyone anymore. I tell you, the *devil* is in him. He's become the devil!"

When Benji was just a teenager, Marco had rescued him from a diamond mine in Sierra Leone. Since then, the kid had helped Marco steal more guns than either of them could count, but Marco had never asked him to fight. Even so, Marco felt defensive. "The general means well. These orphaned boys have nowhere else to go. At least if they serve in his army, they get fed." It was a sad and all-too-familiar story in this part of the world. But giving children guns and calling them soldiers was evil, and Marco knew it.

Benji knew it, too. Parking the vehicle, he muttered, "Think what you want, Chief, but he's the *devil*."

The encampment was a primitive mountain fortress surrounding grass-roofed huts. Even so, with the weapons Marco supplied them, these rebels held their own against the Hutu militiamen—and sometimes even the government. Wearing green camo and military boots polished to a mirror shine, the general approached Marco sporting a brass-tipped baton. A pack of dogs barked at his heels and all his boy soldiers saluted as he passed. His ebony face warmed with a smile of greeting. "Ahh, the Great Northern Warlord has arrived!"

Marco's old friend seemed leaner, gaunter, with a hint more mania in his eyes, but the two men embraced like comrades. They'd been together in Rwanda and seen the horrors of genocide. Now it was an obsession for both of them.

"What did you bring for me this time?" the general asked.

"Ammunition." Marco motioned toward the crates of bullets being unloaded. "We'll parachute the weapons in, but…your soldiers are too damned young."

The general waved away Marco's concern with his baton. "I know it displeases you, my friend, but what can be done? We'll talk business later. First we drink!"

In the general's hut, they sat on patio chairs. Marco almost took a cigarette until he remembered his close encounter with an angel of death. She'd challenged him to quit and he'd said he would. For some reason—maybe because of what he was sure his blood had done to her—it was an unspoken promise he felt compelled to keep. "I'll take a beer instead."

"I stole this from Hutu militiamen," the general bragged, handing Marco a bottle. "It is good, no?"

Marco took several gulps before asking, "What happened to the militiamen?"

"You don't want to know what happened to them." There was an awkward silence. Then the general leaned forward. "Benji, your boss is from this place of mists and rainbows…this Niagara Falls, where everything is soft and covered with dew. He sometimes forgets what life is like in Congo. He forgets what it is to fight for survival in Africa, what it is to make war. But we know, don't we?" Benji looked as if he might crawl out of his skin. "He is scared of me." The general chuckled, poking Benji with the end of his baton. "Boo!"

Marco flexed his bandaged hand. "Leave him alone."

The general smiled enigmatically and blew a ring

of smoke. "Have you never told your boy here how we met?"

Marco wasn't much for show-and-tell when it came to his employees, but the general was intent on telling tales. He pulled an old photograph from his pocket, where it must have been positioned for just this occasion. "Ahh, Benji! You see that soldier in the picture, so proud under his blue beret? That was your boss, upright as a Mountie. In those days, Marco even kept a letter from his betrothed for luck."

Benji stared, amazed, though whether it was at the idea Marco had once been a UN peacekeeper or that he'd once been engaged, Marco couldn't tell. "And do you see that skinny black man standing next to him in the picture?" the general asked. "That is me. I was a teacher then, and twenty little Tutsi children came to my school to learn. The Hutus swore they would kill us all. But Marco promised he would keep my students safe."

Marco stood abruptly, nearly tipping his chair in the process. Several beer bottles clinked together and fell at his feet. "That's enough reminiscing. I need to find a bed."

Marco hadn't had to feign exhaustion; he hadn't slept since the night the woman attacked him in Naples. And now he couldn't stop thinking of her. That night, he'd just learned about his father's prognosis; the knife-wielding vixen had taken advantage of a weak moment, his yearning for an easy connection. He remembered the feel of her under his hands, the way she gave back as good as she got. She'd been perfect, crafted for sex. It made him break into a sweat just to remember.

But it hadn't just been that. There'd been something about the way she looked at him—the way she looked *into* him, as if she could see into every little hidden crevice. It'd made him feel as if one person in the world might finally understand him.

And then she'd tried to kill him.

That night, Marco dreamed of Rwanda again. The Hutus were coming with their machetes, but United Nations forces had been ordered out of the area. The evacuation convoy raced down the dirt road, away from the grenades, which sent plumes of soil into the air. Marco had the wheel when they saw a group of militiamen herding villagers into a ditch.

Stand down, soldier!

He was supposed to keep driving, but Marco jerked the truck to the side of the road, tires shrieking to a stop. He was out of the vehicle, weapon drawn, in one smooth motion. Behind him, another truck stopped and his commanding officer jumped out. Marco had halted the whole convoy. "Get back on the goddamned road!" his commander bellowed.

"They're killing the whole village right in front of us," Marco argued. The murderers hadn't even hesitated at the sight of the UN convoy. Instead, the militiamen opened fire on the civilians with the few guns they had and hacked and dismembered the rest with machetes. From the ditch came the horrific screams and the stench of death.

Marco lifted his service pistol and aimed it at the militiaman giving the orders. He thought his commander might do the same. The villagers were unarmed. They called out for help, reaching for mercy. Blood was in the air like a fine mist of a waterfall, and for a moment, Marco couldn't hear anything but the roar.

Stand down, soldier!

Marco pulled the trigger. Damn the rules, Marco shot first, and a burly Hutu militiaman returned fire. Marco was hit in the left shoulder, but it didn't knock him down, so he lifted his pistol and aimed again.

Stand down, soldier!

His red-faced commanding officer was shouting. "We're observers!"

Observers. They'd been ordered to *observe* while the world did nothing. On the news somewhere, politicians dithered over the definition of genocide and the world was busy with other matters. Citizens didn't want to hear it. So, standing there bleeding while his fellow soldiers tried to haul him back into the truck, Marco *observed* as the killers finished their grisly business. He watched until the last little hand of a village child twitched in its death throes. Then he watched as the militiaman who shot him turned and smiled.

Stand down, soldier!

Later, Marco returned to bury what remained of the bodies. In the empty eyes of a dead woman, he saw his fiancée, her lips twisted in a rictus. In the bloodied face of an old man, Marco saw his father. He saw among the dead even his own face. He was one of them. He was the brother, the lover and the son of the dead.

But he had not been their savior.

Marco woke in a cold sweat, his stomach churning and the taste of vomit in his throat. These were his sins, his crimes, and how he'd come to be the way he was. He wondered what sin the shape-shifting woman had committed to give her the same powers. She was probably dead—his blood had almost assuredly killed her. There was no point in thinking about her either way. Whoever she was, no matter how he had felt about her when they were kissing, she could be nothing but poison.

Chapter 4

In the small guest room above Hecate's shop, Kyra tossed and turned with fever, shivering under a pile of blankets. A beaded curtain separated her sickbed from the kitchen, where Hecate was tending to a teakettle. It shamed Kyra to have her former mistress care for her like a lowly nursemaid, but the hydra's blood had left her as helpless as an infant.

Hecate came into the room bearing a tray and sighed before pouring the dandelion tea. "Drink this. I used to brew so many magic potions we'd have our pick of them, but it's the best I can do for now. If only you'd let me call Ares—"

Kyra shook her head. Daddy was the last person she wanted to see in her weakened state. Hecate pressed the matter, anyway. "Ambrosia would restore you."

Ambrosia. Precious ambrosia. The scarcest resource

in the world. A large dose of it as a child had given Kyra immortality in the first place, and she had her father to thank for that. He kept a secret store of the stuff, but not even for the elixir of immortal life would Kyra want to be indebted to a war god. Not even her father. Perhaps especially not him.

"I don't need ambrosia. I'm getting better on my own." Kyra's words were belied by the fact that she could barely hold her own cup. A little tea slopped over the rim and Hecate had to wipe it away with a napkin. Then the old woman settled into an antique rocking chair with a threadbare cushion and Kyra's weak flicker of inner torchlight revealed that the goddess was decidedly cross. "I didn't know Marco Kaisaris's blood could kill me."

"Of course you knew! You just didn't want to admit it to yourself because now that angels are popular, you have a death wish."

Kyra hung her head. "No, I just wanted to do something good again—something important."

Hecate swirled a golden spoon in the ancient teacup—one of a thousand treasures she'd hoarded in her cluttered shop over the years. "Did you really think that *killing* Marco Kaisaris would make the world a better place?"

"A little, yeah," Kyra cracked.

Hecate took a sip from her cup. "Killing is your father's way."

Kyra hated to be compared to Ares. She might be his daughter, she might have tried to serve him once, but that was only because she'd wanted to forge a relationship with her only living parent; she'd never been one of his bloodthirsty gang. Unlike her other war-born siblings, she'd never ridden with Daddy into battle; she'd only been there to guide the souls of the dead afterward. How dare Hecate pretend otherwise?

But then, it wasn't Hecate's role to guide the dead anymore, was it? *She'd* given up her divine responsibilities long ago. *She'd* never comforted the shades of today's murdered children, their skulls fractured by Marco Kaisaris's bullets. Kyra had. She was only trying to rid the world of a monster.

As if reading her thoughts, Hecate's lips tightened. "Kyra, why can't you settle into your life? I've released you—you're no longer my minion. Yes, you're a *lampade,* but you don't *have* to guide the dead anymore. You don't *belong* in the world the same way you once did. None of us do. I hoped you'd use your freedom to find some happiness, but instead you're off chasing monsters! Do you do these things to get attention?"

Maybe. A little. "I went after Marco Kaisaris because *you* once told me I was destined to destroy a hydra, remember?"

Hecate sputtered, as if some old memory were taking shape. "I said you'd *conquer* one, not *kill* him! When Hercules vanquished the hydra of his age, he used a torch to do it. You're a torchbearer, Kyra. You have a gift. You can illuminate the truth of a human heart, find the wounds and sear them closed—"

"No," Kyra said bitterly. "I'll never do that again and you know why."

It'd been a long time since they'd spoken of Kyra's mother and Hecate's sad eyes showed understanding. "Kyra, that was so long ago. You were such a young nymph and unsure of your powers. You didn't mean to—"

"Condemn my own mother to a life of madness?" Kyra finished, furling her lip at the familiar but bitter taste of the dandelion tea. "I wanted to heal her, but she only saw Ares in me. It doesn't matter what I *meant* to do. It only matters that she was a mortal with only a few years of life to enjoy and I robbed her of them."

"You've seen her shade since then…you know she forgives you."

But Kyra had never forgiven herself. She'd wielded her torch in her mother's soul, trying to cauterize the wounds her father had left—and instead burned new ones there. Even after all these years, whenever she visited her mother in the underworld, there was an awkwardness between them. Perhaps it would've been awkward, anyway. After all, Kyra's mother had been born in a world of togas, grand temples and state worship; she couldn't understand the realities of the modern world in which Kyra would live *forever.* She'd become, for Kyra, a shade in truth. A beautiful stranger.

"I won't use my torch that way again," Kyra insisted. "Marco Kaisaris sides with the war gods every time he sells a gun so he deserves to be destroyed, but he doesn't deserve to live as a raving lunatic. It's kinder to kill him."

"That's the bloodlust in you. Perhaps you really are your father's daughter."

It wasn't fair that Hecate knew exactly how to shame her. *Fine,* Kyra thought. Maybe she could just chain Marco Kaisaris in some dungeon, hide him away, so that none of the war gods could harness his powers. Maybe keeping the man at her mercy was the humane thing to do. Still, the thought of shackles on those strong wrists brought an unexpectedly uncomfortable sensation to Kyra's stomach. "Hecate, if I promise not to kill him, will you help me find Marco Kaisaris again?"

"Beware the obsessive nature of nymphs," Hecate warned. "I don't want you anywhere near this man. He's a danger to you!"

In more ways than one. Most nymphs just had to

worry about broken hearts, but just *touching* Marco's blood had felled her. What if the poison got into her bloodstream? Into an open wound? If Kyra were wise, she'd never come into contact with this mortal man again. But then he might fall into her father's hands and if Kyra had to live forever, there had to be some meaning to it. Otherwise, she was a power without purpose. She had to find some point to her long life other than the bloodlust Ares said she was born to.

Besides, she and the hydra had unfinished business between them. More than just his poison had gotten under her skin. His kiss, his touch, his voice...oh, that voice. "I'll be more careful this time," Kyra promised. "Help me find him. I know you can still work some magic and you don't need a crystal ball to do it."

As one of Hecate's black hounds settled at her feet, the older woman took on the more imperious stare of her gloried past. "I don't want to risk your father's wrath. Think of Ares, won't you?"

"I *am*. If I don't find the hydra before Daddy does, imagine the damage he'll do. He could use hydra blood to poison whole armies. Whole countries!"

The ancient goddess had always been a benefactress of mankind. She didn't relish human suffering. Kyra knew she'd relent, and she did. "You'd have to get on a plane—I know how much you dislike flying."

Kyra *hated* flying. Nonetheless, she was determined. "I'll manage."

"Very well." Hecate sighed. "You'll find the hydra in the New World. He's on his way home, because he's about to lose someone very dear to him indeed."

Niagara Falls in winter, with its thundering gray river, was gloomy as the Styx. Kyra watched the netherworld entrance of mist below the tumbling water of the falls, and waved to the receding shade that had been Marco's father. Kyra hadn't killed him, but she'd guided the stubborn old man a little ways when he died. Giving him some light between the threshold of this life and the next had seemed like the least Kyra could do. She even let him see her as a sweet *angel,* because it seemed to comfort him.

He spoke of his estranged son, how heartbroken he'd been to lose Marco to a world of weapons and war. Kyra didn't add to his burden by telling him that Marco had become a monster in truth and that she planned to cage him for the greater good. She'd built a dungeon to contain him. Now she just had to find a way to lure him there.

Of course, Kyra couldn't just put on a sexy outfit and pick up the hydra in a random nightclub again. He'd be wary of strangers now, and twice as dangerous.

Fading so that none of the mortals could see her,

Kyra made her way to the funeral home. That's where inspiration struck. Marco's ex-girlfriend made only a brief appearance—just long enough to express her condolences to the family. Long enough for Kyra to study her face and memorize its shape.

Ashlynn Brown wasn't the sort of woman that Kyra would've expected to find in Marco's past. The hydra was a fierce warrior; she'd discovered that from painful firsthand experience. So how had he ever cared for someone so delicate? With doe eyes and fawn hair, the woman looked as if she were ready to bolt at the first sign of unpleasantness. It'd be tricky to impersonate such a meek woman, but it was the best idea Kyra had.

Kyra waited until Ashlynn left, then took on her appearance, right down to the prim black dress. The soft eyes, the rosy skin, and the wavy hair that could not seem to commit to being either light or dark. She even disguised her peridot choker as Ashlynn's classic string of pearls.

The hydra might *trust* Ashlynn. He might go home with Kyra if she looked like Ashlynn. Then she could lock him up in the basement dungeon she'd built and Daddy would never find him.

Marco knew that funerals were for the living, so the least he owed his family was to show up wearing the face his mother recognized. Consequently, he eschewed all disguises and made his way down the funeral home's hallway in a dark suit and overcoat, bracing for the inevitable reunion; he just didn't expect it to be with Ashlynn Brown.

His ex was sitting on a polished wood bench by herself. Her hair fell in soft waves over her shoulders, and she still dressed like a society girl, but there *was* something different about her, if only he could put his finger on it. Perhaps it was the confident tilt of her shoulders and the alluring smile. Or maybe it was the way she looked at him like he was some kind of hard candy she wanted to suck.

No. That was the look the angel of death in Naples had given him, just before she tried to kill him. So why couldn't he stop thinking about her?

Ashlynn stood to greet him, a bouquet in her hands. "So sorry about your father."

If they'd been anywhere else, he'd have brushed past her without a word. Ashlynn Brown belonged to another part of his life. Another life entirely. Still, it was his father's funeral, and she'd been good enough to come, so he fumbled for a polite reply. All he came up with was, "Asphodel?"

Ashlynn seemed to suddenly remember the white lilies in her hand. "Oh! They're for your father. I'm told it's an old Greek tradition."

"Very old." In one of her saner moments, his mother told him that ancient Greeks used to plant asphodel on the graves of their ancestors to nourish them in the underworld. But Ashlynn had never been interested in his family's ethnic heritage, so this was an entirely unexpected gesture. "Thank you…"

"Can we go for coffee, Marco? After, I mean?"

It was a spectacularly bad idea. The funeral dredged up enough bad feelings without adding a trip down memory lane to the equation. He'd only come to pay his respects and comfort his mother; then he planned to leave the country. There was a storm coming, and he had a jet waiting under an assumed identity in Toronto. But in spite of everything, the way Ashlynn looked at him, the way she seemed to look *into* him, made it hard to refuse.

Damn it. He was *over* Ashlynn Brown. He hadn't thought of her for years. He wasn't even sure he'd actually been in love with her when they were engaged, so why should he feel a pull toward her now? After all this time, he couldn't imagine what they'd even have to say to each other, but bless her shallow little heart, Ashlynn might be the only person from his past still willing to speak to him.

"Sure, why not?" he found himself saying.

Chapter 5

His father's casket was white. An oddly fitting color. White was stark and cold, intolerant of any blemish. Just like his father had been. And yet, Marco didn't resent the old man. His father had fled from war-torn Cyprus with his wife and child in tow. He'd lived a difficult life, and Marco hadn't made things any easier. *I'm sorry,* Marco thought, reaching out to touch the dead man's cold hand. But his father couldn't give him forgiveness now; he wasn't really here.

Grief tightened in Marco's chest. It hurt so badly, he stuffed his hands into his pockets to keep them from shaking. Just then, his sister, Lori, marched to his side, and after ten years, the first words his sister spoke to him face-to-face were, "You shouldn't be here."

She'd lost weight; her face had become all sharp angles, and her eyes were red-rimmed from crying.

He supposed he hadn't made her life any easier, either. "Lori, can we not do this now? It's a funeral."

"He didn't want to see you even when he knew he was dying," she said, her voice cracking with emotion. "Why would he want you here now?"

Marco had resolved not to fight with Lori today, so he clenched his teeth instead.

"Unless…" His sister's tone lightened with hope. "Have you given up…what you do?"

"I can't," he ground out. "I've told you before, there are people whose lives depend on me."

His sister sniffled. "Then why are you here?"

"Because he was my father, too," Marco said, desperate for a cigarette.

His sister softened and turned into his arms with a sob. He kissed the top of her head, but the tenderness of their reunion was broken the moment she felt his holster. "You're wearing a *gun?*" Lori whispered furiously. "Don't you know everyone's watching you?"

Marco had been in such a grief-stricken stupor he'd hardly noticed the other mourners. Now he realized there was a staring crowd. Were they waiting for him to cry? Or were they watching him because of his notoriety? Even if people didn't know exactly what Marco did for a living, there were rumors. "Bet he's in the mob," he thought he heard someone whisper, and he had to restrain a dark and bitter laugh. Their imaginations just weren't fertile enough.

As the wind outside rattled the funeral-home windows, every cye seemed to settle on the expensive sunglasses that dangled from the pocket of his tailored suit. Every glance felt like judgment, except for one. Ashlynn was there, like some kind of beacon in the midst of a sea storm. As if she had some kind of innate understanding of his mourning. And when their eyes met briefly across the crowd, it unexpectedly steadied him. At least, until he saw his mother sitting by herself. "Ma?"

"Oh, Marco, I've been waiting *hours* to see the doctor," his mother said in Greek. "Can't you speak to a nurse about moving up my appointment?"

She didn't know where she was. Maybe she didn't even know her husband was dead. Marco tried to smile, tried not to alarm her, but he couldn't make himself do it. "How are you feeling, Ma?"

"I'm so sad," his mother said, her scarred cheeks drooping. "I'm always so sad."

When he was a boy, she used to say, "I left my smile in Cyprus." He never understood until he was a soldier. Until he saw for himself how ethnic fighting splintered communities, broke nations and stole the happiness of the survivors. Now, from her wheelchair, his mother reached for his hand. "It's so dark Marco. It's black as night."

But it wasn't. The darkness was inside his mother's mind, and Marco felt it creeping into his own. "I'm sorry about Dad."

"I'm frightened," his mother said, her voice rising in terror. "I'm frightened. I can't find my way!" She lifted her hands, clawing at her face as she retreated back into that shadowy place of madness.

Marco caught his mother's wrists and called for Lori, but Ashlynn got there first. She stooped down and gently took his mother's hands from his. "It's not that dark, Mrs. Kaisaris. If you just look at me, I'll guide you."

Marco wanted to push Ashlynn away. This was none of her business and she should stay out of it. But his mother stopped struggling. "Oh, the light," his mother murmured and in that moment, Marco thought he saw something flicker over the old woman's scarred features. Something like…*grace.* "But you're—you're not Ashlynn, dear."

"Of course she's Ashlynn," Marco said.

As a teenager, his ex had always been polite about his mother's illness, but shied away from her, as if madness were contagious. Now, Ashlynn let his mother grip her hands like they were a lifeline, and didn't pull away even when the older woman's nails dug into her skin. "Ma, let Ashlynn go," he said quietly. "You're hurting her."

"It's all right," Ashlynn said. "She's hurting worse than I am."

Lori pushed forward with a bottle of pills and his mother's nurse in tow. "Both of you get away from her," his sister said, glaring at Marco as if he'd caused his mother's outburst. Ironically, it was the one damned thing he didn't feel guilty about today.

"You're okay now, aren't you, Ma?" Marco asked. "I'm right here with you."

"Please," Lori said, acidly. "She doesn't even know who you are. On the days she remembers you, she tells the doctors that her son was a soldier, a *peacekeeper*. And you know what breaks my heart, Marco? She sounds proud. Ma's mind is so far gone she doesn't have any idea that you've become some kind of mercenary."

He shouldn't have this argument. Not now. Not again. Not here where everyone was listening. But being home again was opening every old wound. "I'm not a *mercenary*," he hissed, voice low. "It's not like I sell weapons to the highest bidder. I *choose sides* in the world."

Lori just shook her head, angry tears in her eyes. "But nobody elected you to choose sides, Marco."

"The people we *elected* are doing a shitty job of it!"

Marco wanted to slam something. He wanted to kick over chairs, or crash the floral displays to the floor. It was only Ashlynn's hand on his arm that calmed him and gave him the presence of mind to fish a check from his coat pocket. "Here, take it."

That's when Lori realized it was a check. "I don't want your money," Lori snapped.

Marco took a deep breath. "Funerals are expensive. You can't afford it with the house, and mom, and the restaurant—"

"Your money is *blood money,* Marco. I think you should go."

And, for once, his sister was right.

Chapter 6

Kyra was shaken.

It wasn't that she thought she was the only person in the world whose mother suffered from mental illness. But in confronting the hydra again, she hadn't expected such a stark reminder of her own past. It made her feel sorry for Marco Kaisaris and, somehow, she was going to have to shake that off.

She'd managed to get the hydra to agree to go for coffee. If she played this right, she could lure him into the basement dungeon she'd built for him, and then neither his poisonous blood nor his bullets could ever hurt anyone again. But Marco didn't look like he was in any mood for a caffeinated beverage. He maybe needed a Scotch on the rocks, not a latte.

Once he'd helped her into the car, he was distant, but showed no signs of suspicion so she must be doing a good job of impersonating Ashlynn. Then again, the man had just lost his father. She had him at his most vulnerable. "No one ever tells you how much smaller a person looks in death," Marco said, pulling out of the parking lot. "It's like something's missing, as if their spirit took up physical space."

"Oh, but it *does*," Kyra said emphatically. But now wasn't the time to give lessons to mortal men on the physicality of the soul. Snow was turning to sleet, and it was good that Marco was driving because Kyra had trouble concentrating on the road. She was too busy watching for signs that Daddy was on her trail. She knew to be alert for the vultures of Ares or Athena's telltale owls, but here in Niagara Falls, Kyra had to be just as wary of the local echo god who once carried Iroquois war cries on the wind.

"Listen, this was a bad idea, Ashlynn." Marco's black-gloved hands tightened on the wheel. "We're not just two old friends going for coffee. You don't know me anymore and, trust me, you don't want to."

"I know you're in some kind of trouble with the law," she replied.

When they stopped at a red light he looked like he wanted to reach for the unopened package of cigarettes on the dash. Instead, he folded a stick of gum into his mouth and crumpled the wrapper. She watched the way his strong jaw worked under his five-o'clock shadow.

"Some kind of trouble with the law…is that what my sister told you?"

"Would she have been wrong?" Kyra asked, avoiding the question.

The light changed, but Marco didn't drive through the intersection. Instead, he abruptly pulled over to the side of the road. Gravel popped under his tires. In the oncoming sleet, traffic cut past them in an angry blur of headlights and windshield wipers. "I can't do this," Marco said. "I can't just pull into some coffee shop and sit down with you in a crowd and act like—"

"You don't have to act like anything."

He sighed, his shoulders slumping. "I can't do it, Ashlynn."

This wasn't going well. If he made her get out of the car, then all Kyra's scheming would be for naught. Scrambling for an alternative plan, she tried to play on whatever sense of chivalry he might have. "Can you at least drive me home?"

Marco gnashed at his gum. If he'd known who it really was beside him in the car, he'd have left her stranded—or perhaps even strangled—on the side of the road without a second thought. But when he finally glanced at her, he nodded.

"I'll give you directions," she said as he pulled back onto the road.

"I remember the way."

"No, I just bought a new house," Kyra said, and that wasn't even a lie. So they drove up Niagara Parkway, mostly in silence. She'd chosen the desolated location carefully—just about as remote a place as one could get and still be in Niagara Falls. But once they were in the hinterlands, he was impatient. "Just how much farther is it?"

"Not far. Up ahead after the turn. You should come in. I can make you that coffee."

"I just need to drop you off, and leave. This time for good."

So that's how it was going to be. Kyra hadn't planned to use her powers right away, but unless she did, Marco Kaisaris was going to disappear again before she could stop him from becoming one of her father's minions, or from putting AK-47s into the hands of another group of child soldiers. Luckily, Kyra saw the guardrail up ahead. Staring intently, she concentrated all her power. Ever since she'd been poisoned, it was painful to do this and she knew it'd weaken her, but she had no choice.

She was a nymph of the underworld, a torchbearer of Hecate; a mortal like Marco couldn't bear the light she cast. Widening her gaze, she flashed her inner torchlight so brightly that it hit the guardrail reflectors and bounced back into Marco's eyes. He brought his hand up as a shield against the sudden glare, but it was too late. Temporarily blinded, he lost control. They hit a patch of ice. He cursed, pumping the breaks, but to no avail. The car spun out and crashed in an explosion of shattered glass.

Kyra found herself face-first in a ditch, covered with shards and pieces of metal. She'd been thrown from the car and something inside her felt ruptured. The pain was so intense, she couldn't catch her breath. She was bleeding. *It shouldn't hurt this much,* she thought, as she fought for air. She should be healing faster. But she wasn't.

Gasping as icy water seeped into her clothes, she thought for a moment she understood what it was to fear death. And having used all her power to cause the accident, it took all the strength she had to maintain the illusion that she was another woman entirely.

Dazed and bleeding, Marco found himself standing in another ditch staring at another motionless body. He was confused, momentarily unable to orient himself in time or place. His instinct was to reach for his gun and radio for air support. It was only the snow that reminded him he wasn't in some war-torn country in Africa. What had happened? Had he hit another car? If so, where was it? He only saw his own rented Jaguar in the ditch. And Ashlynn. She lay half-submerged in the water, bobbing like a beautiful but broken doll.

The sight sent a jolt of adrenaline through him. Climbing over the wreckage, he jumped into the ditch, slush up to his waist. His overcoat fanned out behind him, soaking up water, becoming a heavy drag, and utterly worthless against the piercing chill. Still, he desperately slogged forward.

Grabbing Ashlynn by the shoulders, he pulled her out of the ditch. He managed to push her up onto the snowbank and drag himself out after her. He was grateful to find her breathing and at least semiconscious, but her teeth were chattering. He had to get her somewhere warm. And fast.

He hoped the keys in her coat pocket were for the house at the top of the hill. It didn't really matter; it was the only house around. He'd break the door down if he had to. Lifting Ashlynn into his arms, he carried her up the snowy driveway, his dress shoes sliding on the ice every few feet or so. She made a weak protest but he ignored it. There was no way she could walk on her own given her condition. Besides, as he recalled, Ashlynn wasn't built for adversity.

The key fit and he shoved the door open with his foot. He set her down on the living-room couch, but there was only a throw blanket to cover her with. Whoever's house this was, it was remarkably spare. "Ashlynn, are you all right?"

"You're the one who is bleeding," she murmured

with half-lidded eyes, reaching up to touch his cheek where he'd been cut.

He caught her by the wrist. "Don't touch it," he barked. "My blood is poison." He hadn't meant to say it, and he certainly hadn't expected her to believe him. But she visibly recoiled—as if she knew how afraid she really should be. She blinked in wordless terror and he worried she might actually have a concussion. "Is this your house?"

She still blinked rapidly—too rapidly—but then nodded.

"Where's the phone?" he asked.

"I—I don't have one," she stammered, her wrist still locked in his grip. "I just moved in. The service hasn't been turned on yet."

Something about her answer didn't seem right. Maybe it was the way she stammered or the way her eyes slid away from him, but Ashlynn had never lied to him about the small things. Taking a quick personal inventory of his sodden belongings, Marco found that he still had his gun, but his cell phone was gone. If he was going to call an ambulance, he'd better go find it. Letting go of Ashlynn, he started for the door.

"You're leaving me?"

His steps came to an abrupt halt. She'd asked him that once before, when he was just eighteen. It had been an accusation then, cloying and immature. As if enlisting in the military was something he'd done to ruin their wedding plans. This time was more of a plea—something desperate, and resigned. "I'm just going to look for my phone, Ashlynn. I'll be back."

Kyra hadn't meant to cause such a horrible accident. She'd only been trying to cause a little fender bender. At most, she'd hoped for a broken axle—something that would incapacitate his rental without doing any real damage. She'd never intended to *total* the car. And no matter what Hecate would say, this time she really hadn't been trying to kill the hydra.

The problem was that Kyra had never encountered a storm like this; she hailed from a warmer part of the world. It was the ice that hadn't figured into her plans. Now, she deeply regretted that oversight. Why, she'd been so disoriented after the accident that she'd nearly touched the poisoned blood on Marco's cheekbone!

Fear of death didn't come naturally to Kyra; it was still a reflex she was learning. If he hadn't stopped her from touching him, what might've happened? But he *had* stopped her. He'd even told her the truth about the poison in his blood—at least, he told *Ashlynn* the truth.

She should be healed by now. But ever since the poisoning, her powers of recovery were decidedly slow. She actually felt too weak to get up and follow Marco.

He said he'd be right back, but she was afraid he'd just disappear again into the snow, and every day he was free to sell weapons was another day of death and destruction. Every day he was free made it that much easier for Ares to find him, and bend the hydra to an even darker purpose.

At least, that's the reason she told herself she was afraid Marco would disappear when he walked out that door. But there was another reason, too; she was shaken. Shaken by the accident, and even more shaken by the way he'd pulled her out of the ditch and carried her to safety in a strong and protective embrace. Why had he been so tender with her? Not with her, of course. With *Ashlynn*. She must remember that he was seeing a woman he once cared about. Even so, if a man could behave that way, could he still be a monster?

Marco usually traveled with a driver, but he hadn't wanted Benji or any of his employees nosing around his hometown, so he'd rented the car. Now, as Marco climbed over the twisted metal and fished his ruined cell phone out of the icy water, he counted that decision a mistake. There'd be questions about the wreck when the authorities found it. Meanwhile, he was in the middle of nowhere, alone with Ashlynn Brown for the first time in years and without a working phone. How in the hell had this crash happened, and why couldn't he remember?

He found her purse in the snow and carried it inside. She was still on the couch, but she'd found another blanket. That was probably a good sign—that she'd been able to get up on her own—but she still looked stunned. They were both shivering, soaked to the bone, but he said, "I'm going to have to walk to a neighbor's house and call you an ambulance."

"In this weather?" she asked. "My closest neighbor is a mile away."

Marco glanced out the window with frustration. The snow was really coming down. He'd planned to be well on his way to Toronto by now. But that was before he nearly killed his ex-fiancée in a car wreck. "I don't have a better idea."

"You're not dressed for a hike through a storm," she said, eyeing his ruined dress shoes and sodden over-coat. "And I don't need an ambulance. I'm okay."

"You looked *dead* out there," he said, the memory of it still churning like bile in his stomach. "You looked *dead,*" he repeated, unable to fathom how quickly she seemed to have recovered.

"But I'm fine. I just have a few bumps and bruises. Besides, in your profession, I'm sure you've seen people hurt much worse."

He stooped in front of the hearth to start a fire. "My profession?"

Kyra watched him, noting the way his shoulders tensed. His emotions were like a tinderbox just waiting to flare up. She remembered the dark expression on his face in Naples and the way he'd frightened her, and she wondered what the hell she was doing. This wasn't the way to lure him into the basement dungeon. Still, impulse control had never been her strong suit. "They say you're a gunrunner. I've seen your name on the news."

"Since when are *you* interested in the news, Ashlynn?"

Kyra sighed inwardly. Just her luck to have chosen to impersonate the one clueless woman from his past who wouldn't care about his illegal enterprises. "Maybe I've changed."

Marco arranged a few logs in the grate. "Maybe we both have."

"So, is it true?" she pressed. "Are you an arms dealer?"

He lit a match and started the fire. "It doesn't matter."

"It mattered to your father," Kyra countered.

He rolled his muscular shoulders, but didn't turn to look at her. Still, she knew her arrow had struck true. "You know, Ashlynn, I do what I do so that people like you can live your safe little lives and never have to think about the horrors of the world."

"You broke your father's heart," she said bluntly.

Marco silently stabbed into the fireplace with a poker. Then he exploded all at once. "What else is new? You remember how he was. I wanted to do something with my life so that other people wouldn't have to suffer like my mother suffered, but he couldn't get over the fact that his only son didn't want to work in the family business. The only thing he cared about was that stupid restaurant."

That's crap, Kyra wanted to say. But instead, she kept Ashlynn's sweeter demeanor. "No. Your father just thought he'd escaped a world of war. He didn't want to see his son back in it. But at least he was proud of you when you were a soldier. It was when you amassed your own private arsenal to sell to criminals—that's what he couldn't forgive." Kyra knew this, because these were among the last things Mr. Kaisaris had said before she led him to the entrance to the underworld.

Fortunately, Marco didn't ask her how she knew. He was too pissed. "My father didn't understand and neither do you."

"I understand that you cause wars."

"Gunrunning doesn't *cause* wars. It simply prolongs them."

Ug! He sounded like Ares himself. Wrapping her

blanket more tightly around her, Kyra wondered if he knew how chilling his words were. "And that's better?"

"It *is* better," Marco said, turning to face her at last. "You see, there are some things civilians don't *get*."

Civilians? Did he still think of himself as a soldier? Even now? Fighting some war the rest of the world had forgotten? "Why don't you educate me, Marco."

"Sometimes the only thing that keeps people alive is war. In some places in the world, 'peace' only comes after a massacre. Fighting isn't the worst thing that can happen, especially when it means you live to fight another day."

"How can you say that? You used to be a UN peacekeeper."

"Because when I was a peacekeeper in Rwanda, they killed eight hundred thousand people in one hundred days. Which is how I know peacekeeping is a *joke*."

Kyra opened her mouth to reply, but the fire and his temper weren't the only things burning; where his blood had dripped onto his collar, smoke rose from the cloth. She recognized the potent scent of it and it immediately reminded her of how Marco's blood had literally stopped her heart. Kyra pretended not to notice, but he caught her glance.

"I need to get cleaned up," was all he said.

Chapter 7

While Marco showered, Kyra took his clothes into the small laundry room off the kitchen, and put his shirt and slacks in the dryer—his jacket was a lost cause. He'd told her that once his clothes were dry, he'd hike through the storm to find a phone. Kyra thought he was a menace to himself and society for even considering going out in this weather—wet clothes or dry— but she didn't know how much longer she could keep him here unfettered.

The accident had left him confused and unsteady, which should make it easier to tranquilize him and drag him into the cage in the basement. It also made it easier for her to lie to him about not having a phone. She was lucky her purse had been thrown clear of the wreck, and that he hadn't opened it and found the cell phone inside. Now she flipped it open, made sure it was still working, then tucked it, snug in her ruined coat, into a laundry basket.

Then she went to check on him.

He was in the bathroom with nothing but a towel around his waist. The first thing she noticed was his muscular back—broad, shower-damp shoulders above a perfectly curved spine. The second thing she noticed was that he had a sewing kit on the bathroom countertop, and a needle in his hand.

As he lifted the needle to his face, she gasped. "What are you doing?"

"A bit of quilting," Marco said through clenched teeth. "What does it look like?"

He was giving himself stitches. He was actually sewing together the cut skin over his cheekbone as if he'd done it a hundred times before; as if he had no one else in the world he could trust to care for him when he was hurt. And maybe he didn't. Kyra couldn't help but let her eyes drift down to his hand—the one she'd slashed open with her knife in Naples. She wondered who healed him then. He was mortal, after all; his wounds didn't close up the way hers did. Kyra reached tentatively for the needle. "Let me help you."

"No," he said quietly. "I told you, my blood is poison."

She hadn't forgotten, and yet, she still wanted to help him. Was it just her natural inclination as a *lampade* to guide him? Or did she really have a death wish, after all?

At that moment, their eyes met in the mirror, and before she could guard against it, she briefly glimpsed right into him. She saw him with her underworld nymph's eyes, shedding light on forgotten corners of his soul. She saw his grief over his father. Again, she saw his need to know and be known, to understand and be understood. That same need echoed inside her and, for reasons she couldn't explain, tears welled beneath her lashes.

"Aren't you going to argue with me?" Marco asked, breaking eye contact as he cut the end of the thread. "Aren't you going to tell me it's not possible to have poisoned blood?"

Kyra shook her head. "No."

"I'm HIV positive," he said.

"You don't have to lie, Marco. When you told me your blood was poison, you meant it literally. I saw your blood burning your shirt. I just want to know… why."

"Why?" Marco's dark eyes met hers again, his voice thick with emotion. "I guess it's because sometimes, in war, you see things so horrible, so unforgivable, so *toxic,* that it gets into you…it *poisons* you."

Kyra understood this better than she could admit. With Ares came the vultures and anguished cries of the dying—cries that Kyra endured as part of her duties in the underworld. Like all the war gods, her father fed on bloodlust and brutality. It wasn't just Kyra's family legacy, it was in *her* blood. She could have let her violent instincts destroy her, but she hadn't. She could have given in to her father, but she hadn't. At least, not yet. "It doesn't have to poison you. You can use it to find your purpose."

"I *have* found my purpose," Marco said bitterly. "It's just a darker one than I ever imagined. You see, nobody cares about what happened in Rwanda anymore. It's over, they think. The world has moved on, but I haven't."

He was struggling. Kyra could taste it. She understood it. While Kyra was born to darkness, struggling to live a life of light, for Marco, the reverse was true. "What I mean is that you can use what's happened to you, to change."

"Oh, I change," he replied.

And then he did.

Kyra watched with fascination as his face reshaped itself. She saw the skin age and wrinkle before her eyes. She watched his hair shimmer with gray until he looked like his father. Then, in a horrifying display of malleable flesh and popping cartilage, Marco changed into a series of men Kyra did not recognize until he finally settled upon the face she knew. She startled, captivated by the sight of the lips she had kissed in Naples only moments before stabbing him.

Kyra didn't have to pretend to be upset. No matter which face he was wearing, her inner torch revealed such exquisitely mortal pain, that it shamed her. She'd tried to *kill* him in Naples, like he was only a creature, like he was some sacrifice on the altar of her good intentions. She'd seen only the monster in him, not the man. Maybe she wasn't so different from her murderous immortal family, after all.

With that thought, she turned and fled the bathroom.

In the living room, she stared out the front window. Shadowy tree limbs arched gracefully under the freezing rain, encased in moonlit ice. She'd never seen a storm like this and she couldn't stop shivering, but this time not from the cold.

She heard Marco come up behind her. "Ashlynn, look at me." It wasn't her name, so she didn't turn around. She just pushed her hands against the windowpane and let the cold seep into her. "Ashlynn, it's just me. It's Marco. I promise. I'm sorry, I didn't mean to scare you." He wrapped his arms around her, holding her, trying to comfort her, when she should be the one apologizing. But she couldn't speak. "I think I just wanted someone to know about me," he said softly as the fire in the fireplace crackled behind him. "To know that I can change into people who've hurt me in some way. I'm some kind of... I can't explain it."

Was it possible that he didn't even know what he was? "You're like a hydra," she whispered, suffocating under the weight of her own deceit. He was not *like* a hydra; he *was* one. But how to tell him?

He turned her around so that she was looking at him. "A hydra?"

"Your parents are Greek," she whispered. "Don't you know the old stories?"

"I know them," he said, tilting his head.

Kyra stole a glance up at him from beneath her lashes. "The ancients said that the hydra was a poisonous monster. And it had a thousand heads. If a warrior cut off its head, two more would grow in its place."

"Yeah, yeah," he said impatiently. "Unless the warrior used a torch to cauterize the wound."

How innocently he said it. How guileless. He didn't suspect he was holding a torchbearer in his arms. Nor that she was fated to destroy him. And yet, she couldn't pull away. "I think you're like that, Marco. Like a hydra."

She hadn't meant her words to wound him, but he fell back as if struck. "You think I'm a *monster.*" His face reddened. Then, finally, he nodded with grim resignation. "Maybe you're right. Maybe I am a monster."

Kyra's stomach clenched, as if she could feel his pain as her own. She was only trying to help him to understand what he'd become. "Marco...what happened to you?"

To her surprise, he told her.

He told her about Rwanda. He told her about how he had been shot. He told her about the villagers in the ditch, slaughtered while he stood by. And he told her about the day he buried them. The way his voice flattened broke her heart. Even now, he made fists of his hands as if to keep them from shaking as he finished his tale.

"When I returned to base camp, I looked in a mirror and, instead of my own face, I saw the face of the militiaman. I saw the face of a murderer and somehow it made perfect sense who shot me, because I'm just like him."

Kyra listened to his story in silence, but couldn't contain herself any longer. How could she have been so wrong about him? "You're nothing like those men."

He leaned back against the arm of the sofa, unable to meet her eyes. "I stood by and just watched that massacre happen."

"No, you didn't," she argued. "You tried to stop it and got shot for your trouble."

Reminded of his old injury, his hand went to his bare

shoulder. "Well, that's what soldiers are supposed to do. We're there to take the bullets if we have to. We're there to protect people who can't protect themselves. But in the end, we just *observed*." He said the word with venom.

"You were just following orders."

He winced. "Bullshit, Ashlynn. Since when has that been a defense for anything? But I'm trying to make up for it now. Now I help people fight back. I make damned sure they're *equipped* to fight back. I give them all the guns and the ammo they'll ever need."

He was just like her—trying to do the right thing, and making every conceivable mistake along the way. He was all but naked and she could read it on his skin. He carried inside him a terrible grief, and not just for the mother he'd lost to madness or the father he'd buried today.

She wished she could take it away, make it hurt less somehow. The cords on Marco's neck were tight with emotion and Kyra couldn't stop herself from tracing his chest with her fingers. He watched the path of her touch as if mesmerized, and it encouraged her. Her heartbeat picked up the pace of his. Kyra stroked the scar on his bare shoulder, knowing a bullet fragment was still there in the bone. And yet, that bullet had caused less damage than the things Marco had done, and the things he'd failed to do. He wanted someone—anyone—to understand. And she did. He was only a mortal, so she couldn't imagine how they were so much alike. But there was no denying it. He was a reflection of her. It made her want him.

And why not? She could give him pleasure without having feelings for him, she told herself. She'd done it with countless mortal men before. She was a nymph of the underworld; she could use her skin to soothe his pain. It didn't have to mean more than that.

She drew his hand to her and kissed the still-angry scar. Her lips upon the sensitive skin made him twitch. "Don't," he finally choked out. But Kyra stepped closer and kissed the scar on his shoulder, too. At first, he was still as a stone, but the heat of his skin and the soft hair of his bare chest against her cheek reminded her he was no statue. "I have an open wound," he whispered. "I'm not safe to touch."

No, he wasn't safe to touch. And that, in itself, held a powerful allure. "You're bandaged. It's not dangerous to touch your skin, is it?"

"No," he admitted, sheepish longing in his eyes. "I just…don't want to hurt you."

Mortal men never *wanted* to hurt nymphs, but they always did. And yet, Kyra couldn't turn away from him. Not when he needed her. "Your kisses aren't poisoned, are they?" she asked, lips trailing up to his mouth, achingly soft. She couldn't remember a time she'd ever kissed a man so softly. But the scent of his clean skin and the taste of salt upon his lips made her sigh. He'd been holding his breath, and now his lips parted as he exhaled into her kiss. She took that breath into her with all its stain and sorrow and kissed him again, giving that breath back to him cleansed with her inner light.

Then it happened all at once.

The way he groaned. The way he took her hands, clasping them at the small of her back. The way he crushed her against him, his teeth scraping along the hollow of her throat. It was the grief that drove him, she thought. Mourners often sought solace in physical connection, as if to prove to themselves they were still alive. But she didn't mind. She knew how to make her body malleable for a man's pleasure.

She let him pull her onto the sofa in front of the fire where he laid his body atop hers, pulling her clothes off piece by piece. There was some fumbling with his wallet on the end table where he'd left it, and he sheathed himself in a condom. Then it was all skin and sweat and sighs.

The feel of his arousal hard against her sent little shocks along her skin. The sudden forcefulness of his body as he pinned her wrists over her head made her senses spark like the fire in the hearth. Kyra was no shy maiden nymph in the face of a man's need. No coy

Daphne, to flee from Apollo's lust. This was a threshold that Kyra *wanted* to cross.

Her thighs parted and their eyes locked as he sank all the way into her. She'd done this to comfort him and sate his needs—but it stoked a fire inside her, too. She loved his thickness and the way she stretched to accommodate him. She loved the feel of his muscles as his back arched. She arched, too, to meet him.

He was looking into her as she looked into him; he was inside her just as she was inside him. There was nowhere to hide—and for one magical moment, she was certain that he knew her, that he saw her true face, that he saw her for herself.

But then he closed his eyes.

Gods above and below, she loved the feel of this mortal. The scratch of his beard, the light scrape of it on her cheek that reminded her he was man and she was woman. She loved the rough texture of his scars. How must it feel to have marks that so boldly told the story of his pains right there on the surface of his skin? And she loved his strong arms. Arms long enough to wrap all the way around her. Arms that made her feel as if she were not too wild to fully embrace.

She'd had many lovers before. She'd worshipped the perfect bodies of ancient gods. She'd admired the well-oiled muscles of Olympic athletes throughout the ages. But for some reason, Marco's body, battle-hardened and scarred as it was, suited her perfectly. He *fit* with her, and every time he pushed inside her, the sensation of completion was renewed.

She wanted to make him come—fast and hard. She wanted to move her hips in just the way he liked, and make him forget everything else. But as they moved together, it was *her* arousal that spiraled higher and higher, out of control. The couch scraped against the floor, his chest scraped hers, and it went on and on, as if every stroke exorcised some demon. As if every caress were a confession. She kissed him as they strained together, a kiss broken finally by her own gasping climax. Flickers of light danced beneath her eyelids and she couldn't believe it had happened so quickly or so intensely. His followed soon after, a groan at the back of his throat. He buried his face against her chest as his body convulsed in orgasm, his legs straining between hers. Beneath him, Kyra lay nothing short of astonished.

Afterward, her body tingled with sensation, every single hair seeming to stand on end. They were quiet, her hands stroking the hair from his damp face as he nuzzled her breasts. It'd been a quick release of tension—and now he seemed to want more. She did, too, but she couldn't remember the last time she'd had sex this tenderly. At least, it'd been tender by Kyra's standards, and tender wasn't her way. Somehow, she and Marco had connected. Maybe it was because they were so much alike.

Or maybe it was because she was pretending to be someone else.

The thought was so sobering, so unsettling, that she stopped the trail of his lips down her stomach. "What's wrong?" he asked.

Everything was wrong. What's more, his bandage had peeled away just enough so that she could see the crudely stitched wound. The threads looked frail and tattered as if the poison was eating them away. What if even a little bit of his blood dripped onto her skin again? Just being this close to him, she was taking her life in her hands, and yet, why did she suddenly fear it was her heart most in jeopardy? "It's just…"

"You regret it," he finished for her.

No. She didn't regret it. And that was the problem. "It's just—I'm not sure I'm the kind of woman who does this." What she meant, of course, was that she wasn't the kind of *nymph* who did this. She took lovers, certainly. But this encounter with Marco had the potential to be so much more. And that frightened her out of her wits.

As the silence stretched on between them, his shoulders tensed in the firelight. She could see she'd angered him, broken the thread of tenderness between them. When he spoke again, it was guarded. Sarcastic. "What, Ashlynn? Are you afraid I'm not going to respect you in the morning?"

"Maybe," Kyra said, but that was a lie. She was afraid that, in the end, she'd be just like all those silly, sentimental nymphs who mistook sex for something more, and lost themselves in the bargain. "You wouldn't be the first man to judge a woman in the morning for doing exactly what you wanted her to do the night before."

"I've had too many one-night stands to judge you," he said. So he meant this to be the only time. Kyra wasn't sure why this should've bothered her, but it did. Her disappointment must have shown, because he said, "Look, I know I said some unkind things when we broke up…"

In spite of herself, she was desperately curious about how Marco parted from his ex-lover. "Like what?"

"Don't do that," he said, shaking his head. "I know you remember what I called you. And I'm sorry. You were lonely when I went overseas and you were inexperienced. He took advantage of that. You were an innocent and I blame *him* not *you*."

An *innocent?* Kyra made a mental note never again to impersonate someone like Ashlynn Brown. She couldn't pull it off. In fact, she'd better cut off this conversation quickly. Any trip down memory lane was likely to mess her up. She didn't share his memories and she wasn't the woman he was reminiscing about, but she wasn't sure she could bear for him to realize it so soon after the tender intimacies between them. "Well, we're different people now."

"We are. And though I'm sure you don't like to think of yourself as the kind of girl who gets down and dirty in the middle of the living room…if you ask me, a little naughtiness suits you."

"So you're saying that you like me better now than the way I was?"

If only he hadn't paused to think about it. If only he'd given her any real answer at all. But what he said was, "I'm not sure my opinion matters… I'm hungry. Are you hungry?"

"Charming." Kyra tried, and failed, to keep the acid from her tongue. "Is that how you are with your other women? 'Hey, thanks for last night. Let's order some pizza!'"

Marco arched a brow. "My *other women?*"

"Weren't you just bragging about all your one-night stands?"

His brow arched even higher. "Are you jealous?"

"Should I be?"

"I just take fleeting pleasure where I find it. I don't deserve much more than that."

"That's not true." Now she knew that he wasn't an

arms dealer for the cash or for the power. He was a *crusader;* he had the idiotic notion that what he was doing would help people.

She ached a little at the break in contact as he withdrew from the tangle of limbs and couch cushions, but she liked looking at his body in the firelight. He was as hard and scarred as an ancient legionary, with dark hair that trailed down his chest and thinned out on his belly. She wanted to rub her face against it, and her arousal frustrated her. Meanwhile, he found his towel, wrapped it around his waist and padded barefoot, apparently intent on foraging for food. "I'll cook us something."

She opened her mouth to stop him, tried to spin some quick lie to explain why the fridge was empty, but she was too late. He threw open the door, then looked at her from across the countertop that divided the living room from the kitchen, incredulous. "Don't you eat?"

"I told you—I just moved in."

His eyes narrowed. "You keep saying that, but I don't see any boxes."

"They're still back at my old place," Kyra quickly lied.

That's when he flung open the freezer and found the food rations she'd stored when she'd planned to lock him in the dungeon. She hadn't planned to starve him, after all. "What the *hell?*"

"Doesn't everybody love Salisbury steak?" But she couldn't keep the guilt off her face, and she pulled the blanket tighter around her, anticipating a truly horrible confrontation.

To her surprise, he laughed. And it wasn't one of his dark bitter laughs, either. This one was rich and warm and it made her fingertips tingle. "Ashlynn, you have about twenty trays in here. It's bad enough that you're subsisting off craptastic frozen dinners, but every single one of these is the same!"

So she wasn't caught, after all. "Variety makes me nervous," she chirped in relief.

"I remember that about you." He pulled two boxed dinners out of the freezer and tossed them on the countertop. "This is all congealed gravy and high sodium— you keep eating this stuff, and it's going to kill you."

No, she thought. There was only one thing in this world that could kill her and that was him. "Marco... I'll take care of dinner if you want to clean up. Your bandage—"

It was the wrong thing to say. His hand quickly went to his cheek as awareness dawned in his eyes. For a few moments he'd given pleasure, taken pleasure and laughed. For just a little while, he'd forgotten he was a monster.

Now, she'd reminded him again and it seemed to turn him to stone.

Chapter 8

Marco checked his bandage, relieved to find that he wasn't dripping blood. How could he have been so damned reckless? What if his cut had opened up again while he was on top of her? What if he'd poisoned her? He was usually so much more careful about this. But somehow when their bodies were joined, Marco had forgotten about his poisoned blood. He'd forgotten about wars, he'd forgotten about Africa, he'd forgotten about his many faces, his mother's madness and he'd even forgotten his father's death.

And that was all because of *her*. Because of Ashlynn Brown. The same woman who couldn't even wait until he'd come home from his tour of duty to return his engagement ring and run off with another guy. Ashlynn had wounded his pride, but that was all. He'd been so young that he'd already fallen out of love with her—if he'd ever been in love with her to begin with. Or is that just what he told himself? Because if he'd really stopped having feelings for Ashlynn, how could he explain what just happened?

He couldn't explain it, or maybe he just didn't want to. Furious with himself, Marco riffled through the bathroom cabinets to find a clean bandage. He'd been surprised at Ashlynn's rather well-stocked medicine cabinet. Not just your standard aspirin and Band-Aids, but a full first-aid kit and some pretty heavy-duty sleeping pills. He couldn't help but wonder what kept her up at night.

After he'd redressed the wound on his cheek, assuring himself that he wasn't going to bleed on anything, he looked for something dry to wear. A towel wasn't going to cut it. He went into her bedroom. The bed looked as if it'd never been slept in, but Ashlynn had always been a neat freak that way. He opened the closet and found two bathrobes hanging on the back of the door, neither of which looked as if they'd ever been worn. Also, to his extreme shock and surprise, he found a pair of shiny silver handcuffs.

He actually did a double take, pulled them out and tested them. Yep. Real handcuffs. What the hell kind of life was Ashlynn living now that her bedroom closet contained bathrobes and handcuffs but hardly any clothes?

Something about this house was *so* wrong, and under any other circumstances he'd have marched to the kitchen and demanded an explanation. But did he really have a right to ask? This was his high-school sweetheart he was dealing with hcrc and he had the distinctly uncomfortable feeling that he was intruding in her private space.

Leaning against the door frame, he listened to the wind howling outside. The temperature outside was dropping, and every tree was slowly being trapped in ice. Just like him. Trapped here in this damned house with a woman who was as familiar as a lover, and as mysterious as a stranger.

The last time Kyra had cooked, microwaves hadn't been invented, so she opted for the oven and set a timer. Not long after, Marco came back from the bathroom wearing one of the bathrobes the real estate agent had left there as a welcoming gift. He tossed his bloody bandage—as well as the towels he'd used— into the fire.

"Does that get rid of the poison?" she asked, genuinely curious.

"Hopefully." He didn't look up at her—just stood there watching everything burn. "You know, I'm not sure that I really believed any of it until I changed faces in front of you. Until I showed you, I thought maybe it was some madness. Now that someone else knows…"

It had been a reality check. She could see that it was all hitting him now in a way it hadn't before. It had never occurred to Kyra that he kept this monstrous secret from everyone. She'd always thought a friend might have known, or his family, or even some of the men who worked for him. But of all the people in the world, he'd shown *her*. He'd told *her* everything. He'd trusted *her*.

No… He'd trusted *Ashlynn*. And now she was going to have to keep abusing that trust to keep him out of her father's clutches. It made her sick.

Marco used the poker to push the burning towels farther into the flame. The smell of his blood as it burned was not pleasant, but it seemed to bother him more than it did her. "Ashlynn, when I changed faces in front of you, why didn't you scream?"

The question startled Kyra. "What?"

He leaned against the fireplace. "I showed you something that should've frightened you, repulsed you, and yet…you reached for me."

She'd reached for him because he'd needed her, and it'd been a long time since anyone had. But that truth cut too closely to the bone, so she smiled and said, "Well, there's a storm and I didn't have a phone to call the police, so sleeping with you seemed like my only other option."

Clearly, it was the wrong joke to make. He looked as if her words had dealt him a body blow. He set the poker aside and motioned toward the rumpled couch where they'd been intimate. "So you slept with me because you're afraid of me?"

"Don't be ridiculous." *I'm not afraid of anything,* she told herself. Except for her father. And some of the other war gods. And of Marco's blood. And of the emotions swirling inside her now… "Marco, if I was afraid of you, why would I come anywhere near you?"

"It happens all the time. Women end up in bed with men that scare them." Marco's mind seemed somewhere else. Somewhere like the Congo. "Sometimes women find themselves trapped in a bad situation. Maybe they find themselves captured by enemy soldiers and they think it'll be worse for them if they resist."

Oh, the horrible things he'd seen. The images, the experiences of war, really *had* poisoned him. "But it wasn't like that between us, Marco. I kissed you—"

"So what? Sometimes in Africa, those same women seduce those same dangerous soldiers in the hopes of some gentleness. It's a survival instinct." His voice was getting colder. More clinical. "They take a horrific circumstance and turn it into something familiar, something over which they have some semblance of control. It doesn't make it any less wrong to take advantage of it."

Frustrated, Kyra asked, "Is that what you want to believe happened here tonight?" She was incredibly uncomfortable with her impersonation of Ashlynn Brown. The play-pretend wasn't protecting her emotions, which felt now like they were right on the surface of her skin. He was trying to ruin everything. He was trying to take the one moment of connection she'd felt in centuries and turn it ugly. "Do you think that a *good girl* like Ashlynn wouldn't have sex with you willingly?"

He tilted his head at her use of the third person.

She was so disoriented that she'd nearly given herself away, but she couldn't stop herself now. She was angry and didn't know why. Maybe it would make her feel better if he was angry, too. "Or maybe it turns you on to think I didn't want it."

Marco gave her a sharp look, then the flats of both his hands slammed down on the mantelpiece. "After all these years, you still don't understand the first damned thing about me!"

They stood there, facing each other, he in the bathrobe, she clutching the blanket around herself. Then the beeping timer on the oven split the night. Kyra turned toward the kitchen, but Marco grabbed her by the arm. He was fast, just like he'd been when they'd fought in the hotel. And remembering his strength, how they'd brawled, Kyra flinched.

"You *are* afraid of me. Did you think I was going to hit you?"

Of course, he *had* hit her before. Mind you, he'd been fighting for his life at the time… "No—no," Kyra stammered, unable to spin a quick lie.

Marco swallowed, letting her go. "Get dressed."

"Maybe I don't want to get dressed," she said, nostrils flared.

"Who knows how long you were floating in that ice water before I pulled you out? You could have hypothermia. Put some clothes on."

"Oh, is that an *order?*" she asked sarcastically.

"Ashlynn—"

"You're not a soldier anymore, Marco, and I don't take orders from you. I don't care how much money you have, I don't care how many guns you own and I don't care how many governments you've helped topple—"

He reared back. "Is that what you think I do?"

In spite of their argument, maybe this was an opening for her to persuade him to give up arms dealing. To warn him about Ares before it was too late. Wasn't that the whole reason she was here? "Yes, Marco, that's what I think you do."

He looked as if he were going to deny it, but then he started coughing. "What's that smell?" She smelled it, too. It was smoke. Dinner was burning. "I'll take care of it," he said. "Get dressed."

Kyra fetched a robe while trying to think of what to do next. She hadn't planned to sleep with Marco and now everything had changed. For now, she didn't need to chain him up—the storm had trapped him here with her. But what would happen when it let up? How could she keep Marco away from Daddy and the other war gods who would try to use him for their own purposes?

"So I noticed you aren't wearing a ring," Marco finally said, cutting around the burned edges of his dinner and into her thoughts. "Didn't you marry that asshole?"

Kyra didn't know anything about Ashlynn's life and wasn't sure she could keep faking it. Should she just reveal herself as a nymph now? Marco had told her his secrets, so why shouldn't she share hers? Because he might *kill* her, that's why, and she was every bit as trapped here by the storm as he was.

Kyra stirred the mashed potatoes in the tray. "Things didn't work out."

"Sorry to hear it," he said, taking a bite.

She glanced at him and saw his smug expression. "No, you're not."

"Sure I am…" His body language was all arrogance.

"You're not sorry, Marco."

"Okay, so I'm not sorry. I hated that guy. There's nothing worse than being in a war zone knowing that your buddy is back home stealing your girl. And you know what else? While we're telling the truth here, I don't remember you caring so much about toppled governments. I must've written you a hundred letters about Rwanda, and you never took an interest. All you wanted to know was when I was coming home and what flavor wedding cake we should have. Remember?"

Kyra was developing a distinct dislike for the woman who she was pretending to be. What kind of silly, self-absorbed little girl had Ashlynn Brown been? But maybe that wasn't fair. Marco was remembering a teenage girl, not a woman grown. "Don't you think people can change?"

He stared down at his fork. "Sure. Just not usually for the better."

He was going back to that dark place inside himself where he was so much harder to reach. She had to stop him, distract him. She slid her tray over to him. "You can have the rest of mine… It's all burned and…really terrible. I guess it's not exactly the kind of fare a big shot like you is used to."

"Maybe not, but I've seen too much starvation to turn my nose up at food," he said, taking her tray. "This would be a feast for some kids. And when I'm out in the field, I eat MREs."

As the storm continued to howl outside, Kyra settled farther down into the corner of the sofa, pulling the bathrobe around her for warmth. "An MRE?"

"It's a military acronym. Meals Ready to Eat," Marco explained. "You can eat them cold, or add a little water, or heat them up."

So he really did still think of himself as a soldier; it's just that he was fighting a war all by himself. "Do you steal them from the army?"

There was just enough offense in his tone to let her know she was crossing a line. "I wouldn't steal food from soldiers. You can buy MREs at any good camping store."

"Let me get this straight…" Kyra said, appraising him anew. "You'll steal weapons and resell them, but you won't steal MREs?"

"It's totally different," he said, as if she just didn't get his moral code.

"Why *do* you steal weapons, anyway?" she wondered. "There are enough folks involved in illegal arms trade that would sell them to you."

"I don't want them to profit from it."

She noticed he was rubbing his shoulder again and her guilt bubbled back up. After the accident, he'd been worried about calling an ambulance for her. It hadn't occurred to her she should call one for him. "Do you need some—uh, some medicine? For your shoulder?"

"No. My shoulder always hurts," he explained. "There's still a bullet fragment in there."

Kyra had seen it, sensed it, a little sliver of evil embedded in the bone. She couldn't stop herself from reaching out to touch it, and when she did, his fingers tangled with hers. "Ashlynn, don't."

She ignored his warning. "You insulted me before, when you said that I'd only slept with you because I was afraid of you."

"I'm sorry," he said, his expression sincere. "But you *are* afraid of me. I see it in your eyes."

Kyra looked up, lifting her chin. "There are a lot of things that people want that also make them afraid."

His grave look turned just a little bit smug. "Like what?"

Like love, Kyra thought. Everybody wanted it, and everyone was desperately afraid of taking the risk. But she said, "People are afraid of change. People are afraid of knowing too much about problems that seem overwhelming to solve." That struck a chord in him, she could tell, and when his fingers closed tighter around hers it seemed as if she couldn't pretend to be Ashlynn Brown for even one more second. "People are afraid to tell the truth. I need to tell you the truth about something, but I'm afraid to. I need you to promise…"

"Promise what?" Marco asked, dipping his head closer to her.

What did she want him to promise? Promise not to kill her? Promise not to leave? Nymphs always asked mortal men to make that promise, and they never kept it. Never. Kyra's voice quavered. "I need you to promise that you'll believe me."

He was about to answer her—his lips were actually parted in promise—when a loud creaking noise erupted from the basement, startling them both. "It's your pipes. They might be freezing."

Cursing under her breath at the interruption, she watched him get up. When Kyra bought this stupid old house, plumbing wasn't something she'd worried about. All she'd cared about was whether or not she could fit a man-size cage in the basement.

Oh, no, the cage! "Marco, wait!"

"I'm going to go check your pipes," he said, and in a few purposeful strides he was already halfway there. "Is this the basement door?"

"No!" Kyra nearly shrieked the word, rushing toward

him. She could well imagine what would happen if he went down into the basement and saw the dungeon she'd made for him. No amount of explaining her good intentions would make him forgive her.

Marco's hand rested uneasily on the doorknob. Confusion swirled in his eyes. "It's not the basement?"

"Please, just don't." Here he was, poised at the basement stairs. All she had to do was let him go down and follow him with the knife and handcuffs she'd secreted for just this purpose. But that's not what she wanted. That's not even who she wanted to be anymore. She didn't want to be Ashlynn Brown, and she didn't want to be a hydra slayer, and she didn't want to be Marco's captor. "Just please don't go down there."

Marco searched her face, as if trying to understand. He reached up, tilting her chin to look at her. To look at *Ashlynn*. Never before had holding on to the appearance of another woman been so painful. She wanted to let him see her, the real nymph beneath the illusion, but before she could reveal herself, everything went dark.

Marco found himself plunged into darkness, holding a woman who had looked, only moments before, as if she were going to shatter. "Your power is out," he said, trying to soothe her. "It's just the storm. That's all."

"Don't go," she said, clinging to him fiercely.

An unnamed emotion tightened in his chest. *Don't go.* She'd asked him that when he was just a kid, and he hadn't listened. He wanted to serve his country. He wanted to make sure that the things that happened to his mother never happened to anyone else. He wanted to do something good in the world and Ashlynn had tried to hold him back. He'd judged her for it. But maybe some part of her had known what he'd see in war and wanted to protect him.

"Ashlynn," he said, waiting for his eyes to adjust to the light. "What were you trying to tell me before?"

"You won't believe me," she whispered.

"I'll believe you," Marco said, resolved. "I promise."

In the blackness, all he heard was the sound of her breath, ragged. All he felt was the trembling of her shoulders. All he could smell was her hair, smoky and alluring. And all he could see was a strange, flickering light in her eyes... "I want you," she said.

And he believed her.

This time she led him to the bedroom and there was no shyness, no strangeness, no barriers between them at all. She was different in the dark. She became something wilder, more elemental, something utterly raw. And as she kissed him, all he wanted to do was fling her onto the mattress. Yet, when she reached beneath his bathrobe to curl her fingers around his shaft, the white-hot pleasure of it kept him still. She was wickedly talented with her hands and she gave him sweet, painful tugs that sent him careening toward the edge.

She was all in shadow—only the light of the moon outside showed him the silhouette of her sleek body— and he wanted to take things slow this time, to treat Ashlynn with the respect she deserved. But the way she stroked him filled him with an urgent and burning need. His breath went ragged and his fists clenched at his sides as he struggled to regain control. But then she crawled over him and straddled his hips. He was so hard it was almost painful, and when she teased him, grinding herself slowly along the length of him, he felt her wetness. He found her hair in the dark and made fists of it, pulling her body down onto his cock. She let out a cry as he filled her, and once he was buried all the way, she thrashed atop him with a violent, rocking motion. He was half-afraid she was going to hurt herself, or him, or both of them.

He wanted to flip her over and ram himself into her again and again, but her thighs were too strong around his waist. He tried to guide her with his fingers, letting them dig into the flesh of her hips, but she wasn't something he could tame or control. As she rode him, her thighs tightened like a vice around his hips and her body battered against his. *More combat than sex,* he thought.

As they moved together, he caught glimpses of her in the dim moonlight, which made her skin almost translucent. Atop him, she was some goddess of the night, exorcising his demons, scourging his skin with the hot whip of her dark hair. She was frenzied, but he matched her stroke for stroke.

This side of Ashlynn was one he'd never seen before, and it made him want to consume her. Mark her. Make her his. It wrecked him. Destroyed him. His reason was gone. Every cry, every desperate sound, every undulation, turned him on more. It also made him fiercely protective. This was a side of Ashlynn she'd plainly been hiding from the world. Or maybe just hiding from him, for fear that he'd somehow crush it like he crushed everything else good and beautiful.

"You don't have to hide anything from me," he rasped and her touch faltered, her sweat-soaked belly quivering with pent-up want. He knew she was close to the edge, but she seemed to be trying to make him come first. So he held back and he teased her, liking the sense of mastery that it gave him. She arched her back to take him deeper, balancing awkwardly with one hand on the mattress. He braced her at the small of her back, and heard himself saying, "I won't let you fall. I'll never let you fall."

And then they came together, a throaty cry from her that mingled with his shuddering release.

Chapter 9

Kyra let mortals see only what she wanted them to see and, for her, sex had only ever been a way of filling empty hours. A way of feeling needed, a way of letting the pleasure crowd out all the dark thoughts in her head. Over the centuries, there'd been times when she could've let sex become something more—but whenever the opportunity came, she'd let it slip away. If there was ever a time when telling the truth would've brought about intimacy, she lied. If there was ever a time that letting a man look her in the eye would've shown him her heart, she looked away.

That was how she lived, how she survived, as a *lampade* and a daughter of Ares. As a nymph, anything else was to invite her own destruction. So why did it suddenly make her so sad that the man whose body was tangled with hers couldn't see the truth of who she was? Maybe because Marco—whose breath was finally steady and untroubled as he slept—had no idea who he held in his arms. He had no idea *what* he held in his arms.

She'd called him a monster, but she was a dark creature, too.

Was it so wrong to have let herself feel like a woman, buoyed with airy desire, for just a few moments? Even now, Kyra could feel nothing else but the places on her body where he'd touched. It reminded her of how his fingers had pressed into her hips. The way he'd held her at the small of her back and promised not to let her fall. He'd taken her breath away, and for those precious moments, she'd pretended there were no secrets between them. But that had been a lie. He didn't know that she'd once tried to kill him. He didn't realize that the woman he'd just slept with had lured him here with the intention of chaining him up like an animal. In fact, he didn't realize that he'd had sex with *her* at all. He'd told her that she didn't have to hide from him, but he didn't know she was a nymph, and he'd only leave her if he did.

That's how it always happened. Men came into the lives of nymphs and held them so tightly they thought they could never fall. Then men left and didn't even glance back to watch as a nymph tumbled down, like a fallen angel, crumpled and broken on the ground. Kyra had seen it all before.

Calypso had been sexy and alluring. She'd rescued Odysseus from the sea and loved him. But in the end, Odysseus preferred his modest and mortal Penelope. Calypso wasn't the only one. There was also Clytie—a spirited nymph who loved and lost Apollo, then grieved herself into stone.

That's how love stories ended for Kyra's kind. Men pursued nymphs with urgency, told them they were sexier than mortal women, wild and untamed. Men told them they were loved just as they were…and then abandoned them. One way or another, the love of a man always changed even the strongest, most danger-ous nymphs, transforming them into something harm-less, like a tree, or a cloud, an echo.

Because she was *war-born,* Kyra had always thought herself too strong, too proud, to let love change her into something softer. Nevertheless, the world had changed, and now she was changing, too. She was tired of lying, tired of disguises. Millennia worth of tired. But she'd earned Marco's trust in the guise of another woman. Now she'd have to keep on pretending, and for that, she had no one to blame but herself.

On the pillow beside him, Ashlynn's cheek glowed pink in the light of rosy-fingered dawn. Marco caressed her innocent face, wondering how it could belong to the woman he'd made love to last night in the dark.

They had been good in the dark. Better than good.

Ashlynn had always been a fine-looking woman, but all he had to do was think of the shape-shifting assassin in Naples to remember what pure lust felt like. *That* woman had been half-dressed and wearing brothel perfume. He knew what lust felt like, and this was something better. This thing with Ashlynn was... something else. It was grief-sex. It was need. But it had somehow turned into more than just skin against skin. More than just the taste of her. More than the erotic sounds she'd made above and beneath him. It'd been different. Not just different than the series of trysts that had filled the past years his life, but different than it'd ever been with Ashlynn before.

When they were high school sweethearts, her innocence frustrated him to no end—especially when it made her so vulnerable to guys on the make—but she was no longer a shy ingenue who blushed at the sight of a naked man. No. She'd changed, and for the better.

And she knew his secrets. She knew what he'd done, what he was, and still wanted him.

He'd lost himself in Africa but, last night, she'd found him again. Since Rwanda, Marco had taken on so many different faces that he'd become anonymous to himself; she'd helped him remember who he was. She'd compared him to a monster, but somehow made him feel more human than he'd ever felt before. She'd pulled him free of the darkness as surely as he had pulled her from that icy drainage ditch. She'd been a beacon of light on one of the darkest nights of his life and he didn't know how the hell he was ever going to thank her for it.

Every muscle screamed as he moved, but he rose carefully so as not to wake her. It was a new day. A beautiful day, actually—the sunlight glistening off the ice-encased trees outside to illuminate a winter wonderland. It was the kind of day that made him wonder if maybe the world wasn't quite as irredeemably screwed up as he thought it was. Maybe today, he really could decide to change his life. But whatever he decided to do with this day, it'd have to start the same way. He'd have to get dressed, hike up the road and find a phone.

He slipped into Ashlynn's laundry room to get his clothes and the first thing he noticed was that there wasn't any laundry—just his stuff in the dryer and Ashlynn's coat in a basket. The second thing he noticed was that the coat in the basket was making some kind of music, like a funeral dirge.

With a sense of dawning dread, Marco reached in

and found a pink cell phone with a macabre ring tone. He flipped it open.

"Kyra." It was a man's voice, and it was menacing. "I want you to listen to me carefully and consider the consequences of your actions. Return the file on the hydra and I'll consider forgiving you for what you've done to my armory in Bosnia."

For a moment, Marco felt as if he couldn't breathe. He felt as if something had hit him square in the chest and knocked the air right out of him. He just stood there holding the phone against his ear, all but deaf and dumb. "Do you understand me, Kyra? Defying me would be unwise."

Marco finally broke in. "Who the hell is this?"

Silence. Then a click—the end of the call.

Some instinct—probably the same instinct that had kept him alive in war zones—told Marco to dial information and ask for Ashlynn Brown.

"Hello?" It was Ashlynn's voice. All restraint and sweetness.

Marco just stood there, listening to her breathe, as his worst fears were confirmed. Whoever he'd gone to bed with last night wasn't Ashlynn. It was the shape-shifting assassin from Naples. It had to be. But how the hell had she survived coming into contact with his blood?

Ashlynn's voice rose a bit. "Hello, is anyone there?"

The smart thing to do would be to hang up. He had his answer. That should've been enough. But instead, he found himself saying, "It's Marco."

There was a hesitation on the other end. Did he hear the laughter of children in the background? The scratch of a dog's claws on the kitchen linoleum? He could almost imagine her, coffee cup in hand, leaning up against the countertop with her hair in a tight ponytail behind her head. "Marco, I'm not sure calling me is a good idea."

He forced the words. "I came home for my father's funeral."

"I'm so sorry." There was a precisely measured amount of sympathy in her voice. "I went to pay my respects, but I didn't see you there. We must've missed each other."

So she *had* been at the funeral. Perhaps if he'd arrived a little earlier, everything would have worked out differently. Perhaps he'd be standing in *her* kitchen instead of in some creepy house out in the middle of nowhere with an imposter.

Who was the woman who had lured him to this house? What did she want with him? Why had she gone to bed with him?

"Marco," Ashlynn broke in. "You should know…

your sister told the police that you were at the funeral. The authorities were at my house this morning but I told them I didn't know anything. Which is the truth."

Marco closed his eyes. *Lori.* Swallowing down the bile of betrayal, he said, "I'm sorry you had to deal with that. I really am. I'd have thought with this ice storm, the police would have better things to do."

"They said you're wanted in connection with some missing weapons."

Marco kept his voice low and a wary eye on the bedroom door. "And you want to know if it's true?"

Another hesitation. "No. I don't want to know."

He could have predicted her answer, and it was just as well because Marco had already had this conversation with the woman impersonating Ashlynn the night before and wasn't sure he could do it again. "Are you happy?"

At that, Ashlynn gave a brittle laugh. "I'm getting a divorce."

"I'm sorry," Marco said, and this time, he was pretty sure he meant it.

"He ran off with his secretary," she said, again, very calm. Ashlynn was never one for big shows of emotion. "I suppose you'd have never done that, Marco. You were always the type to stick with a commitment to the bitter end."

Was she trying to pay him a compliment or point

out a character flaw? What surprised him was that he didn't really care. The emotions he expected at hearing her voice didn't come. Maybe it was because he'd already experienced them with a pretender. Maybe it was because he was *over* Ashlynn and had been for a long time, which made what happened last night with the stranger even more inexplicable. And it was something he was going to have to deal with sooner rather than later.

"Take care of yourself, Ashlynn," he said, then hung up the phone.

Chapter 10

Blinking awake, Kyra stretched like a cat in the unfamiliar bed. She reached for Marco but he wasn't there. He was sitting in a chair, fully dressed, his overcoat spread on his lap. She actually smiled at him until she realized he was pointing a gun at her.

"Who are you?" he snapped and before she could lie he added, "I just talked to Ashlynn—the *real* Ashlynn. I called her on the phone you said you didn't have."

So he knew. There was no point in denying it now. With a shudder, Kyra let go of Ashlynn's shape and let him see her true reflection. Her pale skin and the rest of her, too, hair and eyes black as night. To his credit, this time he didn't recoil. He just stared, as if confirming what he already knew. "So it's you again... and you're like me."

"No," Kyra said, mindful of the muzzle of the gun

pointed at her. "I'm not like you. At least, not in the way you mean. You're a war-forged hydra. Your blood is deadly and you take on the faces of people who've hurt you."

"So do you," he countered.

"No. I can look like anyone or anything or nothing at all."

He shifted forward in the chair. "What are you, then? And who sent you?"

"I tried to tell you last night. I—I *wanted* to tell you," she stammered. "I'm a nymph."

"A nymph?" he asked with a dark laugh of surprise. He'd lived with poisoned blood long enough to accept the supernatural, so it must have been something else that surprised him. "Those sweet spirits that live in rivers and woodlands?"

In spite of the night they'd just spent together, he obviously thought she was too malevolent an entity to be one of those. "Woodland spirits aren't the only kinds of nymphs. I'm a nymph of the underworld. The Romans called us *nymphae avernales,* but we're more properly known as *lampades.*"

He looked bemused but didn't lower his gun and she couldn't tell whether he believed her. When he spoke, his lips were curled with contempt. "And just what did you do to get turned into a nymph of the underworld?"

"I was born this way," she said, now eager for the whole truth to come out. "My mother was a priestess of Hecate and my father is Ares—"

"Ares?" He laughed again, but it wasn't a pleasant laugh. She worried he was going to pull the trigger. "From the Greek myths?"

"They're not all myths."

"No?" he asked. "So you're saying, what? Gods like Ares are real?"

"Oh, yes."

Marco pointed to the window. "You're telling me Artemis frolics out there through the ice-covered woods in a loincloth?"

"It's a bit cold here for her," Kyra said, her lips tightening as he mocked her. "But I'd appreciate it if you took me seriously. I'm trying to explain the world to you."

He snorted. "You want me to take seriously the idea that ancient gods exist? How do you know they're not just people with powers, like you and me?"

"They do exist, though not likely the way you imagine them and they're not like us. There are old gods of all kinds. Greek, Norse, Hindu, Native American… It's just that most of the oldest immortals no longer hold any sway in this world because people don't believe. But war is a part of every age. The people still call upon the war gods—even if they don't know their names. And when they call, the war gods answer."

"Well, I didn't call them," Marco said.

"Yes, you did. Every day you ship guns to some war-torn part of the world, you chum the waters for the war gods with human flesh. You feed them."

She expected him to deny or justify it. Instead, he asked, "What do you feed upon?"

She pulled the blanket beneath her chin, suddenly self-conscious of her nudity. "Struggle, I suppose," she murmured.

"What was that?"

"Struggle." Now she lifted her eyes in challenge. "I was a torchbearer of Hecate, dark goddess of door-ways, thresholds and crossroads. Maybe that's why I was attracted to you—why I still am. Because whether you know it or not, you're struggling and you need help. You know what you're doing is wrong and you want to change."

"A torchbearer…" For a moment, she thought she was getting through to him. He lowered the gun and his body language changed like it did when he confessed his secrets. But then something seemed to snap together in his memory. "Torchlight… I thought I saw a torch during the accident. You caused the accident."

"Yes," Kyra said, hoping a ready confession would make up for what she'd done.

But he raised the gun again, his mouth a hard, thin line. "You'd better tell me what game you're playing, or you're not going to live long enough to spin another lie."

"You can't kill me with that gun," Kyra said with more bravado than was strictly called for. Bullets would pass through her, but they'd also hurt like hell. "So just let me explain—"

"Explain what? Why you tried to murder me in Naples?"

She winced. "Yes. Among other things."

"Are you going to explain why you've got a basement outfitted like a dungeon? Who were you going to imprison down there?"

So, her cell phone wasn't the only thing he'd found while she was sleeping. There was no point in answering, but he let the silence stretch on and on until finally she blurted out, "You! Okay? I was going to lock you down there."

His eyes darkened dangerously, and with more than a little arrogance. "But I'm stronger than you, so you needed the tranquilizers, or sleeping pills, or whatever I found in your bathroom. Seduce me, then sedate me. Was that the plan?"

It had *not* been the plan only because she hadn't thought that far ahead. She hadn't known she was going to impersonate Ashlynn Brown until the moment she saw her. But Marco continued with his theory, anyway. "The problem is, I don't trust easy. You had to sleep with me twice before I trusted you enough to close my eyes, and by then, you were pretty exhausted yourself. Putting on such an enthusiastic sex show must have really tired you out."

"It wasn't a *show!*" Kyra sputtered, angrily. He shouldn't taunt her. Really, he shouldn't!

"Why so offended?" He sneered. "That's how you got me alone the first time, isn't it? You literally thrust yourself into my lap so you could stick a knife in my heart."

Heat came to her cheeks. "Yes, that's what happened the first time. But that's *not* how it was last night."

"Right."

Kyra's nostrils flared. "Last night I wanted—"

"I don't want to hear it. I don't know what you want from me, and I don't care."

Fine. It was time to make her intentions as naked as she was. "I want you to be careful of the war gods. I've told you that they exist. What I haven't told you is that Ares is looking for you."

"Why?"

"Because he collects monsters!"

He grimaced, as if she'd cut him again, and she supposed she had. "And you think I'm a hydra. That's what you were going on about last night."

"I *know* you're a hydra—"

"You're wrong. I wasn't born like this. I grew up just a normal man. Like anyone else. It wasn't until Rwanda—"

"You were *war-forged* there," Kyra stressed. "Monsters aren't all *born,* Marco. Some of them are *made.* What you said—sometimes in war you see things so toxic that they poison you—that's true."

"Then why aren't there thousands like me around the world? Millions!" he roared, slamming his free hand into the door next to his chair.

He was angry. Furious. And whether he knew it or not, he had the power to kill her. Kyra should've been terrified of him, but all she could think about was how to explain. "The circumstances have to be right. You were shot. The lead is still inside you, poisoning you. You're Greek…just think about your name… And your mother was—"

"Don't even speak of her," he warned. "And don't tell me I was born of some raping pig."

Kyra bit her lower lip. She waited until his breathing steadied before saying, "It doesn't matter how you became a hydra, Marco. It just matters that you *are* one, and that Ares is after you."

"For what?"

Kyra sighed. Wasn't it obvious? How could he be so dense? "For your poisonous blood."

"Well, he can't have it."

"You may not have a choice if he finds you. He could kill you and drain you of every drop. But more likely he'll try to bind you to him in oath. Daddy's like all the other war gods. They make it seem like what you're doing is just your nature, that it's your own idea, all the while extracting promises from you to turn you into a minion."

"Luckily, I don't make promises anymore," Marco said.

But he had. He'd made her promises last night, with his words and with his body. Some liked to say that skin doesn't lie—but Kyra knew better. And it hurt. She tried to shake it off, as much for his sake as her own. "The gods will want you to pledge to be their minion and they don't care a whit for your consent. They only care about claiming you as their own, so that other gods can't take you away."

"Well, I'm no one's minion," Marco snarled. "Are you?"

"I used to be." Kyra sat up straighter on the bed. "I was given to Hecate as an infant and swore myself to her when I came of age. But she freed me a long time."

He narrowed his eyes, as if trying to figure out what to make of her. "So as a hobby, you now go around assassinating arms dealers?"

She snorted. "You were my first."

He raised a suggestive eyebrow. "Somehow, I really doubt that."

"My first assassination attempt," she spit out. "I've killed other men and monsters in self-defense, but you were the first person I *tried* to kill outright."

"Should I be honored?" he asked, that voice of his low and dangerous.

"Look, Marco, Daddy had a file on you. He was looking for you—actively searching you out. So I took the file, I used it to hunt you down in Naples, and then I destroyed it. Don't make it all have been for nothing."

Something she'd said ignited a spark of recognition behind his eyes. "If Ares really exists, why can't he just snap his fingers and find me?"

Kyra tried very hard not to roll her eyes, and mostly succeeded. "Gods aren't all-powerful. They never were. Do you think Hera would have let Zeus get away with all his affairs if she could've just snapped her fingers and found him anytime she liked?"

Marco sucked slightly at his teeth. "How do I know you're telling the truth?"

She had no answer for that. "I know you think you're doing the right thing, but what you're doing is illegal—it's immoral."

"Yeah? Where were all these laws and morals when

it came to Rwanda?" he demanded. "Some people want to make it seem complicated, but the way I see it is very simple. Where do you think those genocidal Hutu militiamen went after they were kicked out of Rwanda? They went to Zaire, and the people there need guns to fight them."

"That's not what the people there need," Kyra said, though she wasn't prepared to debate global weapons policy in the nude. Since she was reasonably sure he wasn't going to shoot her, she found her underwear and started to put them on. He watched her bared breasts as she slipped into her bra, his face caught somewhere between arousal and contempt. And that's when Kyra heard tires crunching on the snow outside. "Someone's here."

He stood, starting for the bedroom door. "Yeah, I called the people that work for me. I just didn't expect Benji to be here so soon."

"But you can't leave," she blurted.

Marco hesitated only a moment. "Why not?"

There were many reasons, and not all of them had to do with her destiny or thwarting Ares anymore. She wanted Marco to stay because he needed her. Being with him made her feel like she still belonged in this world. But to admit such a thing to a mortal was self-destructive. He'd only leave her, anyway, and then she'd be like all the other sad nymphs who had changed into weeping trees and crying fountains and teardrops of amber. Kyra wouldn't let that happen. Never! "You can't leave because…because I need to convince you to let me hide you from Ares."

Marco snorted. "You can't convince me of anything, *Kyra,* because you've already told too many lies. Is that even your name?"

Kyra nodded, hurt that the first time she heard her name on his lips, it was with such disdain. "How did you know?"

"Because the man who called your creepy pink cell phone gave you away," Marco replied. "Who is he? Another guy you lured into bed?"

Bastard. Unable to look at him, she glanced out the window, her gaze turning as cold and hard as the ice that glittered on every surface outside. "If it was a man on the phone, it was Daddy. It was Ares."

"Right," Marco said, then turned around and walked out.

Kyra was too humiliated to chase after him. Instead, she sat there staring at the world outside the window. At the end of the driveway, in the ditch, she saw a large bird flapping around the crashed car. It'd been useless to try to explain herself to Marco and her mood was as black as that bird against the ice and snow. But the bird wasn't *all* black, was it? Even at this distance and through the trees, Kyra was sharp-eyed enough to see a glimpse of red on the bird's crest. Was that a *vulture?*

Marco was halfway into his overcoat, already bracing for the cold, when Kyra came streaking half-naked out of the bedroom after him. What the hell was wrong with him that his first inclination was to admire her body and her athletic grace? It was only his second thought that Kyra was a dangerous harpy who'd already tried to kill him. Twice.

"Don't come any closer," he said, raising his gun and aiming it at her. She was a few feet away and he was comfortable with this weapon. It was a Browning Hi-Power and there was no way he'd miss if he took the shot. But either she really *was* as immune to bullets as she claimed to be, or she had way too much faith in her sex appeal, because she didn't even break stride.

"Don't go out there!" Kyra shouted, bracing herself against the wall. She peeked out the glass by the door, like she was getting ready for some kind of shoot-out.

Now Marco wasn't sure whether he should be aiming his gun at her or out the window. Not taking any chances, he dived to the other side of the front door using the wall for cover. "Why not? What's out there?"

"It's not your ride. I'm pretty sure the woman outside doesn't work for you."

There weren't many women that worked for Marco, and nobody could confuse Benji's roguish silhouette for a female's, so she was probably right. "Who is it, then?"

It was probably the police, he decided. In the light of day, someone could have reported the wrecked car. But even if the police were here to arrest him, Marco wasn't about to get into a shoot-out with them. If it was the Russians or Chinese, on the other hand...

"It's a vulture," Kyra said.

Was that some kind of code? Marco wondered. "What's that? An exterminator? Was she the one who was supposed to get rid of the body after you were done with me?"

Kyra flashed him an exasperated look. "Just stay away from the door and give me your coat!"

He didn't like her bossy tone, but he was already warier of whatever was outside the door than he was of her. "Who is she?"

"I told you. She's a vulture. She belongs to Ares. If you don't let me shoo her away, she's likely to discover you here."

Was this supposed to scare him? "So what?"

Kyra folded her arms in front of herself, covering up the lacy bra he'd been too distracted to study in any detail the night before. "Okay," she said. "So you're pissed at me for a lot of stuff, including the fact

I planned to imprison you in the basement, right? Do you have any idea what Ares and his vultures could do to you? It'd make anything I'd planned for you seem pretty tame."

Nothing about Kyra was tame. Or normal. Nothing had made a damn bit of sense since his father's funeral and Marco wasn't sure he believed a thing she was saying. But for some reason, he could tell that *she* believed it, and until he had a better idea of what was going on, that would have to be good enough. It was as clear to him as it was to her that he wasn't going to shoot her, so he lowered his gun.

"Now give me your coat, and hurry," she said. "I can't go out there in my underwear."

"What? Suddenly shy?" he asked sarcastically, shrugging out of his overcoat and tossing it to her.

"It's cold!" she said, pulling it on and hastily fastening the buttons.

Then the doorbell rang. Yeah, definitely not his crew. Benji would have picked the lock before ringing the bell. So Marco positioned himself in the hallway, just out of the line of sight, gun at the ready.

As Kyra opened the door, a frigid gust of wind blew snow into her eyes. Then she found herself face-to-face with her father's creature. Kyra hated vultures—both the regular birds and the ones that Ares took for minions. Like *lampades,* vultures hovered at the threshold between life and death, but their purpose was only to feast on the decay. Vultures had no care for the living, nor the shades of the dead. Kyra had even seen them circle over the dying, mocking them. Because of that, and because they were Daddy's special creatures, it was difficult for Kyra to hide her distaste.

Anyone else might see the uninvited visitor as a beautiful redhead, all bundled up in a black ski vest. But Kyra's inner torch revealed a scraggly buzzard's soul with tattered black wings. Luckily, when the vulture looked at Kyra, all she'd see was a little old woman in a bathrobe.

"Can I help you, dear?" Kyra asked, projecting an illusion of frailty.

The vulture smiled beneath her sharp nose. "Actually, I was passing by in my truck and noticed the wreck at the end of your driveway. Do you need me to call anyone? An ambulance? A tow truck?"

Kyra tried not to snort at the vulture's feigned solicitude. Instead, she hunched forward, letting her voice quaver as if she were ninety. "Oh, aren't you sweet to ask, but emergency services have already been called." These kinds of lies came easily to Kyra, and at this moment, she'd have said anything to get rid of Daddy's minion. "They'll send a tow truck later today when the roads are more passable. Thanks for stopping by, my dear!"

With that, Kyra started to close the door. But the vulture stopped her. "It's just that my sister Kyra was driving this way last night. We haven't heard from her today and, after a storm like this, we're worried. I was wondering if you saw the woman in the accident, if you could describe her."

They were certainly not sisters, but the vulture had such an honest look of concern on her face that Kyra had to admire her skill. She was almost as good at lying as Kyra was. Two could play this game. Kyra chuckled, still giving the illusion she was shrunken and old. "Oh, I saw the accident happen from my front window but there was only a man in the car. Just an older gentleman like myself. It's easy to lose control on this ice."

"Then where did this come from?" The vulture's mouth tightened like a sharp beak as she held up Kyra's peridot choker.

Her mother's choker! Kyra must have been too stunned by the accident to realize it was missing. When it had still been around her throat, Kyra had simply disguised it as a set of Ashlynn's pearls. Once it broke free of her body, though, even a stupid vulture could recognize it for what it was. Now it was all Kyra could do to suppress the urge to snatch her choker out of the vulture's filthy claws. "That is a lovely piece," Kyra said. "I hope you can return it to whomever it belongs to."

The vulture came closer in the doorway. The red-haired woman bobbed her head slightly, her nose just by Kyra's ear, and then she sniffed. Kyra let her approach. She wasn't afraid of the vulture. But she tensed nonetheless, knowing that Marco's scent was in the house, on her hair, on her skin...

"Oh, Kyra," the vulture said. "You should know better than to try to hide from me as an old woman. Don't you know I can smell decay?"

Damn it to Hades. Kyra *should* have known better. Vultures like this one could sniff out age and death years away.

"In fact," the vulture said, with a puzzled tilt of her head. "Have you been ill, Kyra? I think you must not be feeling well lately. I swear I can scent your mortal side—not enough ambrosia, *my dear?*"

Enough was enough. Releasing the shape of the old woman, the nymph emerged as herself, eyes fierce as midnight. "Careful how you speak to me," Kyra warned. The vulture might be Daddy's minion, but she was also mortal, and Kyra would enjoy putting her in her place. "What are you doing here?"

"I've come for the file on the hydra," the vulture replied.

"It's gone. I destroyed it. And Daddy's backup, too."

"Pity," the vulture said, her breath puffing steam into the cold morning air, arms fluttering a little impatiently at her sides. "I come with a message from Ares, but I didn't expect to have to follow you all the way to the New World to deliver it. What are you up to, little nymph?"

What was Kyra to say? That she'd come to Niagara Falls as a tourist? "I came to guide someone to the underworld."

"Poor little Kyra," the vulture said. "Always looking for a purpose, never finding a place to belong. Haven't you figured out that no one needs you to guide them anymore?"

The vulture was needling her, trying to get beneath her skin to feast upon the festering emotional wounds there, and Kyra struggled not to let that happen. Even so, the vulture continued to taunt her. "How difficult it must be to live as a cast-off minion whose goddess doesn't even want her anymore." Kyra felt the heat of rage come to her face and the vulture smiled. "Ares would have you serve him…"

"*Never,*" Kyra said. That was never going to happen. "So you can stop following me. How did you find me, anyway?"

The vulture gave another sniff. "I've been on your trail since you destroyed the arsenal in Bosnia."

Kyra supposed she shouldn't have been surprised. Bosnia was very near to where ancient Thrace had been. Near her father's homcland, where his powers were strongest. Kyra had known her interference there would irritate him. In fact, she'd chosen the place *because* it would irritate him. But that was before—when she had no one to protect but herself. "Well, tell Daddy that I'm sorry about that."

"Oh, he knows you're sorry. At least, he knows you will be," the vulture said, reaching out with long, slender fingers to caress Kyra's cheek. "Once I'm done with you."

Kyra swore she heard Marco's breath catch in the hallway behind her and determined to show no fear before this creature. "So he sent you to punish me?"

"Oh, yes, Kyra," the vulture said with relish. "I'm going to chain you down and feast on your liver for days. And you've chosen such a perfect, isolated spot for me to do it. No one will hear you scream."

Kyra's blood ran cold. She could all too vividly imagine how it would feel for the vulture's sharp beak to pierce her flesh, to yank out her insides, to torment her with pain and the stench of dismemberment.

"You've gone paler than usual," the vulture said. "As well you should. For an immortal like you, time passes so slowly. You'll be in agony, of course, but you'll heal, and every time you do, I'll tighten the chains that bind you and tear at your flesh again until you're begging for forgiveness—"

"How original," Kyra snapped, for it'd been one of Zeus's favorite punishments in the old days. "There's only one problem. You're not strong enough to put me in chains."

The vulture must have seen something dangerous in Kyra's eyes, because she took a step back. Not fast enough. In a snap second, Kyra had her by the wrist. The first thing she did was take back her mother's peridot choker—infuriated that it had ever been touched by the vulture's defiling hand. The second thing Kyra did was shove the vulture back against the door frame with all her strength.

At the sudden impact, icicles fell from the gutter and shattered on the porch around them. Meanwhile, the vulture's eyes went wide with mortal fear. Kyra had her by the throat and wasn't letting go. As the red-headed woman struggled for breath, Kyra snarled, "If you want to survive the day, you'll keep your claws off me."

The vulture's scarlet lips parted in surprise, then curled into a malicious smile. "You wouldn't harm me, Kyra," she choked out. "I'm under your father's protection." Kyra's grasp loosened a little and the vulture brought her face so close Kyra could smell her carrion breath. The vulture's eyes lit up with an almost sexual thrill. "Besides, little nymph, Ares commands you to submit to me."

"Maybe some other time," Kyra said, letting go of the filthy creature.

The irony was that Kyra never saw the gun. She'd already spun for the open door—ready to slam it in the vulture's face—when she felt the cold muzzle against her side. "Don't be a tease," the vulture said, poking Kyra with the pistol and shoving her back into the house.

Kyra's hands went stiff at her sides as she found her balance in the threshold of the foyer. Marco was just beyond, hidden behind the archway. She hoped he'd be smart enough to stay there. "Oh, I never tease," she said. With that, Kyra jerked her elbow into the vulture's stomach. With the vulture off balance, Kyra spun and punched her square in the face. The woman's face snapped to the side, blood spurting from her nose. Kyra pressed the advantage, grabbing for the muzzle but just then, the vulture pulled the trigger.

Pain exploded through Kyra's left side, deep into her hip. She felt the crack of bullet against bone, the sickening pierce of the metal as it passed through her flesh in one side, then out the other. Wood splintered behind her as the bullet lodged itself in the parquet floor where Kyra dropped in agony.

Groaning, she put her hand over the wound as blood flowed between her fingers and a pool of it fanned out beneath her. Lying there gasping, the darkest rage welled up in Kyra. She promised herself that when she got up, she'd tear this vulture limb from limb. It was the bloodlust in her. It was the legacy of Ares. She was perhaps her father's daughter, after all, and for just this moment, she didn't mind. "Do you know what happened to the last person who shot me?" Kyra cried, her war-born nature rising with a little thrill at the memory of how she'd gutted the Bosnian who tried to rape her. Oh, yes, she'd enjoy tearing this bird woman apart, feather by feather, with her bare hands. "You might as well put that silly gun away."

"Oh, I know bullets won't kill you, but shooting you slows you down a bit."

Kyra tried to stand, determined to wipe that smug look of satisfaction off the vulture's face, but then she toppled back down into an inelegant heap. What was the matter with her?

"You're not so close to home," the vulture explained, as if reading Kyra's mind. "Your powers aren't as potent here in the New World."

No, something else was wrong. Why was it taking her so long to heal these days?

The vulture closed the front door and circled around Kyra in the foyer. She took her time, too, heels clicking on the wood floor until she was looming over Kyra, ready to fire again. "Hold still, Kyra. This time I'll get the liver."

Kyra braced for the agony of the second bullet, but it never came. Instead, there was a sickening crack—the distinct sound of some heavy object against flesh and bone. The sound a gun made as it struck the back of someone's skull. Then the vulture collapsed on the floor.

Chapter 11

The vulture slumped over and Marco stepped out of the shadows, gun in hand, held like a club. "What the hell did you do?" Kyra cried, her bullet wound finally starting to close up, flesh mending over flesh.

"I saved your life," he growled. "You can thank me anytime."

Saved her life? She had everything perfectly under control before he interfered.

Kyra started to get up, but Marco growled, "You're shot. Stay down, damn it!"

"I already told you, bullets can't kill me," she said as he maneuvered over the prone form of the vulture with the precision of a combat veteran. He pried the gun from the vulture's hands and kicked it out of the way before crouching down to feel for a pulse. "I was going for a blow to the side of the neck, but she turned her head. . . In any case, she's still alive."

"Not for long," Kyra replied, retrieving the gun from the floor where Marco had kicked it. If she could have had a picture of his astonished face as she stood and walked on what had clearly been a shot to the hip, she would have framed it.

Kyra calmly aimed the pistol at the center of the vulture's forehead. Her finger, slick and sticky with blood, found the trigger and hovered over it. She was the daughter of a bloodthirsty war god. Daddy had always said Kyra was born to viciousness, bred for destruction. The vulture certainly wouldn't have been the first person Kyra had killed. So why couldn't she pull the trigger?

"If you shoot her, is she going to heal up?" Marco asked, his jaw sliding forward so that his face held a dangerous serpentine edge.

"No, she's a mortal and a monster. Just like you."

He glared. "Then either kill her or call her an ambulance."

"Why don't *you* kill her? *You're* the one who cracked her skull. I was just defending myself."

"I was defending *you*," Marco said, as if he couldn't remember why he'd bothered.

"Well, I don't need your protection. If you'd let me beat her unconscious myself, she'd never have known you were here. Now, if I leave her alive, she might remember that you hit her and she's going to report everything back to Ares."

Kyra could see that Marco was still having trouble wrapping his mind around everything. In spite of having lived with his own powers, he'd never truly accepted them as real. He'd thought he was mad like his mother, trapped in a hell of his own making. She guessed that now he realized that if he was in hell, he wasn't the only resident.

"So, kill her, then," he said, his eyes narrowed. "You picked up a gun in need, didn't you? In the end, all your fancy lectures about perpetuating violence don't mean a thing in the face of actual danger, do they?"

So he thought she was a hypocrite. And maybe she was.

Marco watched Kyra stand over the unconscious redhead, gun in hand. Her eyes were hard, her nostrils flared and those lush lips were tightly pursed, as if she were afraid she might say something that would tip the balance of life and death. If only the she-devil had shown this kind of hesitation when she tried to plunge a knife into his heart in Naples, he might've been able to forgive her.

"*Damn it.* If you had to get involved, Marco, why didn't you just shoot her in the head?"

"Why should I do your dirty work? For all I know,

you deserve everything she was threatening to do to you."

The woman—the vulture, whatever—was breathing shallowly. He could still feel her pulse at her throat, though he'd opened a wound at the back of her head, which was now dripping onto the floor beneath her. Add that to Kyra's gunshot wound and there was blood everywhere. Thankfully none of it was his, but it was triggering him. He was already seeing blood as it sprayed up from a ditch in Rwanda. He was seeing blood as it flowed red over all of the Congo. He needed to clean this up before he went crazy.

Meanwhile, Kyra lowered her gun. "How badly is she hurt?"

"Concussion probably," Marco said. He wasn't a medical expert, but he'd seen plenty of wounds. He'd been willing to call an ambulance when he thought Ashlynn needed one and the most troublesome questions the authorities were likely to ask were about the wrecked car. He had a false registration for that. He had a false face for that, too. But a shooting was going to involve more than traffic cops and Marco really needed to get out of here. "If you want to be on the safe side, take her to the hospital. I'm sure you've got a car stashed somewhere around here, all hidden away like your cell phone."

Kyra shot him a look, flipping that long black hair

over one shoulder. Now that she wasn't disguising herself, her hair was straight as a razor and sharply cut at the edges—just like her. "I left the car at the funeral home."

Just how many lies had the nymph told him? "Ah, of course. I should have wondered why you needed a ride home. I'm not usually such an easy mark. But then, my enemies have never tried to manipulate me at my father's funeral."

He could have sworn he saw a flash of hurt pass over Kyra's features, but then both of them heard a hideous gurgling noise. The woman he'd knocked out was stirring, but didn't open her eyes. At just this small show of life, Marco saw Kyra's stark look of panic. No matter what she said about not needing help, Kyra was obviously in some kind of danger. Truthfully, the redhead didn't look like much of a threat, but what did he know? Until this morning, he thought Kyra was Ashlynn, so looks could be deceiving.

Kyra was still wearing his overcoat, which was now bullet riddled and bloody, and she put the gun in the pocket. Then she crouched behind the vulture woman, grasped her beneath the armpits and began dragging her toward the kitchen. Marco was fascinated. "What are you doing?"

"Getting her into the basement," Kyra said, stopping every few feet to take a deep breath. "I don't know if she brought any of her friends with her and I don't want them looking for her. At least, not until you're safely away from here."

He knew better than to trust anything Kyra said to him, but her story about Ares and the war gods was all starting to take a dreadfully consistent shape. After all, the man on the phone had threatened Kyra, and it was a message Marco hadn't delivered. If he'd warned her about the phone call, maybe she wouldn't have been shot.

"Let me help you," Marco said, grabbing the unconscious woman's arms.

"I told you I don't need your help," Kyra said, as she staggered and fell. He caught her before her hands hit the carpet.

"What's wrong with you?" Marco asked, trying, but failing, to keep the genuine concern from his voice. "I thought you said bullets can't hurt you?"

"They *hurt* me a lot. They just won't kill me," she said, steadying herself and pushing him away. "Anyway, just go. Get out of here before Daddy's vulture wakes up and sees you."

It was sensible advice. So why wasn't he taking it? It was still icy outside, but he could just start walking. Better yet, he'd take the unconscious woman's car. He went over to her body, found the keys in the pocket of her ski vest and pocketed them. Now he could leave this damnable nymph of the underworld alone to deal with all this. But instead, he asked, "What if her friends come looking for her?"

Kyra lashed out like a wounded animal. "I dunno. But I have her gun. Guns solve everything, right? In any case, I'm fine by myself."

She was not fine. There was clearly something wrong with her. Though he wanted nothing to do with whatever drama Kyra had gotten herself into, he remembered all the threats the vulture woman had made about eating Kyra's liver. With an irritated grunt, he picked the redhead up into his arms, letting her bloody head loll back, and carried her to the basement door.

Kyra followed him down the stairs and kept her mouth shut until he reached the bottom stair. "Just put her in the cage," Kyra said, obviously winded.

Marco snorted. "How stupid do you think I am? You think I'm just going to walk into that cage and let you slam the door shut behind me and lock me in with her?"

"The last thing I want is to lock you in there with her. I don't want her to know you even exist!"

"Yeah, well, you can drag her the rest of the way yourself."

"So that you can slam and lock the door behind *me?*" Kyra asked.

Oh, this was rich. *She* didn't trust *him?* Marco

shrugged, setting the vulture woman down. "Guess you're just going have to take that chance, *Angel*."

She glared at him, and the two of them stood there, in this basement, the tension thick between them. This was the same woman who had tried to kill him. The same damned woman who had seduced him not once, but twice, in the guise of a former lover. It made him feel violated and furious. He wasn't giving in.

With a frustrated sound, Kyra grabbed the woman and dragged her a few feet into the cage. For a moment—just a moment—Marco considered slamming the door on both of them just as she'd feared he would. Then he could get some semblance of control over this situation. But he had no idea what powers the vulture woman had and whether or not she could really hurt Kyra the way she'd promised to.

Besides, he didn't like to think of himself as the type to reward trust with betrayal.

Kyra dragged the injured vulture only a few feet into the cage, then jumped back out and slammed the door to shut. "Go upstairs before she wakes up," Kyra said, pushing Marco, insistently. But it was too late. The vulture was already scenting the air. A few moments more and the vulture's eyes blinked rapidly as she looked directly at him. Thankfully, the bars were too close together for her to escape, even in her vulture form. "Let me out of here!"

"Give me one good reason why I should," Kyra panted, double-checking the lock.

"Because your father's vengeance will be terrible," the vulture threatened. "You know how much Ares enjoys punishments."

"Maybe he won't find out. Vultures disappear all the time," Kyra said, trying to instill a little fear of her own. And it worked, too.

When the vulture spoke next, there was a touch of panic in her voice. "You're not just going to leave me down here…"

"Sure I am," Kyra said, slumping back against the steel support beam for a breath. Being shot had weakened her far more than it should have, and she didn't want the vulture to know it.

But the witless creature was now fixating on Marco. "Who is the man?"

"If I were you," Marco answered. "I'd worry less about who I am and more about being nice to Kyra. She has your fate in her hands."

"Fate?" The vulture shuddered, as if her feathers were ruffled, then gave Marco a penetrating stare. "She can't let go of it, can she? Poor little lost nymph. Has she taken you for a lover to distract her from her troubles?"

"Yes," Kyra said quickly. There was no reason for her father's minion to know who and what Marco was. As long as Marco didn't take on another face right in front of the vulture, or bleed his toxic blood, no one had to know that he was the war-forged hydra Ares was looking for. Let the vulture think Marco was just a lover.

"Isn't he a pretty little pet?" Kyra asked, sidling up alongside Marco and tilting his face down so that she could kiss him. She felt him go stiff, anger brewing just below the surface of his skin, but he didn't pull away. He let her kiss him, her real lips against his real lips. And if she didn't know better, she would swear he kissed her back. The taste of him, the smell of him, the feel of him, brought back memories of the dark night before. But once again, it was all pretend.

When she pulled away from Marco, the vulture looked unimpressed. "Oh, Kyra, you've taken up with *another* mortal man?"

Marco's body went rigid by her side. Was it jealousy or stung pride? Remembering the way he'd accused her at gunpoint, mocking her in the very bed in which they'd been intimate, Kyra decided to make it sting a little more. She put her hand to Marco's cheek, luxuriating in the feel of the stubble there as it scratched her fingertips. "How could I resist these dark good looks? He looks like Narcissus in the right light."

Marco glowered as if he might break her hand if she touched him again. Even the vulture picked up on his foul temper. "You," the vulture called to him. "I can smell the irritation on you. You're already tiring of the nymph...you're angry with her. You don't have to do as she commands. Let me out of this cage, and I'll give you a reward."

"I've already got more money than I can spend."

"Then do it for spite. You know you want to get away from her," the vulture told Marco. "That's always the way with nymphs. They're so exciting at first, aren't they? So intense, so raw, so hard to resist. But they always get too attached, too emotional, too much for a mortal man to handle."

Kyra's jaw clenched, pained by the truth in the vulture's words, and a little dizzy, too. This weakness couldn't just be that she was in the New World. She'd been away from the Mediterranean before, farther away than this, and never felt so powerless. This was more like she'd felt after she was poisoned with Marco's blood. She was so tired. Too tired even to respond to the vulture's taunts. There was no point in it, anyway. She had to get Marco away from here—get him away from Ares.

Kyra turned toward the stairs and started to climb, motioning for Marco to follow. But before he could, the vulture continued, "Oh, I'll grant you, Kyra's a little different. She comes from the line of Ares—she's harder than most nymphs, less likely to be overcome with love than bloodlust."

Kyra's voice tightened over the lump forming in her throat. "Don't listen to her. She doesn't know anything about me." But why should it be so important to her that Marco knew the truth of her heart? He was just some criminal, some monster, some arrogant mortal man.

"Oh but I've known Kyra all my life," the vulture insisted. "She hasn't experienced the all-consuming obsessions so typical of her kind. But she was born a nymph, and it's a nymph's lonely fate she'll have."

All Kyra wanted was to get up the basement stairs, but she felt trapped by the fate of her kind—as trapped as if Marco had locked her in that cage.

The vulture crowed, "Of course, if you're really special to her, you'll change her when you go. Everyone knows that a nymph's lover never stays. Even she knows it. Why do you think she's fleeing up the stairs to hide her broken heart?"

Oh, if Kyra had her knife and just a little more strength, she'd carve this vulture up like one of those New World Thanksgiving turkeys!

"That's enough," Marco growled.

But the vulture ignored his warning. "She'll end up

some sad plant, mark my words. Maybe she'll go mad, like her mother."

That was one taunt too many. Marco slammed one hand against the cage. "Shut up! Just shut the hell up."

Kyra held her breath. Was Marco actually *defending* her? Or was it just that they both shared that special pain of losing a mother to mental illness? Marco took her arm and steadied her on the stairs. "Come on. We're going."

The vulture banged against the cage, her voice coming out in a series of woofs and chuffs distinct to her species. "You can't just leave me down here!"

"Why not?" Kyra returned. "You should die slowly, suffering, waiting for the rats to pick the meat off your bones. Isn't turnabout fair play?"

Marco helped Kyra up the last few stairs and locked the basement door behind them.

Flattening herself against the locked basement door, Kyra fastened her peridot choker around her neck where it belonged. Marco was coming toward her, impossibly close. In spite of everything, his proximity was potent. She could actually feel the heat of his body. She took a deep breath, fighting down her gratitude to him for having defended her against the vulture. Fighting her desire to be near him. Did he remember that this was the body he held in his hands, last night? That this was the skin he had kissed? That these were the eyes that guided him in the dark? Not Ashlynn's body, but hers?

But as always, Marco's mind was on weaponry. He thrust his hand into the pocket of the borrowed overcoat she was wearing, pulled the vulture's gun out and tucked it under his belt with his own weapon. "Nice friends you have," Marco said.

"I thought it was pretty obvious that vulture isn't my friend. But that's just the kind of person you're going to turn out to be if you fall into the clutches of a war god. They turn their minions ugly—uglier than they were before."

If her words were getting through to him, he wasn't letting it show. "Ah, I see. So you only tried to kill me to save me from such a horrible fate."

Damn him. "Aren't you ever going to let that go?"

"What? That you tried to kill me?" He gave an incredulous snort, lifting his hand to show off the jagged scar she'd left him that night in Naples. "No, I'm pretty sure I'm not going to let it go. Even if I could get past it, there's still the fact that last night I slept with a woman who looked like my ex-fiancée, but who turned out to be a homicidal maniac with Daddy issues, relationship baggage and a penchant for locking people in cages."

"I'm not a homicidal maniac!" Every fiber of her

being seemed to scream out in protest against that accusation most of all. "I'm not really going to leave the vulture down there to die, you know. As soon as we're both far away from here, I'll make an anonymous call."

Marco sighed, but didn't argue. Instead, he took a kitchen towel and walked into the foyer, where, to her amazement, he stooped down to wipe up the blood.

"Haven't you been listening to anything I've been saying?" Kyra asked. "We need to get out of here! Ares could come looking for his vulture at any minute."

"I'm not leaving the place all bloody like this. Besides, I need to wipe the house down so that none of my fingerprints are left behind. It's bad enough we're leaving her alive to give a description of me."

Kyra was so frustrated. In her day, no one ever had to worry about things like fingerprints or DNA. Now with the humans cataloging everything and keeping track, technology was intrusive enough to make immortals despair of retaining their divine mystery. "If you'd just done what I told you, the vulture wouldn't have seen your face."

"I stopped following orders a long time ago," he said.

She watched Marco methodically clean, erasing himself from the place as if he'd never been there. As if he wished he'd never touched anything, or anyone, in this house. Kyra bit her lip, an ache in her chest that went well beyond exhaustion. "I'll finish up here, Marco. I'll make sure there are no traces of you—I owe you that much. You can go. Get out of here before the police come or more vultures arrive."

"I'm still waiting for my ride," Marco said without meeting her eyes.

Kyra dug into the bullet hole in the floor with one toe. "Now who's lying? I saw you snatch the vulture's keys from her pocket."

He actually looked abashed. That surprised Kyra. She wouldn't have expected that a man like him—one who lived in a world of thieving, lawbreaking and as-sumed identities—could be shamed by being caught in a lie. But he was. "I'm going to take her car and leave, but I want to make sure that you're okay first. I don't believe almost anything that comes out of your mouth, but it *does* sound like some guy's got it out for you. If he finds you, what's he going to do to you?"

"Don't worry," Kyra said with as much bravado as possible. "I won't tell my father that you're the hydra he's been looking for. I hold up well under torture."

"He'd torture you?" Marco's lips thinned and he shoved his hand through his dark hair. "Look, let's both just get the hell out of here, then. If you clean up and get dressed, I'll take you with me as far as Toronto."

He'd take her with him. Kyra's heart beat just a bit faster and she muttered a silent curse at herself. It was always this way for nymphs. Reading far too much into a man's words. Wanting to believe they meant something they didn't. "Marco, after the way I tricked you, why would you help me?"

"Because you helped my mother."

Chapter 12

Marco put on his sunglasses to guard against the glare, then eased the SUV down the icy driveway. In the passenger seat beside him, Kyra was quiet. The only sound was the snow and glass crunching beneath the tires; they were leaving a whole lot of wreckage behind—and not just the smashed-up car in the ditch.

Underneath it all, he was still filled with rage. Last night, he'd trusted her. He'd shared with her his darkest secrets and she'd betrayed him. He'd never had an inherent distrust of women—not even after what happened with Ashlynn. But right now, everything about Kyra seemed like an embodiment of sexy feminine deceit. And as if that weren't bad enough, she was annoying him by adjusting and readjusting the side mirror. "What the hell are you doing?"

"I'm watching for kettles of vultures," Kyra said, as

if this were the obvious answer. "Or really, any suspicious birds. Daddy and the other war gods like them. Eagles, owls, vultures—almost any kind of raptor..."

She sounded batshit crazy, but he was starting to believe her. Or maybe he just *wanted* to believe her because it made him feel like less of a dupe. What she'd done to him wreaked havoc on his emotions. But he'd enjoyed himself, hadn't he? Last night he'd made her scream in pleasure and it should've made him feel smug, but it just made it difficult to keep his hands steady on the wheel.

He tried to forget the way her wild abandon had affected him. He tried to force out of his memory the way it had felt to be inside her. She'd been pure sex, pure need. It had felt like the most honest thing he'd ever experienced in his life, and it had wrecked him. In fact, it must have bewitched him; how else could he explain why he'd *really* taken her with him?

He wanted a cigarette. Badly. But he'd be damned if he'd let her see that weakness in him so he grabbed a stick of mint gum instead. Probably for the better—he needed both hands on the wheel. Nobody should be driving in these conditions, but that meant the roads would be empty and that was a good thing.

When he passed up the ramp to the highway, Kyra said, "I thought we were headed for Toronto."

"We have to make one stop first."

He could have sworn that his brusque tone made crystal clear that he wasn't going to discuss it, but that didn't stop her. "Marco, don't you understand that we have to get as far away from here as possible? Do you *want* Daddy to hunt you down and turn you into one of his pets? I know I told you Ares isn't omniscient and all-powerful, but that doesn't mean he can't follow a trail."

Tension thumped behind Marco's temples. "My mother buried her husband yesterday and I don't know when, or if, I'm ever going to see her again. I'd like to say goodbye."

That shut Kyra right up. He could see she wanted to argue. Her lips parted—goddamn, those killer lips of hers—but then she snapped her mouth shut again and...turned into Ashlynn Brown. Her skin didn't reform itself—she just looked different whenever she wanted to, and it pissed him off. "Stop that right now."

Kyra obediently, and apologetically, shimmered back into her own form. "I just thought that if we're going to see your mother, I should look like someone she knows. She shouldn't have to see my real face."

"What's wrong with your face?"

"It's different," she replied.

In Marco's line of work, he'd seen a lot of unusual faces. Hell, he'd *worn* a lot of unusual faces. Faces of white men and black men. Asians and Arabs. He'd worn the faces of Tutsis and Hutus. And in the end, none of them were that different—though sometimes people treated him as if they were. "There's nothing wrong with the way you look, Kyra."

She wound her fingers in her lap. "My face frightens some people."

Glancing sidelong at her, he supposed he could see why. Her eyes weren't just dark, they were completely black—without pupils—like some kind of starless night. Her lashes were dark, too, as if someone had smudged them with permanent eyeliner. And when he wasn't too busy thinking about how hot her lips felt on his body, he could see that they were shaped like an intimidating archer's bow. But he liked them. He couldn't imagine anybody not liking them. "You have the face of an ang—"

"Don't say it," she snarled, turning in the seat to face him. "You were going to say that I look like a fucking angel, weren't you?"

He was caught off guard by her vehemence. "You sure don't talk like one."

She tensed in the seat beside him, her voice dripping with sarcasm. "So sorry that I'm not more like your demure little Miss Ashlynn in pearls and basic black with a perfect manicure."

That was a vivid—and accurate—description of

Ashlynn. And in truth, he should've known the difference between the two women last night. But the combination of nostalgia for his old flame paired with Kyra's fiery personality had been so potent, he hadn't wanted to question it. He'd just wanted to hold her down and spend himself inside her. Part of him still felt that need. He had to get it under control. "So why'd you pick Ashlynn to impersonate, anyway? If you can look like anybody, why her?"

Her silence, her reluctance to answer, hung like gunpowder in the air between them. Kyra just stared out the window, and for a moment her gaze was so intense he feared she was going to do whatever it was she did before to cause the car accident.

"Is that your mother's street?" Kyra asked as they came to the empty intersection—the one with only a few tire furrows in the snow. "Because the police are there."

Of course they were. Marco worked his jaw. "My sister called the authorities."

"I'm sorry," Kyra said, and actually sounded as if she meant it.

But Marco didn't want her pity. "What would you know about it?"

"I have siblings, too," Kyra confessed. "Most of them, more terrible than I could ever describe. My brothers—Deimos and Phobos—are the literal incarnation of dread and fear. I haven't spoken to either of them in centuries…but *your* sister is actually trying to do right by you. She might not know how to express it, but she's worried sick about you and the life you've chosen."

Marco snorted.

"It's true," Kyra said. "I saw it when I looked at her. And I don't just mean that I saw emotions in her eyes. I can see deeper than mortals with my powers."

"You're telling me you can see through people's bull-shit?"

"I can see through *anything* if I concentrate."

Marco actually hovered at the intersection, not sure if he should let the police arrest him or not. He hadn't chosen the life of an arms dealer to hurt his family. He'd chosen it because he'd made a promise to the victims of Rwanda. They had no real voice, no one to fight for them but the general, and even *he* couldn't do anything for them without the weapons Marco provided.

Marco kept driving.

After Kyra left an anonymous message with authorities that there was a woman locked in a cage in the basement, Marco used Kyra's cell phone to call Benji and tell him to turn around. As soon as they pulled into the parking garage beneath the Grand Palace Hotel, Benji was waiting with a crew, ready to dispose of the stolen car and get Marco out of the country. "We have a new mobile phone and papers for you upstairs," Benji said when Marco stepped out of the car. "You can be at the airport and on a flight within the hour."

"Good work," Marco said, tossing Benji the keys—though he probably didn't need them; Benji could hotwire a car in his sleep, but his attention was riveted on Kyra.

"What about the pretty girl, Chief?"

Marco watched as the young West African looked her up and down and gave her a flirtatious wink. Marco didn't like it. He also didn't like that the nymph was in disguise again. But Benji had asked the question of the hour. What the hell *was* he going to do with Kyra?

He'd kept his promise to her—he'd taken her as far as Toronto. He'd gotten her out of immediate danger. If he had any sense, he'd part company with the woman—nymph—right here and right now. But instead, he found himself saying, "Take her upstairs."

When Marco's young tough opened the passenger side and hauled Kyra out, it took everything she had to keep from slamming the kid's head against the hood of the car. But he had a gun and Kyra didn't relish the idea of being shot again today. In fact, this was the third time in one day that someone had her at gunpoint, and the mortal hubris was starting to infuriate her. The sudden flash of murderous rage must have shown in her face because Marco said, "Careful, Benji. She's a hellcat."

Benji grinned at her, trying to charm, rather than frighten her. "What fun is being careful?"

The young man's flirtation didn't surprise her—after all, he couldn't see her true form. When Benji looked at her, she made sure he saw some pretty thing who might welcome his attentions. What *did* surprise her was the way Marco's eyes darkened with a possessive warning. *She's mine,* they seemed to say. Then he actually reached out for her arm and physically yanked her away from Benji and into the elevator.

Why did that flash of petty human jealousy please her so much? She should have been offended by his blatant attempt to claim her. But if she'd learned anything about him in the past twenty-four hours, it was that the things Marco claimed as his own, he protected. The people, the places, the causes. And she couldn't help but wonder what it would feel like to have him care about her that intensely.

No. She couldn't let herself wonder that. That was just her nymph's nature trying to grasp at straws and turn them into hearts and flowers. Pathetic. She had to shake it off. "Just where are you taking me?"

"Behold my innermost sanctum," he said wryly. Just

then, the elevator doors opened to a luxurious suite. A quick glance around showed that it had an excellent view of the snowcapped Toronto skyline and the retreating storm clouds. Carved wooden masks adorned one vaulted wall, and the decor was done all in black, green and tans. The colors of Africa.

"You live here?"

He loosened his tie as the elevator doors shut behind them. "Sometimes."

Kyra rubbed her arm—he'd yanked her away from Benji so roughly that it actually still hurt. "It's a little extravagant, isn't it?"

"I suppose you live in poverty up on Mount Olympus, or wherever…"

"I live in a villa apartment."

Then she wished she hadn't said it, because it clearly made him curious. "In Greece?"

"No. In Italy. Where we met. I was born there near a shrine to Hecate."

One didn't reveal such things to mortals, and with good reason. His lips twisted in mockery. "And I suppose your villa apartment is just a modest little place. Just a comfortable bed for you and whatever guy you've picked up at the local nightclub."

Damn him. "I don't bring men there. I don't bring *anyone* home with me. Ever."

With that, Kyra stormed back to the elevator and

punched the buttons, since it seemed to be the only way out. Unfortunately, it also seemed to need a key. "What am I? Your prisoner now?"

Marco was already pulling off his rumpled jacket. "Turnabout is fair play. Isn't that what you said to the vulture, *Angel?*"

"Don't call me that." Kyra punched the elevator button again, for good measure.

"You can't escape that way," Marco said, pulling his tie free of his collar. She wished she didn't like the sound the silk made as it passed over his rough hands. "Even if the doors opened and you took the elevator to the ground floor, you'd just have to deal with one of my men."

It struck Kyra for the first time just how extensive Marco's organization was. He wasn't just a lone gunrunner. He had people who worked for him—probably all over the world. He'd made for himself his own little empire. "One of your men? Like the goon who stuck a gun in my ribs? What's his name? Benji?"

"He's harmless. I've known the kid since he was a teenager in Sierra Leone. He can crack a safe in seconds. He can smuggle a crate of rockets past customs officials in any country in the world without getting caught. But at the end of the day, I don't think he could ever hurt anybody."

"But I could," Kyra insisted. "I should have broken his arm."

He unfastened his shirt buttons, one by one. Gods, she loved the way he moved. "Are you really that vicious?"

"You don't want to find out," Kyra said, nostrils flaring. "I didn't have to come up here with you, you know."

"I know," Marco said, working at his cuff links. "But I knew you'd come peaceably."

"That was a risky assumption on your part."

"Not that risky." He stalked toward her, eyes locking on hers. She tried not to stare now that he had his shirt all the way unbuttoned. His chest was bared to her. "I knew you'd come. After all, we have unfinished business between us."

They certainly did, but the way he was closing in on her made her think that another discussion about arming the downtrodden peoples of Africa was not foremost on his mind. His hand came to rest on the wall behind her and he leaned in. His closeness was making her nervous and excited at the same time. So much so, that Kyra found her eyes dropping like some shy damsel.

He caught her by the chin and forced her to look at him. "I know you're not Ashlynn. You don't have to pretend you're demure."

The feel of his callused fingers brought back such sharp memories of pleasure that Kyra felt weak at the knees, just like in all those mortal movies where the fair damsel swoons away. And it wasn't just arousal; she could have handled that. No, this feeling was something different from lust, and wholly unfamiliar. She felt as if she was being turned inside out and it was more than she could bear.

He was going to kiss her. If she didn't stop him, he was definitely going to kiss her. And she *wanted* him to. But nothing had changed. She hadn't fulfilled her destiny. She hadn't conquered the hydra within him. She hadn't killed him. She hadn't captured him. And she hadn't even persuaded him to give up arms dealing. Everything Kyra had tried to do had failed, and she couldn't add a humiliating love affair to the list.

So when Marco tried to pull her into the kiss, she fled—actually fled—to the opposite side of the room. She had thought herself no coy Daphne to fly fleet-footed from a suitor, but now she was starting to understand why so many nymphs ran. He would change her—hell, he was already changing her. The only safety was in retreat. And yet, there was nowhere to go. She was stopped by the glass window that showed her the dizzying height at which she was being imprisoned. Staring out the patio doors that overlooked the city below, Kyra felt like she was in the sky, so high up, higher than Olympus—a discomforting height for a nymph of the underworld. It was why she hated flying. She didn't belong up here. And she didn't belong with this man.

"Afraid of a little kiss, *Angel*?" Marco chuckled.

"Aren't you in a hurry to get out of the country?" Kyra asked. "Do you really have time for this?"

Marco put a mocking hand over his heart. "Oh, I'm sorry. I wasn't aware that you were the kind of girl who needed leisurely wooing."

Kyra was about to make a scathing reply, but then he came up behind her and the words died on her lips. "You're an excellent actress," he said with his mouth by her ear, that incredible voice unraveling all her resolve. "But even you can't pretend you don't know where you want to end up."

"Where's that?"

"Underneath me," Marco said.

She found herself exhaling a breath she hadn't known she was holding. Maybe it was his words, or the sound of his voice, or the intimate sensation of his mouth that made a wondrous flutter go through her. A *flutter,* damn it! It was like some exquisite swarm of winter butterflies had been unleashed inside her, all vivid and angel-winged.

Gods above and below, Kyra had to put a stop to this. She was the siren seducer of men, not the seduced.

She took lovers and discarded them at her whim. Kyra broke away and turned to face him again. "I think you're a little too sure of yourself. What happened between us last night was—"

"What?" he broke in, his eyes narrowed in challenge.

It was nothing. It was fake. It was a ruse. It was just to trick you into my dungeon. There were a thousand lies she could have spun, but she couldn't seem to say any of them. Face-to-face with him like this, his breath warm on her cheeks she couldn't coax even one more lie to pass her lips.

This time he *did* kiss her and she let him. Really, there was not much choice in it. It might be the only thing that would stop her heart from slamming out of her chest. Besides, it was only a kiss. It couldn't possibly make her as vulnerable as she'd felt last night with him in the dark. *They'd been so good in the dark.*

Kyra closed her eyes at the taste of his mouth—some combination of mint gum and sorrow. Swaying with the sensation of his lips on hers, Kyra's arms went limp and it comforted her when he took her wrists and put them at the small of her back. He'd done that before, the first time he'd taken her to bed, but this time, he didn't pull her closer into his embrace.

Instead, she felt the cold bite of metal on her wrist.

"What are you doing?" she asked, half-dazed,

rousing herself too late to stop him from handcuffing her to the handle of the sliding door.

"I found these in your bedroom. Think of it as foreplay," he said, and for a moment, she almost believed him. She could feel the ridge of his arousal beneath his pants, hard against her thigh, but she didn't think this was sex play. Kyra gave a good tug, only to find she was well and truly fastened to the door.

She'd set out to capture him and now she was the one in chains. She started to struggle, but as he caught and cuffed the other wrist, his kiss smothered her angry protest. Her fury only ignited a scorching heat across her skin as he took full advantage of her arousal. His strong hands cupped and kneaded her breasts.

She tried to get her hands free to push him away, but when she tried, the cuffs only rattled against the door. If he'd been any other man, she would've bitten him and forced his tongue out of her mouth. But if she broke Marco's skin—if she made him bleed that toxic blood of his—it could kill her.

With his tongue tangling with hers and her nipples aching at his touch, she was completely at his mercy and it was sweeter than she could have ever imagined. She groaned when his hand trailed down her belly. There was no way of escaping the insistent fingers that slipped under the lace edge of her panties and stroked her. Even if there'd been a way to move out of his reach, his hand at the nape of her neck held her still. And gods help her, she liked it.

A sharp clench of sexual need tightened her belly. She swayed where she stood as he etched slow circles over the slick source of rapture between her trembling thighs. It wasn't right, it couldn't be right, to want a man this much. To have him touch her, arouse her, give her pleasure without being able to do anything in return…it made her so vulnerable she couldn't breathe. She started to inhale in short, panicked bursts.

And that's when Marco finally let her go. The sudden break of contact was like a gust of frigid winter air between them and she could see now that he'd only been toying with her. She yanked on the handcuffs again, to no avail. "You…you tricked me," Kyra rasped, blinking her eyes as if she could hardly believe a mortal had dared. "With a kiss!"

"Sure I did," Marco said, leaning against the sliding door as if he needed to steady himself. She watched as the temperature of the glass under his hand seemed to replace all his heated raw sexual power with something colder and angrier. "I tricked you into the handcuffs. I manipulated you, Kyra. And if it makes you feel even a fraction as violated as I feel because of what you did last night, then maybe you've learned something."

"But I wasn't trying to manipulate you last night!"

"No? What would you call impersonating another

woman so as to seduce me?" Marco shrugged out of his dress shirt and replaced it with a short-sleeved linen button-down that some helpful servant had left for him on the couch. She could plainly see that he was still aroused, but he continued to dress as if it were of no consequence. As if he'd mastered his sexuality in a way that she couldn't.

"It wasn't like that," Kyra argued. "After you told me what happened in Rwanda. I just wanted to reach out to you and make it better, to make it hurt less."

"Well, you did for a little while," Marco muttered, grabbing his coat and starting for the elevator. "But now as much as I'd like to stay and teach you all the other lessons you so richly deserve, I have a plane to catch."

Why wouldn't he even try to understand? Furious, Kyra yanked on the door handle until the handcuff bit into the skin of her wrist. "Where are you going?"

"Where I'm needed. One of my men will free you after I'm gone. But don't bother trying to rough him up for information. Only Benji knows where I'm going, and he's coming with me."

"But, Marco," Kyra protested. "Ares is looking for you. And if he finds you—"

"Kyra, I've heard you out. Thanks for the warning. But nobody is going to use me. I've made a commitment, and I've got to keep it. So don't look for me. Don't follow me. Just stay away."

And with that, he left her standing there chained to the door.

Chapter 13

The snow-laced streets of Sarajevo were disgracefully peaceful. How was Ares supposed to enjoy his coffee without even the occasional snap of a sniper's rifle to start his day? Worse, his vulture had returned with nothing but excuses. The sharp-faced redhead whined, "Kyra refused to submit to her punishment even after I told her it was at your command! And she says she's destroyed all the information you gathered on the hydra so that we can't even find him."

Ares put the coffee down and took her chin between his thumb and fingers, turning her head slightly to the side as her eyes fluttered down in submission. There was a gorgeous bruise on her face, livid and dark. "Kyra did this to you?"

"Yes," the vulture said. "Just before I shot her."

Ares admired the injury, delighting in the swelling,

sighing with satisfaction at the broken blood vessels and damaged skin. This little bit of violent art, painted in bold strokes of deep purple was a much more satisfactory start to his day.

"And this?" Ares asked, letting his hand trail up the vulture's neck to the bandage at the back of her head. "Kyra did this, too?"

"No," the vulture said, her eyes still on his feet. "I was surprised from behind by the man with her."

"A man?" Ares asked. "A mortal man?"

"Her latest lover," the vulture replied with a nod. "I could smell the attraction between them. Kyra was all but naked when she answered the door. And she had that sad look of a nymph who is falling in love."

The god sat bolt upright. *Kyra in love?* The possibility was so awful that Ares actually groaned. If his daughter had taken up with a satyr, a local river god or even some foreign deity he wouldn't have had as much cause to complain. But nymphs never chose sensible lovers. How had this come to pass? He knew Kyra was struggling to find her role in a changed world, but he'd been sure that, one day, she'd take her rightful place beside him in his war chariot. That would never happen if she let herself fall for some feckless mortal man.

She was a nymph; love would change her like it did all her kind. Love changed pretty Galatea, who turned into a fountain of tears when her mortal lover died. Pitys's heartbreak transformed her into a tree that weeps whenever the wind blows. And who could forget Salmacis? She was so desperate with love for Hermaphroditos that she melded her body with his and became a new creature, half woman, half man!

These were the fates of nymphs in love, and Ares was not about to let it happen to Kyra. She was his progeny. His blood flowed through her veins. How would it reflect upon him if his daughter were to meet such an end? "Who is this man she's taken up with?"

"I tried to find out," the vulture said, eager to please. "But he uses false names wherever he goes. He's a mystery. No one knows."

Ares let go of the vulture with grim determination. "Oh, I think Hecate knows."

Chapter 14

It'd been only a day or so since Marco's men had released her from the handcuffs, and having failed at her mission again, Kyra had nowhere else to go but home. She called upon her old mistress, but like the priceless wall hangings and ancient artifacts that littered the room, Kyra now felt as out of place in Hecate's crumbling shop as she felt everywhere else. Outside, tourists strolled past. People laughed, shopped and ate at the bistro across the street. The little Italian city was alive with color and life, but Kyra watched with a puzzling detachment. This was the bustle of the world, as it had been for centuries and it would be for centuries still. She was trapped in its endless cycle of passing time without purpose. She hadn't conquered the hydra as her destiny foretold—and feeling about Marco the way she did, she no longer wanted to.

"You look no better than last time," Hecate said by way of greeting. "So what's wrong with you now?"

"I don't know," Kyra said, afraid she might burst into a maudlin display of nymph's tears. Was it the poison still at work in her system, or was it just Marco Kaisaris that had gotten under her skin? "I lost the hydra."

She hadn't meant to speak of it, but she couldn't think of any other excuse for her behavior and now Hecate was eyeing her shrewdly. "You're thin," the goddess said.

"Food doesn't interest me." It was quite possible that the last meal she'd eaten was that half-burned boxed dinner with Marco. "Is this what it was like for you? Did you just wake up one day and find that you weren't as strong as you used to be? That your powers weren't as potent? That whatever made you a goddess—whatever gave you purpose—was suddenly with you in only half measure?"

"No," Hecate replied. "For me it happened very slowly. And I haven't lost all my powers, you know. I can see that you're hurting."

Yes, that was a good way to put it. Kyra was hurting, inside and out. "I don't heal as fast as I used to. I get tired. I think I'm damaged in some way."

Hecate's mouth tightened. "I was afraid of that. Achilles was half-mortal. Hercules was half-mortal, too. Both men died because the hydra blood ate away at what let them live forever. I fear it's the same with you, that this Marco Kaisaris—this monster—has taken away your immortality."

"He isn't a *monster*," Kyra protested. "He's just fashioned himself into one to fight a battle everyone else has forgotten."

Hecate settled into her rocking chair. "Well, you told him the way of the world. He should know better now."

Yes, Marco really should know better than to keep flooding Africa with cheap guns and ammo. More importantly, he should understand that Ares could hunt him down and use him for more nefarious things than that. But Marco was angry and bitter over having been tricked, and she had no one to blame for that but herself. "Hecate, he's so close to seeing things the way they really are. I was starting to open his eyes. If only he'd listen to me—"

"That's the trouble with mortals. We try to guide them at the crossroads, but sometimes they still choose the wrong path. Now I think you must stay away from the hydra and make amends with your father. Ares will give you ambrosia—and then you'll be as good as new."

"But I can't stay away from Marco. You have to help me find him again."

"Oh, Kyra, listen to yourself. You sound like a besotted nymph!"

Hecate was right, but if what she felt for Marco was even a fraction of how other nymphs felt, she could understand how all their sad stories came to pass. She understood Marco, understood the part of him that kept fighting when everyone else had given up or turned away. And if she let herself, she could love him. *Really* love him. How was it that she'd never known how strong and immortal a force love could be, in its own right?

"Marco needs me. He's struggling so hard and he's never had anyone in his life strong enough to struggle for *him*."

Hecate sighed. "I fear that when it comes to the hydra, you've already done all that you can do."

"No, I haven't. I can't have. You said I was fated to conquer a hydra. You said it was my destiny."

"But I don't think you want to conquer him anymore, Kyra. I think you want him to conquer you."

Marco knew it was still snowing in Niagara Falls, but the Congo was hot as a furnace. Everything was burning. Children burned with fever, villages were put to the torch, and Marco had passed a funeral pyre on his way in, piled with corpses so mangled and crisped they were barely recognizable as human.

Inside the general's hut, Marco's old friend peered into the crate. "What is this?"

"Kevlar vests," Marco answered in the face of the general's furious glare. "Consider them a gift." After all, Marco had made enough money in this business. He'd be very rich even if he never made another dime.

The general twitched his baton at his side and Marco wondered when he had acquired it. When the general was a schoolteacher in Rwanda, hadn't it just been a ruler he wielded in the classroom? Perhaps the war had changed them both beyond recognition. "*Where* are the guns?" the general demanded. "*Where* are the grenades?"

Marco didn't flinch. "*Where* is the peace treaty you were supposed to sign with the government?"

It'd obviously been a long time since the general had been questioned by anyone. He kicked a chair at Marco, who ducked out of the way. The chair crashed into some cook pots and sent a rooster skittering. Then the general exploded. "Do you know what the Hutu militias do? They take the women, rape them and cut off their ears. When they kill my people, they eat—they actually eat—their hearts and livers. And you want me to make peace with the weak government that allows it?"

Marco worked his jaw. "Maybe if you made peace

with the government, it'd be strong enough to stop these things, but I think you've grown too fond of killing."

The general took off his beret, his mask of rage falling away. He shook his head as if profoundly hurt by Marco's accusations. Then his old chameleon charisma came to the fore. "How can you listen to these lies about me?"

"Are they lies?" Marco asked. "My men keep an eye on things. They talk to the local authorities. Just last night, your soldiers shot a teacher in the face with one of my bullets because they thought he might be an enemy sympathizer. A schoolteacher. Just like you used to be."

The general stared at Marco with hard, obsidian eyes. "What is wrong with you?"

"Nothing," Marco said, taking a small flask from his shirt pocket. Water wasn't strong enough for this conversation. It was going to have to be Scotch. Marco unscrewed the cap, took a swallow and let it burn all the way down. Then he searched his pocket for another stick of gum, and found he was all out. All the while, the general watched him like he was a thing of curiosity.

Then, suddenly, the general gave a great booming laugh. "Ha! It is a woman, isn't it? Ahh, I know the signs, my friend. It was like this before, with your Ashlynn."

No, it hadn't been like this before. He'd been a kid when Ashlynn broke things off. What he felt now, since meeting the nymph, was different. Being with Kyra had been the first peace he'd known in his adult life. But it had all been a lie. Even so, he couldn't shake the memory of her. She'd been no wide-eyed innocent to the horrors of the world. Whatever he'd seen, she'd seen worse. Whatever he told her, she could handle it. Whatever he needed, she could give. She was strong, capable and no depthless ingenue, either. He could still remember the way she smelled, the way she sounded when she rode him in the darkness. Somehow, she'd gotten into his blood like a new kind of poison altogether.

"Whatever is bothering you, you must snap out of it," the general said, reaching for the flask that Marco gladly relinquished. "I'll give you two weeks to bring me the grenades and guns."

It was the practical thing to do. It was their arrangement. And yet, none of it made sense anymore. Sure, when they'd started all this, the killings here in the Congo were ethnically motivated. But just as often now, the fighting had to do with mining. It was about who was going to be rich. And whoever won the conflict was going to win using all these child soldiers—just like the ones guarding the general's hut. Little boys who, through fear, hunger and desperation could be molded into murdering, raping thugs.

"I don't think I can get you your guns." Marco hadn't meant to speak the words out loud, but once he had, they felt right. "I'm done with this. With all of this." And with a sidelong glance, Marco admitted, "I think we've turned into the monsters we once tried to slay."

The general's eyes smoldered like coals now. Benji had called him the devil, and Marco was starting to believe it. "Marco, only one of us is a monster. *You* are war-forged, but I am war-born."

War-forged. It was the same term that Kyra had used. Marco's expression must have betrayed his alarm, because the general grabbed his wrist before he could reach for his gun. The man's grip was like iron. "Come now, Marco. Did you really think I was a simple schoolteacher all those years ago? I'm older than you know—ancient in this land. The people here still call for me."

The hairs on the back of Marco's neck bristled. He couldn't tear his eyes away from the gaze of the man who held his wrist in a bone-crushing vice. Was this Ares? Could it be?

"I'm *Ogun,*" the general whispered, flashing those bright white teeth. "And I have waited a very long time for a creature with your powers to come along."

Marco knew only enough African mythology to know that Ogun was a war god. So here it was. Just as Kyra warned. "My powers?"

"You are a hydra, my friend. I have seen you burn your bandages. How you shy away from anyone touching you when you have an open wound. Do you think that here in Africa we don't know how people behave when they know their blood is tainted? We fear even the ones we love. And we know the signs."

Marco swallowed. The sweat was now rolling down his cheeks and he was shaking from the pain as the general continued to crush the bones of his wrist.

"Besides," the general continued, "the Hutu who shot you—I knew that man, Marco. I know how he died. And yet, his face lives on. They tell ghost stories about him now in Rwanda, because it seems everyone has seen him. But that is only because he shot you, and now you can wear his face, no?"

Marco didn't answer.

"What a wonderful gift you have, and it has been useful to me. You can smuggle to me any weapon in the world and no one would catch you."

Marco's nostrils flared, anger cutting through the pain. So he *was* being used. Perhaps he'd been used all along. For once, Kyra had told him the truth, and he hadn't wanted to listen. But he was listening now, and he was horrified.

"Do not look at me that way," the god said. "It was not I who made a monster of you. Mortal men make wars. We immortals are simply at hand to feed off the misery you create."

Marco's joints creaked beneath Ogun's fingers. He feared the bones might snap at any moment. "But you're leading rebels—"

"They called, so I serve. And so will you, as my minion."

"I'm nobody's minion," Marco said through clenched teeth.

"You will be mine, or I will cut your hand off," the god said, and Marco could see now that his baton was a machete. Perhaps it had always been a machete. Perhaps everything Marco had done in Africa from the start had been a lie. A mirage. All for nothing. He'd failed the people in Rwanda and now he was failing the Congolese. Why should he meet a different fate than the people here?

"So cut off my hand," Marco growled. "But you'll get my poisoned blood all over your rebel fortress. It might not kill you, but I have it on good authority that it burns like hell."

His bluff called, the god threw the machete aside. "I don't need to cut you, Marco Kaisaris. I can crush you to dust. I have seen you fight mortal men. You are strong, but no match for me. Which is why you will bring me the guns. Which is why you will bring me the grenades. Which is why you will forget about Kevlar, because nothing can kill me."

At last, Marco yanked his hand free of Ogun's grasp. The blood vessels were all broken and his wrist throbbed angrily. But it was still attached to his arm, so that counted for something. So why were the war god's eyes twinkling with surprise? As if Marco should be saying or doing something other than trying to get his bearings? "Ahh, Marco. You are not as shocked by all these revelations as you ought to be! I reveal myself as a war god, and not even a hint of doubt rises in your eyes. Someone has been telling tales. Perhaps the woman you pine for. Who is she?"

Marco wasn't going to tell him about Kyra. He didn't want to put her in danger, even though he wasn't precisely sure what kind of danger there could be for someone of her kind. "There is no woman."

"You're lying," the god said. Then he smiled a terrifying smile. "You went home to bury your father, yes? You saw her again. Your Ashlynn. And now you want to be with her once more."

Marco spat out the words. "I told you, there is no woman."

The general chuckled. "Stay at the hotel in Kinshasa tonight. I will send a girl to your room. Two girls.

Maybe three. They will make you forget all about this woman, whoever she is."

Marco agreed with a silent nod. He had no intention of sleeping with prostitutes, but it gave him an excuse to leave. He'd never willingly spend another night here.

Marco checked into the Hotel Venus and half expected to see some incarnation of Aphrodite behind the counter. Instead, he was greeted by Benji and a clipped warning. "A woman is looking for you, Chief."

"Only one?" Marco asked, remembering Ogun's promised prostitutes.

"A *white* woman. She's been showing your picture to the locals."

Kyra. She was here looking for him. It was the only explanation. It should've annoyed him. It should've infuriated him that the nymph of the underworld was stalking him. But he found himself somehow relieved at the thought he might see her again. Especially since she'd been right. About everything.

"Let's get out of this miserable country," Benji said.

"Start without me." Marco checked and rechecked his gun. He had no idea what immortal powers Ogun had, and it made him more paranoid than usual. "I'll catch up."

Benji looked reluctant. "I know you have some

trick—some disguise, some way of fooling people at the borders into thinking you're someone you're not—but…"

"I'll be fine," Marco reassured him. After all, it was safer for both of them if they weren't seen together now. "I have my phone and you know the number."

Benji didn't need to be told again. He took a few cartridges of ammunition out of his backpack and tossed them to Marco, then slung the bag over his shoulder and exited the building amid a group of tourists, pick-pocketing one of them along the way.

Once the kid was gone, Marco found a shadowy corner behind a potted plant in the hotel atrium and transformed himself. He chose a face that wouldn't stand out. It was the face of a dark-skinned Congolese man who had struck him in a drunken brawl in Matonge. He just hoped it was a face that Ogun didn't know.

It was three days before he found Kyra. To be more precise, it was three days before she found him. He recognized her voice as it floated up from the hotel lobby. It was the same throaty voice that she'd let him hear, undisguised, when she cried out underneath him. It'd been a voice that he should've known wasn't Ashlynn's. A voice, perhaps, he *had* known wasn't Ashlynn's.

Leaning over the wrought-iron railing of the court-yard-style hotel, he caught a glimpse of her below. He reminded himself that she'd tried to kill him—twice—and she might be back to finish the job. But that way of thinking was starting to ring hollow even to him. Still disguised as a Congolese man, Marco waited for her to leave then followed her into the city streets, keeping his distance as the sun began to set. What surprised him was that, but for a pair of sunglasses, she was undisguised. Her sleek dark hair was gathered at the nape of her neck, exposing her peridot choker, and the too-pale skin of her back and shoulders.

Closing his eyes, he tried to push away his desire. In spite of everything she'd done, he still wanted her, and it made him angry. Then again, why *couldn't* he have her? She'd seduced him twice under false pretenses—she ought to learn how it felt.

Chapter 15

The old witch made Ares wary. Even though she'd adopted this wretched gypsy guise, Hecate still retained some of her powers. She didn't seem the least bit surprised to see him—though that might have had something to do with her infernal barking bitches. Ares picked up her crystal ball, tossing it between his hands, liking the weight of it. It could easily crush a woman's skull.

One of Hecate's dogs growled at him. "In Sparta, men used to sacrifice dogs to me at night," Ares pointed out, and with a flick of his wrist the creatures turned snarling eyes upon one another. If Hecate hadn't shooed the dogs out of the room, they might have attacked one another. That would've been fine sport, but Ares would have to save his enjoyments for later.

"How can I help you, my lord Ares?" Hecate asked. "Would you like some tea?"

Ares snorted. He wasn't about to take any of the old witch's potions. "I've come for Kyra and her lover. I think you know where they are."

"Why should I know?" The older goddess spread her arms wide, a helpless gesture. "Kyra isn't my minion any longer. I released her from her vows."

"And I haven't forgiven you for it! Someone like Kyra needs a firm hand. She needs direction. Or do you *want* her to end up like you, no good to anybody anymore?"

"Why, Lord Ares," Hecate crooned, shambling over to her stove to put a teapot on. "I assure you, business is brisk. Even in this day and age, someone always wants guidance over the thresholds of life. Why, even you, the great god of war, have deigned to darken my humble doorstep. I must still be good for something."

It annoyed Ares that she chose this aged appearance. She was a *goddess*. She could've appeared to him as a beautiful maiden, forever young. But whenever he glanced at her, Hecate was always in her crone aspect, as if to hide her beauty from his plundering eyes. One day, when he had no rivals, Ares would make Hecate appear to him as he pleased. For now, he'd settle for some answers.

"Who is this latest man that Kyra has taken up with?

Is he some wastrel musician? An undertaker? Another depressive poet?"

Hecate busied herself at the stove, rummaging through a tin of various elixirs. "This one is different. You might even approve. He's an arms dealer."

An *arms dealer?* Ares felt his lips curve upward into the semblance of a smile. So, Kyra's war-born nature was coming to the fore just as he'd always predicted. If it was the bloodlust that fueled her fascination for this mortal, perhaps he ought not interfere.... No, best not to chance it. "I'm going to kill him, whoever he is. Men are fickle creatures, and if she falls in love with him, you know what can happen."

Hecate shuddered—actually shuddered—her hands going still on the handle of the teakettle. "I wouldn't kill him if I were you."

"Why not?" Ares came up behind her, and put his hand over hers on the handle of the teapot, which began to swiftly boil. The steam burned his fingers, too, but it was worth it to see the old crone in pain. He kept his voice low. "Don't test me, Hecate. I can make every day of your very long life a torment. What aren't you telling me about Kyra's lover?"

In days past, he would never have dared to threaten Hecate. But now, she was weak. She reacted to him with fear, as she must. "Kyra has already fallen in love with him," she whispered. "And if you kill him, in her grief, she may turn to dust on the wind. She's a nymph. They—"

"Change!" Ares exploded, flinging the teapot off the stove where the boiling water hissed and fizzled against the tile floor. He didn't need Hecate to lecture him on the nature of nymphs. He knew well what this could mean. "How could you let this happen?"

To her credit, Hecate looked genuinely remorseful. "It isn't only mortals who come to crossroads in their lives, and Kyra's always been one to forge her own path."

"We'll see about that," Ares hissed. "Tell me where I can find them."

Hecate shook her head, starting to back away, but he snatched her by the throat. "Oh, good, you plan to resist me…I don't mind. Either you'll submit to me now, or you'll submit to me once I've boiled the flesh from your old bones and watched it grow again. But either way, you're going to look into your tea leaves or gaze upon your crystal ball or resort to whatever witchery you must to tell me what I want to know. Where can I find Kyra and this lover of hers?"

Kyra had never been this far into the heart of Africa. The city of Kinshasa was a teeming sprawl of shantytowns and urban decay spreading along the banks of the Congo River. Matonge was the city's party neighborhood, a tangle of traffic, tattered store-fronts and dingy outdoor tables that passed for res-taurants. Prostitutes plied their trade, drunken men in tattered sneakers stumbled down the street to the music of Papa Wemba's soukous band and pickpockets worked the crowd.

It felt wrong to be among the mortals without dis-guising herself; it would've made her feel less exposed to walk down the street naked. But if she came upon Marco, she wanted him to recognize her. She wanted him to see that she wasn't hiding from him anymore. Or from herself.

The scent of grilled meat kabobs reminded Kyra that she was hungry, and she stopped at a vendor to buy a skewer. French was the official language of the coun-try, so she held up Marco's picture and asked, "*Avez-vous vu cet homme?* Have you seen this man?" It was twilight, and the vendor squinted over the smoke of his grill to look at the picture, then said no. "What about this man?" Kyra asked, showing him another photo of one of the many faces Marco wore. The vendor didn't know that one, either, and Kyra was close to despair. It'd never been easy to find Marco, but she'd done it twice before. She could do it again, she told herself. She felt certain he would be here in the Congo.

The drumbeats from the rooftop of the nearby hotel called to her, an insistent throb at her temples. Guided by little but instinct, she made her way to the roof where revelers danced close together in the popular outdoor club. Laughter and flirting abounded, and Kyra was astonished to find that even in this country, amid the poverty and brutality, there were still pockets of city nightlife.

This mortal resilience of spirit was like a siren's call to her. She ordered a beer, and pressed the cool bottle against her cheek when it came. Did she belong here, in this mortal world, all exposed, looking so human but not *quite?* Had the time for her kind passed? She stood out, and not simply because she was a nymph or because she was a lone white woman in Africa. She was also underdressed, wearing her street clothes— a tank top and shorts—whereas the dancers wore their best, some in western dress, some in traditional African garb. The press of bodies reminded her of the first time she met Marco in Naples. How she slid into his lap and something had ignited between them so naturally that it ached to remember.

But she did remember. She remembered everything about him—even the shape of his soul, the way it looked when her inner torch illuminated it. So her heart leaped a little to see that same shape now. He was coming toward her. Marco was wearing another man's face, black-skinned and curly-haired, but she knew him, and she tried not to look as happy to see him as she was.

"Has no one told you that it isn't safe for beautiful women to be alone in this country?" he asked in French.

Kyra took a deep breath. He'd missed her; she could see it. "Good thing I'm not alone anymore, then."

Marco sat down next to her. "So what brings you to our country?" he asked, affecting a perfectly authentic Congolese accent.

Kyra stared. What was Marco up to? Didn't he realize she knew him? Didn't he realize that as a nymph of the underworld, she could see through all his masquerades? Even if she had no powers at all, she seemed certain she'd know him by his voice alone. "I—I'm looking for someone," Kyra stammered, her fingers drifting over the photo.

Marco glanced at it, then shrugged as if he didn't recognize himself. "Forget about him. Dance with me instead."

Kyra took a swallow of beer, trying to decide how to respond. Was he pretending for her benefit or was he hiding his identity because he was being watched? When he extended his hand to her, she took it, and let him pull her into the crowd of dancers. They swayed together, her ear against his chest where she heard his heartbeat louder than the drums. She liked the way his now-ebony fingers twined with her pale ones, familiar and strange, but it didn't matter whose skin he wore. The moment he touched her again, she knew they fit together, like the final piece of a puzzle sliding into place.

The last time they had been together like this, she'd been the one pretending. Now she was letting him see her true self, and feeling incredibly vulnerable. As if sensing it, he slid his arms around her as they danced. "The man I'm looking for," Kyra whispered, afraid to break the spell. "Will you help me find him?"

Marco tilted her chin up so that she couldn't look away. "What's in it for me?"

"What do you want?" Kyra murmured, breathless as their thighs pressed together.

"I think you know what I want," he said, stooping to kiss her. These lips were fuller than his real lips, but Kyra found the fiery kiss was the same.

Except for the strings of overhead party lights, it was dark, but people still danced around them and Marco was not discreet. He openly groped her. It was rude. Lewd. Inappropriate. Yet she didn't stop him; after all, she cared little about mortal notions of propriety. She could only think that it wasn't fair that she should want him this much, that she should be so easily swept away by mortal longings. But there was no point in pretending otherwise.

Even in the night air, perspiration pooled beneath her shirt, trickling over her tightening belly. She bumped her hips forward against him with every bang of the drum, losing herself in the rhythm. She groaned as he pulled her by the waist, forcing her to rub against his thigh. It was suddenly as if they were having sex, even though he wasn't inside her, and there were clothes between them. He sensed it, too. "Are you going to come for me?" he whispered in her ear, like it was a dare, like he was driving her to it.

She shook her head and tried to pull away.

He held her fast. "Yes, you are. Right here, on the dance floor."

"Don't," she said, but she couldn't keep her hips still. The music was in her, and she couldn't stop moving. Neither could he. Soon the thin fabric of her shorts was pressed tight between her legs. She was close to orgasm—so close. His mouth was at her neck and the muscles of his shoulders rippled beneath her hands. The drums seemed louder, pounding through her like galloping horses. His shirt was clinging to his chest with the heat of the night but he only grinded harder. He was as merciless, as relentless, as the drumbeat.

She was going to come right here in the middle of a crowd, and she couldn't stop it. She didn't *want* to stop it. When the explosion came, Kyra bit her lower lip and squeezed her eyes shut, sparks bursting beneath her eyelids. Her climax was sharp, almost as painful as it was pleasurable. She was glad that he was kissing her, so that she didn't scream.

Wilting in the aftermath, she let him steady her and she slowly became aware of the other dancers. Her knees were weak and her breath erratic. The look he gave her was lurid. "If I help you find this man, will you go to bed with me?"

She didn't trust herself to speak, so she simply took him by the hand. They went to the lobby where he paid for a hotel room. There could be no mistaking Marco's intentions toward her—his hand was possessively at the small of her back. The desk manager smirked knowingly, and some part of Kyra wanted to wilt in embarrassment, but she was too far gone now for that.

Her nymph's need, her fierce desperation to touch him, to be with him, was more than even Kyra's pride could struggle against. She was, in the end, no different than Calypso, Echo or Clytie. No different than any other nymph, after all. And it was too late to stop.

The hotel room was nothing like the plush accommodations of Marco's penthouse in Naples, but there was a clean bed, a chair and a water basin. It was all they would need. His big hand was at the small of her back, arching her body toward him as he kissed her. His groans were urgent and filled with need.

I know it's you, Marco. The words were on her lips but now that they were alone, he could've taken on his own shape again. He could've told her why he was pretending to be someone else, but he didn't. Maybe he wanted his revenge upon her for having fooled him before. Maybe he no longer felt safe with her in his own skin.

If she told him that she knew, would she break the spell? Would she lose him again? Surely she'd lose him sometime, but not now. Not now. For whatever reason, he wanted it to be this way, he wanted to take her this way, and she'd let him.

He sat her down on the mattress. But he didn't cover her body with his the way she had expected. Instead, he pulled back, leaving her by herself on the bed while he sat across from her in the chair. "Now it's my turn," he said, his hand rubbing lightly between his legs. "I want to see you take off your clothes."

Panting with the unexpected break in skin-to-skin contact, Kyra glared at him. He was trying to shame her. And maybe she deserved it. She wasn't exactly dressed for a strip tease, but she unzipped her shorts and yanked them down her thighs, kicking them in his direction. He caught them in one hand, then laughed a rich laugh that reverberated down her spine. "Slowly," he commanded.

Kyra narrowed her eyes, pulling her dark tresses

behind her shoulders. *Fine.* He'd seen her face—her true face, her pale nymph's face. It was time for him to see all of her, the real her. Kyra was taking off more than clothes for him; she was peeling away the protective layers she'd worn for centuries. She tried not to show how her hands trembled at the hem of her tank top. She tried to strip it off her body with bravado, with the sensuous confidence she used to bring to all her sexual exploits. But for some reason, she hesitated.

"Don't you want me to help you find the man you're looking for?" Marco asked.

Yes. She did. Especially since he was sitting right in front of her. With a deep breath, Kyra slid her top over her head, and revealed her moonlit breasts. As he looked at her, something in Marco's expression changed and softened. "Come here." He reached out a hand to her. She took it, and he drew her into his lap in the chair, his dark fingers stroking her as they kissed. Then he let out a sigh.

"What is it?" Kyra asked.

He lowered his forehead to touch hers. His eyes were filled with emotion and Kyra's own throat tightened in response. This was the moment. This was when he was going to reveal himself for who he was, and they would be alone together, with no disguises between them.

And that's when a ringing phone ruined it all.

Chapter 16

"Your phone is ringing," Kyra whispered in his ear.

He wanted to ignore it. He wanted to tell her that it wasn't important. He wanted to tell her that cell phones were half to blame for the violence in the Congo, anyway, and that he felt like pitching his out the window. But only *one* person had this number and that was Benji. Disentangling from Kyra, Marco flipped open the damned phone with a growl. "What?"

"Hello, my old friend!" Ogun's big distinctive voice boomed on the other end.

"How did you get this number?" Marco feared that he already knew.

"I have Benji," the god replied. "After a little persuasion, your boy told me what number to dial. Now I am calling to remind you that the clock is ticking.

You will bring me the grenades. You will bring me the guns you promised. Or Benji will pay the price."

Marco tapped his fist against the unpainted plaster wall and forced himself to say, "So what? Benji means nothing to me."

"You are not getting any better at lying, my old friend. The boy is like a son to you, and he is still alive for now. Would you like to talk to him? Here, I will give him the phone." Then the war god laughed. "He is still afraid of me, you know. All I have to do is shout, *Boo!* He jumps every time."

Benji shouted into the phone. "I told you, he is the *devil!*"

Not the devil, Marco thought. Not exactly. But close enough. "Are you hurt?"

"Not badly," Benji said. "But I'm not alone. There's a woman here, too. The general says she's *your* woman." Dread filled the pit of Marco's stomach even before Benji said, "Her name is Ashlynn."

Marco squeezed his eyes shut as he heard Ashlynn scream in the background. What had he done? What the hell had he done? The general was on the phone again. "Ahh, Marco. She is so soft, your Ashlynn. So pretty. She would not live long here in Congo, no? How is it that the Great Northern Warlord could love someone so timid?"

Marco breathed. "She has nothing to do with this."

Again the war god laughed. "It was not easy to abduct her from Niagara Falls, but I will let you take her back home to her safe little life in the New World. But first, you will bring me my grenades. You will bring me my guns. There is one flight from Kinshasa to Goma tonight. Be on it. You can find your way to Rwanda from there. The clock is ticking."

Then the line went dead.

Marco didn't remember punching the wall, but the reverberations of pain and the hole in the cheap plaster convinced him that he must've done just that. And there was the nymph, standing there watching him rage, without batting an eye. As if she'd seen the dark side of men before. He'd never have to worry about frightening a woman like her. She was gutsy. She was *fearless*. But he wasn't about to drag her into the mess he'd made.

"I have to go," Marco said to Kyra as she dressed. "This thing between us, whatever it is, was obviously not meant to be, but I hope you find the man you're looking for."

Kyra blocked his path. "I've already found him, Marco," she said, taking his throbbing fist gently into her hands. She'd guessed who he was, then? He could feel that penetrating gaze of hers already halfway into his head, and besides, he hadn't been very concerned about hiding his identity while he was on the phone. In light of what had happened to Benji and Ashlynn, it now seemed like a stupid game of pretend, anyway.

"I don't have time for this, Kyra," he said, pulling his hand away. "Do you have any idea who that was on the phone? It was an African war god. He's been using me all along. Just as you warned me. And if I don't get his shipment of weapons to him in the next few days, he's going to kill Benji or Ashlynn or both of them."

Her momentary gasp of surprise allowed Marco to push past her. He flung open the door and started down the hall. How the hell was he going to get to the airport in time? Kyra was on his heels, her long strides matching his. "Did you promise yourself to Ogun as his minion? Did you offer yourself up in any way?"

Marco shook his head, keeping pace with her. "I made no promises but the one at the start—to protect the Tutsis from the Hutu militiamen. That's what I thought I was doing all this time, but I guess you get the last laugh."

They reached the stair landing, and he started taking them two at a time. Kyra did the same, just one pace behind him. "I've never laughed at you, Marco. When I tried to kill you in Naples, I thought you were a monster. I wanted to do something, *anything,* to be useful again. But you're not a monster and you're not Ogun's minion. Not yet. Not if you haven't pledged yourself to him."

Marco burst out the doors into the dark African street. Shrill traffic whistles screamed into the night air and he was so frustrated he wished he could scream right along with them. "Why didn't you tell me about him—about Ogun?"

"I know the Greek war gods best. This isn't my part of the world. But I did try to tell you that there were other war gods, lots of them, from all over the globe."

"Yes, you did," Marco snapped. "And I didn't want to listen. Now it's too late. Ogun doesn't seem like the type to take no for an answer. If it was just my life at stake, I'd let him kill me before I'd sell him even one more bullet. But he's got one of my men, and he's got Ashlynn. In any case, it's not your problem."

"You're wrong," Kyra said, breathless as she all but ran alongside him. "I care about you. I care about what happens to you. Your problems are my problems."

It was really too much. He was already so raw, so angry, so betrayed. He couldn't take one more lie. He came to a halt right there in the middle of the street, and took her by the arms. "Stop it," Marco said, shaking her. "Just stop what you're doing."

"What am I doing?" Kyra asked, her eyes as deceptively wide and guileless as he'd ever seen them.

"I get it, okay? If I can get away from Ogun, I will.

After Benji and Ashlynn are safe, if I can find a way not to sell another gun for the rest of my life, I'll take it. You don't have to keep trying to manipulate me into doing the right thing by pretending that you have feelings for me."

"I'm not pretending," Kyra insisted. "I *do* have feelings for you."

Something tightened in his chest and he'd be damned if he could explain why. "You lie so much, Kyra, you don't even know when you're lying. If you felt anything for me, you wouldn't have offered to go to bed with me when you thought I was another man."

"I *knew* it was *you*," Kyra argued, her cheeks flaming at his accusation. When he started to protest, she bowled over his words. "How do you think I always find you, Marco? And did I seem even the slightest bit surprised when you dropped your Congolese accent?"

She had him there. He paused; whatever spiteful words he'd been about to say just faded away. His grip on her arms went lax.

"I *knew* it was *you*," Kyra repeated, more gently. "I've told you before. I have an inner torch that lets me see into mortal souls. I always see the truth. I see the real you. Is that so hard to believe?"

Her black eyes glittered with unspoken emotion and Marco felt himself softening. He fought against it.

That way lay danger. Trusting people hadn't worked out very well for him before now, and given the way he felt about her, she could just be the final nail in his coffin.

Marco turned and walked away from her, raising his arm to hail a cab. The traffic on the streets of Kinshasa was thick, even at night, but if he managed to grab a taxi to the airport now, he might be able to catch the last flight out. And maybe that would get him there soon enough to save Benji and Ashlynn.

But Kyra—stubborn, infuriating Kyra—grabbed his arm. "I know you've been let down before. They made you stand there and watch murder and forbade you to do anything about it. Your family didn't understand. But I do. I understand you, because you're like me. You can trust me."

A cab pulled over and Marco reached for the door handle. He had to get to an airport right now. "Kyra, after everything that's happened between us, how could I ever really trust you?"

"Because you can kill me," she said. "And you're the only thing in the world that can."

That his blood could kill her was the second most dangerous confession Kyra could've made to Marco. The other, of course, being that she was falling in love with him. She hadn't been brave enough to tell him that. She could be reckless with her life, but not with her nymph's heart.

Now he was staring at her and she had a pretty good idea what he was going to do. Marco was a hard man. He'd had a hard life. He was going to tell the driver to take off. He was going to leave again. She was sure of it. But instead, he said, "Get in."

As she settled into the seat beside him, Marco's brow furrowed. They stared at each other for a moment, the silence between them deafening. The cab driver seemed to sense the tension, and when Marco told him to head toward the airport, he bobbed his head in time to the radio's music and turned it up full blast.

Marco brought his mouth to Kyra's ear and, for one dizzying moment, she thought he was going to kiss her, but instead he whispered, "What do you mean I can *kill* you? Bullets pass through you. I thought you were *immortal*."

"I am—I was," she stammered. Kyra had only told Marco that he had the power to kill her so that he would trust her, but now she could see that she was going to have to tell him the rest, and she was grateful that the radio was too loud for the driver to overhear. "When I was poisoned by your blood…it almost killed me."

"My blood…" Marco winced, jerking back his

hand from her as if he could poison her just by touching her.

Kyra tried to explain. "My mother was human. My father gave me ambrosia to keep me alive forever. But your blood counteracts that." He stiffened. He looked so brittle, she was afraid to say more. Afraid to break him. But Marco needed to know the truth. "Since your blood poisoned me, I've been weaker. I'm aging. That's why the vulture was able to hurt me. That's why it takes me so long to recover from every wound. I used to heal up right away."

His expression went slack with guilt. "My blood can do that to you?"

She put her hand over his, and gently stroked the pads of his dark fingers. "Marco, your blood can kill demigods. It could slay whole armies. Ogun could bleed you and use your blood to wipe out the Congo without firing a single gun. I'm surprised he hasn't thought of it yet. He probably has—he's just enjoying the shooting war too much."

The color drained from Marco's borrowed black face until he was gray as ash. His dismay told Kyra that he'd never considered the fact that he could, himself, be turned into a weapon more deadly than those he sold. "So I've killed you... You were some perfect deathless creature and I—"

"I could get better with ambrosia," Kyra said quickly.

"Then why the hell are you here chasing after me? Why aren't you off somewhere drinking it, or eating it, or whatever?"

"Because ambrosia is very rare and I don't have any."

"What about your father? Can't he give you some?" Marco asked, and she could see he was the kind of man who was going to methodically explore every possibility. He wanted—needed—to find solutions. And it endeared him to her more than ever.

"My father might be able to find some, but it isn't easy to come by. Especially now, with the world the way it is. Besides, I'm not sure I want to be immortal anymore."

His head jerked up at that. "What do you mean?"

As the cab turned the corner, his thigh brushed against hers. The same thigh that had been pressed between her legs not long ago on the rooftop, driving her forward to the drumbeat, into an abyss of pleasure. But it wasn't just the pleasure; it was that he'd made her feel as if she belonged in his arms—in fact, it was the only place she'd ever felt as if she *belonged*. Certainly, it felt more right than the life she'd been living. So why not be honest about it? "I'm not sure there's still a purpose for me as a *lampade*," Kyra said, a little breathless to be admitting it aloud, even to herself. "I don't belong in this world. Hecate doesn't need me. The people don't call upon my kind anymore. What's the point of living forever if no one needs you?"

"Don't say that," Marco said, his hand sliding over her shoulder and gently cupping her cheek. "The world needs more people like you. You don't close your eyes to anything. You see how screwed up the world is, and you want to do something about it. You're not afraid to stare right into the heart of darkness."

"I'm a torchbearer," Kyra said.

"That's what I mean. You're no Miss Mary Sunshine spreading false cheer. You're more like a beacon in the night. You say people don't need you anymore, but you're wrong. You're an ange—"

"Don't say it," she warned.

But he wasn't cowed. "I *will* say it. You're an angel. A dark angel. The kind that carries the fire of redemption in one hand and a knife in the other. You want to right wrongs."

"Nobody needs that anymore. Nobody needs me."

"I needed you." He hadn't meant to say it, she could tell. And now that he had, he almost blushed. His shoulders tensed and he stared out the window at the lights of the airport as they came into view. "In fact, I still need you," he said. "I need you to come with me to Rwanda."

Chapter 17

The nymph was unusually quiet beside him in the crowded plane. A light sheen of perspiration made her bare shoulders shine in a way that reminded him of how heatedly they'd danced together on the hotel rooftop. He'd enjoyed having such a powerful creature give herself over to him. She wanted, she needed, she *connected,* in the most beautifully raw and primal way. But now, she was wound tight.

"Are you all right?" Marco asked her as her hands tightened on the armrests.

"I'm fine," she snapped.

She was not fine. "You're knuckles are turning white."

She mumbled in reply, her cheeks coloring. "I don't like to fly."

Marco loved to fly. The sky was the one bloodless,

untainted place left in the world. He couldn't imagine why someone like Kyra wouldn't love it, too. "What's wrong with flying?"

"I'm a *lampade*," she whispered. "I wasn't made to look down on people. I was made to walk with them on the earth…or under it."

So, Kyra wasn't entirely fearless, after all. There were cracks. Vulnerabilities. And if what she said was true, the poison of his blood had caused some of them. If he'd never touched her, if he'd never come near her, maybe she would have lived forever. But he'd infected her. He was nothing but poison to Kyra and every other woman in his life. Look what he'd done to Ashlynn.

Marco sighed. What had Ashlynn ever done to deserve being kidnapped and caught up in this mess? Whatever happened, Marco had to get her released. He just hoped he could get the weapons shipment to Ogun in time. Luckily, Rwanda was just over the border of the Democratic Republic of the Congo and it'd be a relatively short flight. It was time to wear his own face again.

Marco seemed to have no fear of being arrested here in the warm night air of Rwanda. He made his way through the crowded tarmac with self-assurance. He'd obviously been here many times before. He knew the country, he knew the people. Within a matter of moments, they were ushered past customs officials and let through.

Kyra was oddly reassured by Marco's competence. She stayed close to his elbow as he made a few calls. Shortly afterward, a government official picked them up in the dead of night. It was only once they'd arrived at some sort of military compound—some set of buildings that looked like barracks—that Kyra whispered, "How much did you have to pay him?"

"Nothing," Marco said, helping her out of the car. "I'm a friend of the Rwandan government."

Darkness posed no obstacle for her—she could see all the buildings quite plainly, and the weapons inside them. What she couldn't tell was whether or not the guards were Rwandan soldiers or if they were in Marco's employ. They certainly treated him deferentially enough. As for her, the guards all stared. She could feel their heated glances as they swept up and down her long bare legs, but none of them spoke to her. "Is this place yours?"

Marco shook his head. The corrugated metal door screeched in the night as he pulled it closed behind them. Then he turned on a single lightbulb that swung from a wire overhead. "It's a government stockpile. The Rwandans want the weapons to reach the general, and they're happy to let me bring them over the border."

Kyra's mouth actually fell open. "But why? What has Rwanda to do with the killing in the Congo?"

"I told you before," he said, hefting a crowbar. "After the genocide here, the guilty fled to Zaire—er, to the Democratic Republic of the Congo. They hide out in the jungle, never having paid for their crimes. Worse, they continue to commit atrocities against the Congolese."

"Someone should stop them," Kyra said, starting to see Marco's frustration. "Marco, wait. Are you saying that the government of the Congo is harboring these... these—"

"*Genocidaires,*" Marco finished for her. The word echoed off the walls. Kyra hadn't known there was a word for such men. And she hadn't thought that any government in the world would harbor them. She didn't know what to say. But for once, Marco seemed willing to do the talking. "The Rwandans want justice but the government in the DRC can't seem to give it to them. The general promised that he'd give them that justice. So did I."

It was all starting to come together now. This was the war Marco couldn't stop fighting. The war that he'd promised to fight. But look where it had led him. "Are you giving them justice, Marco, or revenge?"

"Maybe a little of both," he said, prying the top off a crate to reveal a row of Kalashnikov assault rifles.

AK-47s. Cheap to make. Easy to use. The gun of choice in civil wars around the globe. Kyra knew because she had seen them in Daddy's armory. Hell, these guns could have actually come from one of Ares' warehouses. And the thought made Kyra sick.

"Ogun isn't interested in justice and you don't have to give him these weapons. He's blackmailing you and you don't have to give in to it."

"What options do I have? Can I defy a god?"

"I do it all the time," Kyra said, but Ares was her father. He'd only torture her; he wouldn't kill her even if he could. They might not have the most loving father-daughter relationship but they were kin. The same couldn't be said for Ogun.

"Can Ogun be killed?" Marco asked. "Maybe with my hydra blood?"

Kyra shook her head. "No. Your blood only affected me because my mother was a mortal woman. Ogun is a god. The worst thing you can do to him is deprive him of the forces that he feeds upon. War. Violence. Wrath…"

She might as well be asking him to ensure world peace, and he knew it. "Can Ogun be *captured*, then?" He couldn't look at her while saying the word. "Can he be chained?"

Kyra bit her lip. The fact that she'd once intended to lock him up was still a fresh wound between them and she wondered if it would ever heal. "Perhaps, but not forever. And not by us. He's a god of Africa. This is his realm. He's most powerful here, and his bloodlust is obviously well nourished. Maybe if another god opposed him, or an army came against him..."

Marco threw the crowbar on the floor and it bounced on the cement with an angry clatter. "Then I have to do what he wants. I have to get him the weapons."

"He'll only use them to escalate the civil war."

"I have no choice, Kyra."

"Yes, you do. You could run. I know places in the world that Ogun would fear to go. And you can wear a thousand different faces. He might never find you."

"Run? If it was just my life on the line, that'd be one thing. But he has Benji and he has Ashlynn."

Right. *Ashlynn.* She took a deep breath knowing that Marco was going to blow his one chance to escape, because of the woman Kyra had all but single-handedly brought back into his life. He could run—he could even run away with her—but instead, he was going to go back for his simple mortal woman. Kyra tried to make her nymph's heart cold and hard. "So you still love her."

He didn't confirm or deny it. "Ashlynn's an innocent in all this. I can't let her be hurt because of me. I can't live with that."

And Kyra couldn't live with Marco becoming the

minion of a war god. If he gave in to Ogun this time, he'd have to give in to him the next time and the time after that. Kyra knew how the gods were. She'd gone after Marco in the first place to keep Daddy from using him. She couldn't give up just because another war god got there first. "Marco, I could infiltrate Ogun's stronghold. I could free Benji and Ashlynn."

He looked dubious. "You can sneak into an armed encampment?"

"I've done it before," Kyra insisted. "As long as I'm careful and paying attention, I can make mortals see whatever I want them to see. Or nothing at all. I can fade so that none of the mortals would see me even if they looked straight at me."

"What about Ogun? He's not mortal. Can he see you?" She didn't want to lie to him. She didn't want to lie to him ever again. So she said nothing. "No. It's too dangerous," Marco said with a note of finality. "You said yourself that you're not as strong as you used to be. In the morning, we'll load up the plane and I'll fly it in to Rwanda. And I'll need you with me."

"For what?"

"I'll tell you when we get there," Marco said before leading her out and pulling the warehouse door shut. "If we're going to save Benji and Ashlynn, we have to leave at dawn, so we'd better get some sleep."

In truth, Kyra was exhausted. She was hot and

sweaty and wanted nothing more than a bath and a soft bed. But the closest thing to be had was a hammock in one of the empty barracks. She settled into the coarse net, not liking the way it suspended her body in the air. She let Marco find her a blanket and pillow, then watched him take a seat on an empty crate. His hands came to rest loosely between his knees, and in one of them was his gun. "No good-night kiss?" he asked.

She narrowed her eyes suspiciously. "Do you want a good-night kiss or are you just trying to find a way to handcuff me to the door again?"

He smirked. "Which would you prefer?"

Kyra didn't dignify that with an answer. "Aren't you going to sleep?"

"I've got too much to think about. But I'll make sure no one bothers you."

She pulled the blanket over her, ignoring its musty scent. "Why would anyone bother me?"

"You didn't disguise yourself on the way in. You're an exotic, scantily clad woman surrounded by a bunch of soldiers. They'd be all over you if they didn't know that you came with me, and that I'd put a bullet in any man who touches you."

It was a possessive and territorial thing for him to say—and she wasn't sure how she felt about it. But she might have liked it. "That's a little extreme, isn't it?"

Marco let his irritation show. "They all eyed you like wolves eye a sheep."

"Well, this sheep bites back."

"I remember." He leaned back on the wall behind him, ejecting a magazinc from his gun, then replacing it with another he fished out of his shirt pocket.

"I can handle myself, you know. It's not like I'm some wide-eyed virgin. I've had plenty of men before you."

Marco tapped the discarded magazine against the wood crate a few times, as if it was a habit. Then she realized it was annoyance. "Why would you throw that in my face?"

Had she thrown it in his face? Maybe she had. She couldn't say why. Maybe it was because the memory of Ashlynn, his sweet ingenue, kept tap-dancing on Kyra's last nerve. "You started it."

"When?"

"Back in Niagara Falls. The morning after we—" She stopped herself. What was it they'd done? It had felt like making love... "The way you accused me of tricking lots of men into bed. You've taunted me about it several times—as if you're some paragon of purity."

"I was angry." Marco tilted his head back, eyes on the industrial ceiling. "I was a jackass. I was just trying to hurt you."

He was actually admitting that he was wrong? Kyra couldn't quite believe it. "No, I remember the way you looked when the vulture was taunting us about all my mortal lovers. What she said bothered you."

"No. It bothered *you*."

Kyra held her breath. Try as she might, she couldn't come back with a smart-mouthed reply. There had been men, yes, many. But she'd lived for more years than she could count. It was foolish to wish he'd been the only one.

"Kyra…you don't owe anybody an explanation for who and what you are. You're wild. Primal. Beautiful."

She didn't want to hear him say it because she'd heard it all before. This is what all men loved about nymphs but it never held their attention for long. Once a nymph let a man do everything to her that he could've dreamed of, he inevitably returned to a woman like Ashlynn. Kyra glanced away, her emotions a jumble.

"Look at me." His tone demanded obedience, so she met his eyes. "On the rooftop, when we were dancing…the way you moved against me. The way your face looked when you came. You didn't give a damn what anybody thought. I've never seen anything sexier, and nobody has any right to want you to be different. Not even me."

"But would you *want* me to be different?" Kyra asked. "If I *could be?*"

He didn't even hesitate. "No. But I wish *I* was different."

"You can be...you weren't always a gunrunner."

"I wasn't always some face-shifting, doppelganger monster, either. My blood wasn't always poisoned." He rubbed at the stubble on his chin and they were both silent until he said, "You said I was *war-forged,* Kyra. Is there a way to...to unforge me? Or is killing me the only way to get rid of my poisoned blood?"

Again, she was silent because she didn't want to lie. But neither did she want to tell him the truth. If she tried to explain to him about her inner torch—about how she might be able to use her powers to destroy the hydra within—she'd have to tell him about her mother, and she wasn't sure she could bear it. But Marco's eyes were so intently searching hers that she had no choice. "There might be one way."

He sat up straighter, his boots flat on the floor. "How?"

"In the ancient stories, the only way to destroy a hydra was with a torch and a blade. The hero would chop off the monstrous heads and cauterize the wounds with a torch. I'm a torchbearer. I might be able to use my powers to illuminate your soul, to step inside you and cut away the poisoned parts and sear them shut with my flame."

That sent him to his feet. "So do it!"

Kyra shrunk down into the hammock, sorry she'd mentioned it. "Don't you remember what happened the last time I shined my torchlight into your eyes?"

"Yeah. I blacked out and crashed the car. But we're not on the road now and if I fall unconscious the worst thing that'll happen is that I'll bump my head on the cement floor."

"That's not the worst thing that could happen. I caused that accident with just a short burst of light into your eyes—and reflected light at that. If I shined directly into your eyes for as long as it would take to find your inner hydra and vanquish him, it would…" She couldn't say it. She just couldn't say it. She fingered the peridot choker at her throat and tears welled in her eyes. "Look, I've tried this before and it ended badly."

"Given the alternative, how much more badly could it end?"

Kyra sighed. "There are worse things than death, and you know it."

He didn't believe her. He wasn't going to listen; he wasn't going to understand unless she told him the whole truth. So she did. She told him how Ares took her mother as a war prize, how he raped her, how he made her carry his child. She made Marco understand that if he was *war-forged,* Kyra was *war-born* in every sense of the word. "I only wanted to help her," Kyra finished. "I only wanted to burn away the pain, but instead I left my mother blind and alone in the darkness of her own mind. She never recovered. She wasted away, a screaming wraith of herself, so lost and afraid. And I did that to her. Now the only thing I have left of her is this peridot choker."

She realized that Marco was holding her hand. The silent aftermath of her story stretched on so long that her tears had dried in salt streaks down her cheeks. She hadn't even remembered crying them, and it embarrassed her that he should have seen them.

"That's why you were so compassionate with my mother at the funeral home."

Kyra bobbed her head in answer. She'd like to think she'd have been compassionate either way, but she couldn't deny how much Marco's mother had reminded her of her own. "I don't know which mental illness has your mother in its grasp, but even if I vanquish your inner hydra, you may end up just the same way."

He nodded quietly. They both knew that a proud man like Marco would rather die than go mad.

The hot sun sliced into the horizon over Rwanda as the soldiers finished loading the belly of the small cargo plane with weapons. Marco gathered an envelope full of materials that Kyra assumed were the necessary documentation they'd need at the border. He also made a point of asking for two shovels.

She could see the tension in his shoulders and the terrible resolve in his eyes as he walked around the craft, checking the fuselage. But it probably wasn't the olive-green-painted plane he was worried about; they both knew that by returning to the Congo, Marco was walking right into Ogun's clutches.

Finally, Marco slapped the side of the plane. "Time to go."

It was the first thing he'd said to her all morning. She'd discovered a lot of things about Marco since that first night she tracked him down in Naples. But almost none of them surprised her as much as learning that he knew how to fly a plane. Strapped in next to him, she tried not to show her unease at the array of gauges and switches in the cockpit. She watched Marco go through his takeoff checklist, calm and levelheaded, but it was only a veneer over the stress. He was chewing gum again, the muscles of his jaw bulging with every bite. "Do you need a smoke?" she asked, pretty sure she'd seen a pack tucked behind her seat.

Marco put on an aviation headset and handed her a pair. "I quit, remember?"

Kyra didn't argue. Instead, she put on her headset

and watched him press buttons and turn knobs with crisp efficiency. "What are you doing?"

He squinted. "Calibrating the instruments."

A few moments later, Kyra wondered, "Why did you have them load shovels into the planc?"

"Can you just—can you let me concentrate?"

Kyra's lips drew closed and she nodded. Then he turned on the engines one at a time, running them high. But they weren't yet moving and the plane started to shake. This was so much worse than a passenger plane. It couldn't be normal for a plane to shake this much. She knew she was supposed to be quiet but she asked, "*Now* what are you doing?"

"Kyra!"

She shut up, but as the plane rumbled its way down the pitiful excuse of a runway, Kyra had to squeeze her eyes closed for takeoff.

"You really don't like heights, do you?" Marco asked, once they were up in the clouds. His voice came loud and clear in her headset, over the noise of the plane, and it soothed her. It may have been the only thing that could. *Gods above and below,* his voice was a thing of wonder.

When Kyra thought of Africa, it was the desert browns and hard-baked soil that came to mind. But peering over the propeller, she saw nothing but lush greens and blues. The clear water of Lake Kivu was nothing short of astonishing, and Kyra rapidly blinked as if she could not quite take in so much beauty all at once. Verdant mountains sloped gently into the water and palm trees swayed along the shoreline.

She realized that he must have done this before. He must have made flights into war-torn countries hundreds of times before. But never like this. Never with the knowledge that he was trading with a war god. Never with the certainty that the lives of two people he cared about hung in the balance. She admired his steadiness, because her own palms were sweaty.

"I don't belong up this high," she said. "The sky is for the gods. For the winds. Not for nymphs like me."

"You belong wherever you want to be," Marco said.

As the sun kissed the mist-covered jungle mountains below, Kyra asked, "Should I be worried about being shot down over Lake Kivu?"

"The DRC doesn't monitor their airspace. That makes it easy for people to fly in with weapons and fly out with diamonds, or other precious minerals. Like the stuff that goes into your cell phone. They're stripping the country."

"Who is?"

"Everybody," was Marco's reply.

"It's a shame. It's beautiful."

"Looks like heaven," Marco said. "But it feels like hell."

"That lake is so peaceful, though."

"Looks can be deceiving. It's volcanic. It's sitting on top of toxic gas. The whole lake could erupt any time…just like the Congo."

And they were going to be a part of it. By bringing these guns to Ogun, they were going to set off a man-made eruption and they both knew it.

Chapter 18

Marco's gaze was on the airplane graveyard below where carcasses of abandoned and crashed planes rose up from the tall grasses. Cracked steel and broken glass littered the ground. It was a wasteland of bent propellers, rusty turboprops and twisted landing gear. And unless everything went according to plan, the plane he was flying now would probably join them. The strip should be just over the horizon so he banked the plane to the left, into the wind, then lowered the flaps.

"What are you doing?" Kyra asked. "I don't see an airport."

"You think the DRC is just going to let me land a plane full of weapons in one of their airports?" he asked. "We've gotta land here."

Kyra's lips trembled behind the mouthpiece of her headset. "But it's just a—a field!"

"Look a little closer and you'll see the dirt road if we're lucky. Otherwise, I'm going to have to put this tub down in the grass."

"Are you insane?" Kyra asked, legs tensed in anticipation.

"Keep it together, *Angel.*" Marco angled the nose up and pulled back on the throttle. He wanted to slow the plane down as much as possible, and he didn't like how muddy things looked. If the ground was too soft, if a wheel hit a hole, they could be in real trouble. They descended and Marco tilted toward the wind. The plane began to rattle. The wind buffeted the plane madly, as the ground rose up before them.

It was a close call. The wheels hit the mud and skidded, an eruption of smoke and dirt billowing behind them. He brought the plane to a jerking stop, and then there was silence. "I told you I'd never let you fall," Marco said, feeling smug.

To Kyra's credit, she never screamed. But now her eyes were glassy and dazed, as if she were sick with fear. "This was revenge for the car crash, right?"

"No, I forgive you for that." He thought, in that moment, he might have forgiven her anything, but she had to push her luck.

"What about pretending to be Ashlynn?"

"Still working on it. Now, listen," Marco said, once he'd shut down the plane. "I need to hike into Goma, and I want you to stay here with the plane. I don't think anyone saw us land, but if you hear anyone coming, don't do anything brave. Just hide."

She ripped the headset off. "Wait, you're doing what?"

"I'm hiking into Goma. It'll take me a few hours."

"Why can't you just call Ogun to arrange for a swap? Your weapons for his hostages? You can call him. I know he has Benji's phone."

"I have to do something first, and there's no time to explain."

Red anger rose to her cheeks. "So you're leaving me here?"

"It's safer this way."

"For who? There's a UN mission in Goma. If you hike into that city, they're going to arrest you!"

Marco almost laughed at her naiveté, but he didn't have the heart to. "I'm more worried about Ogun. He has spies everywhere. If I'm spotted in the city, I want to be seen alone. I don't want him to see you."

Kyra turned to him in her seat, flipping that sexy dark hair. "Now, *you* listen to *me*. Ever since Benji and Ashlynn were kidnapped, I've let you run the show. I've followed you around and done everything you said like a good little girl. But it's not my nature. And I don't like your plan. You can't expect me to sit here in the middle of the Congo without you."

"Kyra, if someone captures one of us—mortal or god—wouldn't it be better if the other of us were free?"

She clenched her teeth, then stared gloomily out the window. "So you're just going to leave me."

Damn it, he didn't have time to argue with her. "Kyra—"

"Fine," she said, giving him a shove. "Just leave me like Odysseus left Calypso on the sands, so you can go off to rescue your pretty, proper Penelope!"

Penelope? He'd have liked to have known what the hell she was talking about, but a quick look at his watch told him that he needed to get going. He cupped Kyra's cheek, trying to calm her down. "I'm *not* just leaving you here. I'm coming back."

"How do I know that?" Kyra asked.

"Because I'm giving you my promise. I'm giving you my word." He leaned forward and kissed her, hoping it wouldn't be his undoing.

"Why am I even here?" she whispered when he withdrew, her lips set in a near pout. "Why did you even bring me back with you?"

He put his hands in her hair, stroking it back behind her ears. "Because, when Benji and Ashlynn are safe, I'm going to need you to bury me."

He'd tried to say it as gently as he could, but the shock of his words sent a shudder through her. Marco couldn't let her see even a hint of doubt in his eyes. "When this is all over, Kyra, we're going to dig a hole in the sand. I'm going to climb into it and you're going to shoot me in the head and bury me. This way, none of my hydra blood will ever hurt you or anyone else again."

He couldn't be serious…but then she saw that he was. He wanted her to kill him and hide the body. She pulled away, horrified. "You can't mean that!"

"It's the only way," Marco said. "You've always known that. That's why you tried to kill me in Naples."

Acid boiled up in Kyra's stomach. She thought she might retch. She was as sick at the thought as she had been when his blood had first poisoned her.

"You said it was your destiny to rid the world of a hydra, didn't you?" Marco asked. "We're both Greek, Kyra. We both know we can't cheat fate."

He was right, about everything. She had only one argument, and it was the one she dared not make. She didn't *want* to kill him. She loved him and wanted to be loved by him. But those words would not come, no matter how hard she tried to summon them.

"I have to go," Marco said.

He pressed a gun into her shaking hands, she shoved it away. "I don't want one of your stupid guns!"

"Take it for your own protection. In case anyone comes while I'm gone."

"I prefer knives," she insisted, but she didn't expect him to actually produce one.

Fumbling in a case in the back of the cockpit, he drew out a blade. "It's a Glock field knife. Take it."

She let her fingers curl around the hilt as he made his way out of the plane. She sat there with the weight of it in her hand as she watched him tuck an envelope into his shirt, sling a backpack over one shoulder and take off into the bush. It might be the last time she ever saw him, and she was acutely aware of it. She tried to burn the memory of him into her mind—the way his linen shirt clung to his back with sweat. The way his strong shoulders moved as he cut a swath into the jungle, like Odysseus working the rigging of his ship.

He'd promised to come back, but the promises of mortal men were nothing nymphs could cling to. In the end, Marco was going to save Ashlynn and the two of them would find their way back together. That is, if Kyra sat here and did nothing.

In Kyra's defense, she tried to do as Marco asked. She sat in that plane for several hours before deciding to take matters into her own hands. She told herself it was his own fault for giving in to Ogun's blackmail without considering *all* the weapons he had in his arsenal. Kyra was a deadly weapon in her own right and she wasn't about to wait around for Marco to rescue his damsel in distress when she was perfectly capable of doing it. And she didn't need Marco to lead her to Ogun's rebel encampment, either; this place was filled with the shades of the dead, many of whom were eager to tell Kyra what they knew.

Ares held the cell phone to his ear. "Hecate swore we'd find Kyra there!"

"Maybe the old witch lied to you," his vulture said hurriedly on the other end of the line. "I've been sitting outside the UN mission in Goma for days and I haven't scented Kyra or her lover."

Ares supposed it was possible that Hecate had lied to him. Oh, the once-mighty goddess had cried out in pain as he burned her. Her sweet shrieks still echoed in his mind and gave him an erotic thrill. But perhaps he hadn't let the delicious torture last long enough to ensure she was telling the truth.... No, Hecate dared not lie to him. Not about Kyra. "Listen, my little buzzard, do I have to come there myself?"

If he had to go to Africa himself, he'd make someone pay dearly. He hated the idea of roaming so far from his home. There were still-standing temples to him in North Africa, but the Democratic Republic of the Congo was much farther than his ancient influence had reached. He didn't relish the idea of trespassing on the realm of another war god, but he was getting very tired of his minion's incompetence.

"Wait," the vulture replied. "I think I smell him!"

"Then you know what to do," Ares said, and snapped the phone shut.

As Kyra moved silently among the huts, she came upon several child soldiers who purported to be guards. The sight of them, wearing chains of bullets around their little necks like tribal toy beads, was disturbing on more levels than she could name. Two of the boys were crouched, taunting a third, who was crying. The shades had told her to expect this—to know that some of the boys had come willingly to this warrior's life, and others had been forcibly abducted from nearby schools and pressed into the general's army. Drugged, beaten and forced to kill. And if Marco gave Ogun the guns, that's what would happen to the crying boy. He'd kill or die. And Kyra couldn't live with that.

With renewed purpose, Kyra faded and slipped past the boys. They didn't see her. Even so, she was cautious, staying low and creeping from hut to hut until she found them. Kyra almost didn't recognize Benji. His eye was swollen shut, and a gag held his jaw in a distended position. Ashlynn sat beside him on the floor, her face in her hands.

Kyra was surprised by the sudden surge of protectiveness she felt toward Ashlynn. She'd expected to want to claw the woman's eyes out in a jealous fit of rage. But Ashlynn was someone who Marco cared about, someone he'd once loved, someone he might love still. And though she couldn't explain it, that made Ashlynn somehow precious to her. So Kyra was gentle when she put her hand over Ashlynn's mouth and whispered, "Don't make a sound. I'm here to help you."

Then she let herself be visible and Benji's eyes flew wide. Once she was sure that Ashlynn wouldn't scream, Kyra cut the ropes and realized that Benji had already managed to slip halfway out of his. He was every bit as resourceful as Marco boasted. "I'm here for your boss," she said to Benji. "There's a car by the checkpoint at the bottom of the mountain. Marco tells me you can steal just about anything. Can you hot-wire the car?"

He nodded, still wide-eyed.

"And you'll take Ashlynn with you? You'll make sure she gets out okay?"

Benji nodded again. Could she trust him? A gentle illumination into his soul showed her the outlines of his devotion to Marco and she decided that would have to be good enough. "You might need to bribe some people to get out of the country." Kyra wanted to give them money, but didn't have any cash in the pockets

of her cargo shorts. She thought it might just kill her
to do it, but she unfastened the peridot choker at her
throat and handed it to Ashlynn. "Please don't sell it
unless you have to. It's antique, and very expensive."

Priceless, in fact. It hurt more than just about anything to give her mother's necklace to the woman.
Especially to *this* woman. But Kyra's mother had been
a priestess of Hecate. She'd have wanted her jewelry to
help guide another to safety. That helped her let it go,
even though she had to strangle a sob in her throat to
do so.

"What are you?" Benji asked, pulling the gag from
his mouth. "You look like…an angel."

"Well, I'm not. I can't flap my pretty white wings
and fly you out of here. I can only create a distraction
outside to let you get away. So, when you hear an explosion, start running."

As the daughter of Ares, Kyra had a preternatural
sense for weapons of war. Ogun's rebel cache of grenades wasn't hard to find and since mortals couldn't
see her, she simply walked past the guards into the
warehouse and pulled a few pins.

The resulting blast was cacophonous. Numbing.
Mesmerizing, really. The sight of dirt plumes in the
jungle air made soldiers come running from all directions. No one's eyes were on the hostages; if Benji had

an ounce of sense, he and Ashlynn would be well away by now.

Kyra stopped to appreciate her handiwork—a riveting show of fire and shrapnel. Daddy wasn't *entirely* wrong when he said she was bred for destruction. But it was always her undoing. As Kyra turned to flee, a meaty fist closed around her throat. Clawing at an iron grip that left her no room to breathe, Kyra found herself staring into cold obsidian eyes.

"Now what manner of creature do we have here?" Ogun asked.

And then he laughed.

Chapter 19

The last thing Marco remembered was stuffing an envelope under a door at the mission of the United Nations Organization—the world's understaffed and outgunned attempt at peacekeeping in the area. Inside that envelope was everything Marco knew about the general's rebellion. He'd given maps, locations of encampments and an inventory of every weapon he'd supplied for the past decade. He hoped they'd put it to good use.

But now he had no idea where he was. Blinking awake, his eyes made out the fuzzy outlines of a beach house. The scent of eucalyptus trees and volcanic ash let him know he was still in Goma. The lake outside had to be Lake Kivu. Steadying himself on the mattress he saw the shape of a woman standing over him. He could see she wasn't a stranger, either. She was the vulture and she was eyeing him like he was a rotting corpse in the sun. "Oh, you woke up. Such a pity."

"What do you want?" Marco reached back to rub the sore spot on his head and was relieved to find that he didn't have an open wound.

"I knocked you unconscious. I wanted a little payback," the vulture said, and he could see she had his gun. "Mmm, well, you are a tasty morsel," she said, bringing her face close to him and digging her talons into his arm. "Let me just have…a little bite."

"You're not my type," Marco snapped, jerking away.

She leaned forward. "Is Kyra?"

Marco ground his teeth. It was hard enough to make sense of the feelings he had for Kyra. To speak of them with this woman, this creature, seemed somehow obscene.

"More importantly…" The vulture knelt in front of him, licking her lips in a pornographic mockery of an act a man might otherwise welcome. "Are you *Kyra's* type? Or are you merely an amusement? You see, my master hopes that you're just another one of his prodigal daughter's playthings—in which case, I'm going to kill you very slowly and eat your innards at my leisure."

The vulture didn't know! She didn't know he was a hydra, or that consuming his blood would kill her. She was so dumb, she really thought he was just one of Kyra's lovers. "And what if I'm *not* just another one of Kyra's playthings?"

"You mean if she actually loves you? Then I hope you don't bore easily, because your life is about to become much, *much* longer." The vulture drew a syringe out of her pocket, holding it up so that the fluid shimmered in the light. "This is ambrosia. The rarest and most valuable liquid in the world. A little bit will heal you, a little bit more will extend your life, and a little bit more will make you immortal."

Ambrosia. "Give it to Kyra. She needs it."

"Oh, this isn't for Kyra," the vulture said. "This is for you. *If* she's truly set her nymph's heart upon you, my master doesn't want to see it broken by your fragile mortality. You see, nymphs are ridiculously dramatic. Love changes them, ruins them, and Ares has plans for Kyra. He's not about to let her transform herself into some babbling brook or melancholy wildflower on your account."

Was it possible that Kyra loved him? What did it matter? He was going to die soon enough, but with Ashlynn and Benji's lives on the line he really didn't have time to die *today.* "Look, I don't have time for this. I have an angry African war god waiting on me."

In his frustration, he'd only meant to be flip, but

the vulture recoiled. Panic flittered over her face, and her arms flapped nervously. "Which war god?" she squawked.

"Ogun," Marco replied slowly.

The vulture took three steps back and lowered the gun. "You're Ogun's minion? I—I had no idea. But you seemed so ordinary."

He didn't know what sort of divine rules of etiquette were at play, but she seemed distinctly less intent on feasting upon his innards now that she assumed he had Ogun's protection. She had jumped to the wrong conclusion, but it had changed the equation in his favor and he wasn't about to contradict her. "Looks can be deceiving."

"I'm only here trespassing in Ogun's realm because Ares sent me," the vulture said. "The nymph is his daughter, under his protection. So, you see, it's Kyra's fault. She shouldn't be here. This isn't her home. She shouldn't even care what happens in Africa. She doesn't *belong* in Africa."

"Maybe you people should stop trying to tell Kyra where she belongs," Marco growled. "Now, if you'll excuse me, I have a shipment of weapons to transport." He got to his feet and walked toward her, free hand extended for his gun. He wasn't about to leave without it.

And she even seemed inclined to surrender it to

him, too, until he got close enough, and she tilted her nose up in the air, taking a faint sniff. "Is something burning?"

"It's Africa, something is always burning." But he was suddenly and acutely aware of the small scratch she'd left on his arm and the little dots of toxic blood that were boiling at the surface of his skin.

"Your blood, it's—"

He caught her by the wrist before she could touch it. "Careful." As much as he loathed the creature and the carrion stench of her breath, Kyra had told him that the vulture was mortal. In spite of everything she'd done, she probably didn't deserve to die just for curiosity's sake.

"You aren't an ordinary man at all," the vulture said, her eyes widening. "You're the *hydra*. She found you."

"That's right," he said, seeing no advantage to denying it. "My blood can kill you. And it *will* kill you if you stand in my way. So, give me my gun, my cell phone and that syringe of ambrosia."

She swallowed audibly, yanking her wrist away, and took another two steps back. "Not the ambrosia." Her long red fingernails closed around it. There were apparently some things she feared more than death. "I'll give you the rest, but you can't have this."

244 Poisoned Kisses

"Why not?" Marco asked. "You said it was for me, didn't you?"

"There were conditions," the vulture hissed. "Ares said I was only supposed to give this to you if Kyra truly loves you."

Marco found it vexing that the Greek god of war should care anything about true love, but then again, he *was* Kyra's father. "Just give me the syringe. Maybe she does love me, though I'll be damned if I know why."

"Then where is she? If Kyra loved you, wouldn't she be by your side?"

Marco frowned, remembering the way Kyra had asked him not to leave her with the plane.

"No answer for that?" the vulture asked, tossing Marco his gun and his phone.

Marco took one look at the display and saw the text message from Benji. He muttered a string of expletives in just about every language he knew.

Damn it. What had Kyra done now?

Chapter 20

Marco locked the vulture in a closet, then returned Benji's text, telling him to bring Ashlynn to the beach house. Meanwhile, he was grateful the scrape on his arm was a shallow one that scabbed over quickly. He bandaged it, anyway, just to be safe.

When Benji and Ashylnn arrived, the sight of Kyra's peridot pendant was like being doused in ice water. He knew what that necklace meant to Kyra and what a sacrifice it must have been for her to give it up. It made him more afraid for her than ever.

Ashlynn was only a little bruised but more than a little traumatized. She held her head in her hands, whispering, "I didn't know there were places like this, people like this. I never wanted to know."

She wouldn't have ever *had* to know if it weren't for Marco. Racked with guilt, he tried to tell her that she was safe now—or at least she would be safe as soon as he could get her away from Ogun. But he should've felt something for her beyond guilt, shouldn't he? Instead, he kept eyeing the bruises on Ashlynn's arms with a different kind of regret. Those bruises proved that she wasn't Kyra pretending to be Ashlynn—and that, for once, he wished she were. "Where is Kyra?"

Ashlynn wiped her tear-streaked face with her hands. "Is that that…that pale creature with the crazy black eyes?"

Creature. Kyra had saved her life, but Marco realized that Ashlynn thought of her as something alien, something outside her experiences, something apart. And it angered Marco more than he could say. "She's not a *creature*," he growled.

"I don't care what she is," Ashlynn whispered. "I just want to go home."

From the closet, the vulture called out and banged on the locked door, which made Ashlynn jump. "Who is that?"

"You don't want to know," Marco said.

From the panoramic view of the beach house, Marco stared out at the water, then at the patchwork of jungle, dirt roads and pasturelands beyond. Kyra could be anywhere. Anywhere at all. Marco had promised the nymph that he'd return, but it hadn't occurred to him to make her promise she'd stay with the plane. And now

Marco was ready to put his fist through another wall. "Benji, where the hell is Kyra?"

Benji shrugged helplessly. "I thought she'd catch up after the explosion, but—"

"Marco, she seemed like she could handle herself," Ashlynn interrupted, her voice tempered. "She was invisible. She could be in this room for all we know."

That's right. If Kyra wanted to disappear, she could. He'd never see her again even if she were standing right beside him. A pain shot through him at the thought. It was a longing so unbearable that he had to actually brace himself against the door. No, Kyra couldn't be here. Maybe it was just his ego talking, but after the lengths Kyra had gone to chase him down, he couldn't imagine she'd just disappear. She was in danger. Ogun had her. Marco was sure of it. "Benji, take Ashlynn to the United Nations mission. Walk her right in and tell them who she is. They'll help get her back home safe."

Benji—whose eye was still swollen—managed to scowl at Marco under a crust of blood. "They'll interrogate me, Chief. About you. They'll be looking to arrest you."

"Tell them whatever you need to. It doesn't matter anymore."

Ashlynn stood, still trembling. "You're not coming with us?"

"I can't leave Kyra behind."

Now Ashlynn was angry—or at least as angry as he'd ever seen her. She'd been kidnapped and threatened on his account, so he could hardly blame her. But what she said was, "Why is there always someone you think you have to save? Why can't you just come home where you belong?"

If he belonged anywhere, it was with Kyra. He only wished he'd realized it before this very moment. Marco leaned over and carefully kissed the top of Ashlynn's head. "You'll be safe with Benji," he said, and before he withdrew, he unclasped the pendant from around Ashlynn's neck. It was the only thing Kyra had of her mother—and now it might well be the only thing he had left of Kyra. Clasping the glowing stone in his hand, Marco said, "Benji, get going."

"But what about the woman in the closet?" Benji asked.

Marco snorted. "She can take care of herself."

As he watched Benji and Ashlynn make their way onto the crowded and dusty streets of Goma, he made the call. He figured that he could make a simple trade. Ogun would get his weapons. Marco would get Kyra. But when Ogun didn't answer the phone, he suspected everything had changed.

He let the vulture out of the closet and asked, "What would Ogun want with Kyra?"

"To hurt her," the vulture said without hesitation. "If he finds out that she's a *lampade*—if he finds out about her powers—he may use her to speak to shades in the underworld. But mostly, he'll amuse himself with her for a while. Maybe with pleasure, definitely with pain."

Marco felt his poisoned blood boil inside him. The idea of the general's hands on Kyra was bad enough, the idea of him hurting her was worse. He'd seen for himself that she could feel pain. Why the hell couldn't she have just stayed with the plane like he told her? Why had she risked herself for the sake of two people she didn't even know? "We have to go after her," Marco said.

"Why are you so ready to rush into the breach and risk your beautifully sculpted flesh for a nymph? Do you think you'll rescue her and live happily ever after? That's not how the stories of nymphs end."

"I promised I'd return for her," Marco said. "I'm not leaving her behind."

"We're mortals. We don't stand a chance against a war god and now that I know where Kyra is, it's time for me to return to Ares. You should come with me. My master has always wanted a hydra of his very own." She licked her lips again in a blatantly sexual way. "Besides, there could be side benefits."

Ignoring her propositions—and not knowing which

one was more offensive—Marco fastened upon the most important part of the statement. "You're leaving? Look, I don't pretend to understand all the perverse reasons Ares sent you after me, but wasn't part of it to protect Kyra? You said he has plans for her. She's his daughter."

"And Ares is a god," she said. "He's patient. His plans will wait."

"Wait for what?" Marco asked.

"For Ogun to tire of torturing her," the vulture said. "After a decade or so, Kyra will heal and return to Ares chastened by this experience."

"You don't understand," Marco growled. "She doesn't have a decade. Kyra isn't immortal anymore. My blood has made her vulnerable. I've changed her!"

He couldn't tell if the vulture was listening to him. She was too eager to return to her master. If she heard him at all, she was too stupid to know what to do about it without getting Ares' opinion first. If Marco was going to save Kyra, he was going to have to do it on his own.

Ogun's blade opened a thin red line down her arm. Her pale skin parted and blood quickened to the surface, flowing onto the sheets of the bed to which she was chained. Kyra groaned through the pain, waiting for the flesh to close back over the wound, knowing that when it did, he'd only cut her deeper. "Ah, my sweetling, are you ready to tell me what manner of creature you are?" Ogun asked, with a menacing smile. He'd already shot her—amused at how the bullets passed through her. He'd already pounded a nail through one hand to watch her body slowly expel it. He'd already choked her, made her gasp for breath, made her fight for every gulp of air.

But she wasn't healing as quickly as when the torture started, and soon, she wouldn't heal at all. That she was becoming mortal was ever more apparent, both to the war god and to her. But it had all been worth it. She'd saved the people Marco loved. She'd given him the chance he needed to break free of this life. That was the best gift she could give him, wasn't it?

Ogun brought his mouth close to Kyra's ear, a flesh-crawling kiss upon her neck before he sank his teeth into her pale skin. Kyra screamed, feeling as if she were in the jaws of Cerberus himself, wondering if he was going to devour her chunk by chunk. And now Kyra was in so much pain, she couldn't remember why she'd refused to tell the African god what he wanted to know in the first place. "I'll tell you!"

Ogun released her and she felt the warm flow of blood behind her head as it dripped from her ear down her neck. And he was looking at her with expectation.

Shaking her sweat-soaked hair, Kyra let out a choked sob of defiance.

"If I cut all the way down into the tendons...if I sawed through the bone and cut your hand from your body, would it grow back again? I am so curious, Sweetling, because my skin is like iron. No blade can cut me, no weapon can wound me. Shall we try it, or will you tell me what you are?"

"I'm a *lampade*," she spit out, furious at her own weakness, but willing to do anything to make the pain stop. "I'm a nymph of the underworld!"

At this, Ogun's smile of triumph was short but terrifying. "Ahh, another Hellene, just like the hydra. And just what are you doing so far away from home?"

"I'm on safari!"

Ogun laughed. "The mortals only come here for the gold, for the diamonds and for the coltan that they use in their cell phones. But you are here to see the giraffes? I think not." Ogun stabbed her again, this time in the chest, where the blade pierced her lung and it hissed. Then he pulled the knife back out and Kyra coughed. She couldn't breathe, and when she did exhale it was with a spray of blood.

"Now, again, Sweetling," Ogun said, "Why are you here?"

"She's here because of me," a voice said from the door. Kyra's eyes swam in tears of agony. She must have been hallucinating because what she saw was another version of Ogun himself, all tall and ebony and elegant as the Congolese soldiers so often were. He was even wearing camo and carried a rifle over one shoulder.

When Kyra lifted her head from the blood-soaked pillow to illuminate his soul, she found herself too weak to do it. Still, somehow, she knew it was Marco.

No! He couldn't be here. After all the pain she'd endured to set him free, he couldn't possibly have walked right into the god's clutches. Kyra let out a helpless moan. It was the only sound she could make until the wound in her chest healed. But she wished she could shout. She wished she could scream that this was all wrong. Marco wasn't supposed to come back for her. Mortal men never came back for nymphs.

Ogun stood quickly, a bloody machete flashing at his side. "Ahh. The Great Northern Warlord has returned!"

"Release her, Ogun."

"Why should I? This creature is almost as interesting as you are."

"If you let her go, I'll give you your shipment of weapons."

Kyra tried to pull herself upright, only to be yanked back by the chain around her throat she'd forgotten was there. She was in such horrible pain, and to hear Marco make this offer only made it worse.

"Marco, my old friend, why do you behave so foolishly? When it was just your timid Benji and your soft little Ashlynn that I held prisoner, weapons for hostages was a worthwhile trade. But now? I want to know what this creature can do for me."

"She's not going to do anything for you," Marco said, grabbing the keys off the wall. "She belongs to Ares. She's his daughter."

How could Marco be foolish enough to mention Ares? If they involved her father, Marco would never escape. Between the two war gods, Marco would be a prize to be fought over—a deadly arms race between divine forces that would only end catastrophically. Her father was no better than Ogun, and possibly much worse. The mention of Ares was also the first thing— the only thing—that gave Ogun pause.

"Ares, the Thracian?" the African asked with a bitter twist of his lips, and perhaps a touch of alarm. "Is it true, Sweetling?"

"No," Kyra forced herself to rasp. "I don't know Ares."

"She's lying," Marco said. "She's a very accomplished liar, trust me. She *is* the daughter of Ares, and she's here because of me. You see, you're not the only god who wants his very own hydra."

"Ares is powerful." Ogun scowled. "But I think I am more powerful still. Have you made your pledge to the Thracian war god?"

"Not yet. But if you let Kyra go, I'll make my pledge to be your minion instead."

Marco couldn't do this, Kyra thought. He wouldn't do this! Not for any reason. After all they'd been through, he couldn't betray her like this.

A booming laugh came from Ogun. "As you would have it, then, my friend."

With that, the iron collar around Kyra's neck snapped open. Freed, she tore at the chains that clasped her, scrambling to stand. The knife Marco had given her was on the table, and she might be able to get to it if she lunged for it. She wouldn't be able to overtake a war god even if she had all her old immortal strength, but perhaps she could buy time for Marco to flee. That was the only plan she had left.

But Marco must have seen the lethal gleam in her eye because just as Kyra took the knife, he grabbed her. Just the sensation of his skin against hers—a touch she'd never thought she'd feel again—was enough to dizzy her. Though it hurt to speak, she forced herself to whisper, "You can't give your pledge, Marco. Not after everything—"

"Kyra, remember what we said on the plane. We can't cheat fate."

So he'd just given up, then. He'd given in. He thought it was his inescapable fate to be an instrument of death. He really believed that he was no different than the killers in the ditch in Rwanda all those years ago. "Don't you realize what's at stake?"

"I do," Marco said, his eyes trying to make a connection with hers.

Perhaps if she could've used her torchlight…but she was too weak. Her powers were all but useless, but she still had fierce determination. "I'm not leaving you," Kyra said, clinging to him stubbornly, even though he wore the face of the war god she feared.

Marco thrust her away. "I've made my choice, Kyra. Ogun is an old friend and we both see things the same way."

It made no sense. She didn't believe him, but she was in such pain. Everything was swimming before her eyes. Maybe she was imagining it all. "He's not your friend. He's a *war god*."

"And I'm a war-forged hydra," Marco said. "I've been fighting in Africa for more than a decade and I've made a lot of money doing it. I'm not going to give that up. Not even for you."

Could the money have meant more to him than she'd realized? She'd seen his penthouse in Naples. She'd let him kiss her in his luxurious suite in Toronto. Marco drove expensive cars, wore expensive suits and was a man with the power to look however he pleased, go where he pleased, to do what he pleased, to have who he pleased. "What about for Ashlynn?" she asked acidly. "Would you give it up for her?"

Marco shrugged. "She won't have me, so it doesn't matter. War is the only thing I know."

"You're lying," Kyra said. He *had* to be lying.

"No. You're the expert when it comes to lies. Everything between us was deception, Kyra. You're blisteringly hot in bed, but when it's over, all I'm left with is the illusion. I guess that's how it is with nymphs."

Shocked, she stumbled back. His words were as poisonous as his blood, and she could hardly believe they'd come from his lips. "You—you're hurting me."

"You're tough," Marco replied coldly. "You'll get over it. You'll take another lover and move on. So will I. Now go."

It was as if he had backhanded her. She felt the sting and could almost taste the blood in her mouth. She'd thought he was struggling to be a better man, she thought she knew him, but Hecate had been right. No matter how clearly you tried to illuminate the crossroads, mortals sometimes still willfully took the wrong path. And it broke her heart. It broke *her.* She felt as if she was looking at him for the first time. Hell, he'd even taken on the face of a war god. How blind had she been? Like every other silly nymph in history, she'd seen in Marco only what she wanted to see. The reality was that he'd been a soldier, a warrior, and the bloodlust was in him. He'd make a perfect minion, after all.

"I hate you," she grated. "I wish I'd killed you in Naples."

It wasn't true, but she wished it were. His betrayal would hurt so much less.

Marco's eyes were unreadable, but what he said was, "Me, too."

Then he tossed her the peridot choker. She caught her mother's pendant in one hand, gripping it with fury. Then she turned and stormed out past Ogun's boy soldiers with what little dignity and strength she had left. Kyra stumbled down the mountain trail, tears and confusion blinding her. It was only dusk, but Kyra was so weak that she couldn't see through the trees.

She pushed her way through thickets of bamboo, and stopped there, wondering if she might not just become part of them. Right here on this mountain, felled by grief, she could transform. She felt ready to sink down into the earth and become a new sort of tangled, strangled vine. No. Something with wings. She hated to fly, why not punish herself? Why not become like an angel or some creature that could fly far away from a world in which she no longer belonged? That was her fate.

But Hecate had said her fate was to destroy a hydra.

Kyra's heart missed a beat. Marco had told her to remember what they'd said on the plane, that they couldn't cheat fate. He'd said it when he was trying to think of ways to escape Ogun. He'd said it because he wanted her to kill him. To fulfill her destiny. Was that still what he had in mind? Had everything else he'd said in Ogun's hut been a lie designed to make her leave?

In either case, Marco had said one true thing to Ogun. Kyra *was* the daughter of Ares. She could smell war before it came, could hear the explosions before they happened, like the crack of her father's whip over his chariot.

And war was coming now.

Chapter 21

The first explosion went off in the middle of the general's pastureland, sending up a big cloud of dust. Marco heard the jingling of frantic bells as goats and livestock ran. The force of the second explosion was much closer and nearly threw Marco off his feet. A wooden beam collapsed beside him, but he wasn't afraid. Better that he die this way, crushed. And better that he die swiftly so that he wouldn't have to live with the memory of Kyra's tear-streaked face as she left him. He'd been sure that she'd see through his lies, that she'd look into his eyes and know his intentions. It hurt him to think that she might never know how he felt about her, but at least it got her to leave before the bombs started falling.

Outside, panicked men shouted, but even though the shelling had blown a hole in the roof, the war god only laughed. As debris fell around them, Ogun stood in the midst of the destruction, upright, his eyes alight. "Does your little nymph think the same thing will work twice? That a few grenades will make me take my eyes off of my prize?"

Ogun reached for Marco, but Marco leaped away. "It's not another distraction, and those explosions aren't grenades."

"If not a distraction, then what?"

"Something you'll like a lot better," Marco said, lifting the machine gun he'd taken off one of Ogun's guards. *"War."*

With that, Marco pulled the trigger and sent a hail of bullets toward Ogun's chest. Ogun stumbled back, clutching at his torso and Marco felt the brief rush of triumph. But then the general spread his hands, sprinkling the broken bullet fragments like deadly fairy dust. And he began to laugh again. Acrid smoke billowed around them and Marco pulled his sleeve over his face so that he could breathe. Another explosion rocked the ground; it broke the glass and took off part of the front wall with it. Far off, Marco could hear the rumbling, and Ogun could, too.

"Tanks." Ogun's expression lay somewhere between fury and delight. "What have you done, my old friend?"

"What I should have done a long time ago," Marco

said. In the envelope he'd delivered to the UN, Marco had given a complete account. Maps of every strong-hold and fortress. Inventory of rebel weaponry. Everything.

Ogun's soldiers burst in. "An army is coming!" they shouted, then pulled up short, not knowing which man was truly the general. He pulled back. Behind Marco, the smoldering hole in the wall beckoned. As another explosion shook the ground, he dove through the open-ing, rolled to his feet and bolted. He heard the staccato burst of a machine gun behind him and little divots of earth came up around his feet as he ran, but better that he was shot than captured alive—Ogun would still harvest his toxic blood, but at least there'd be a limited supply.

"Don't shoot him, you imbeciles!" Ogun cried, his long elegant strides easily closing the distance. There was no way Marco could outrun the war god, but it just wasn't in him to surrender.

Behind them the battle raged. UN and government forces were clashing with the rebels and the scent of war was in the air. It was the one thing—perhaps the only thing—more tempting to Ogun. "I want to fight. I want to taste the gunpowder, to see the destruction, to feast upon the forces of war!"

"Then go back and enjoy yourself!" Marco shouted.

Vines and thorns lashed at him as he ran and behind him, he heard the god's frustrated cry.

"You'll never find your way out of this jungle in the dark, my friend. I'll win this battle and have you in my hands again by morning."

Probably so, but Marco kept running. At first it was the slim hope of escape that kept his legs pumping and led him to ignore everything but the slope of the mountain as he fled. Then as time passed and darkness fell, he knew it was simply adrenaline that kept him going. He didn't know how long or how far he ran. He was so disoriented he wasn't even sure he was going the right direction anymore. He stopped when it was so dark that he couldn't see anything in front of him. That's also when he hit a patch of wet earth. The ground dropped out beneath him and he slid through the mud, rocks and fallen branches, bruising him all the way.

Momentarily dazed, he checked himself for wounds. Miraculously, he wasn't bleeding anywhere, so he just lay still listening to the rumble of government tanks as they assaulted the general's stronghold. Maybe for once, the world would do something right in Africa. Maybe the information he'd provided the UN would be more valuable than the weapons he'd sold. Only time would tell. He probably wouldn't live to see it, but he felt strangely at peace with that. The important thing was that the people he loved were safe. Ashlynn and Benji were on a plane out of Africa, and hopefully, so was Kyra.

She hated him now—he'd *made* her hate him. He'd never forget the rage on her face when she'd told him so, nor the pain that shot through him when she said it. But he'd saved her, and it might have just been the only good thing he'd managed to do with his life.

Waiting for his eyes to adjust enough that he could make out the shape of the night in front of him, Marco held up his hands. But between his splayed fingers, he saw a brief flash of green, like a firefly from the summers he spent in Niagara Falls as a boy. Then he saw it again, that green glow. Peridot.

No. His eyes must be playing tricks on him. It was just that he *wanted* to see her. Surely he'd pissed Kyra off enough that she'd gotten off this damned mountain and out of the war zone. But what if she hadn't? "Kyra?"

She didn't answer him. She didn't pause to wipe the mud from her hands or cheeks. She simply pushed through the foliage and threw herself into his arms, kissing him hard, desperately. Maybe it was the feel of her that he recognized in the dark, but soon his mouth enveloped hers in that feverish way that robbed her of all reason. And for a moment—just a moment—it seemed as if their gasped breaths were louder than the war that raged in the distance.

"Damn you," Marco finally said, shaking Kyra. "Why are you here? Why didn't you go?"

"Because I love you," Kyra admitted with a sob. It was the last thing she'd wanted to say, but the words wrested themselves from her and left her utterly defenseless. He could cast her away. But he crushed her against his chest, steely arms around her waist as if he'd never let her go.

"Kyra, you said you hated me."

"I lied!" Kyra cried bitterly. "Isn't that why you're always so angry at me? Because I lie and I lie and I lie. But you lied, too, you hypocrite." She pounded her fist against his chest. "Tell me you were lying!"

"Ow! *Damn it.*"

"Don't you hear the war raging up there, Marco? The bloodlust vibrates beneath my skin because I'm the daughter of Ares. But if I can turn my back on it, so can you. Tell me you didn't mean what you said in front of Ogun. All those horrible, *horrible* things you said. Tell me you lied."

"Of course I lied!" Marco barked, pulling her against him as if he couldn't decide whether to hug or throttle her. "You said you could look right into my eyes and see my soul—that you'd always know me, always see the truth!"

Kyra took a sharp breath. "But I didn't have the strength. He'd been torturing me, and I was using everything I had left to heal my wounds. I couldn't use my inner torch…and I couldn't understand why you came back."

His fingers locked around her wrists. "I came back for you, you witless nymph!"

"Oh, Marco—"

"Shut up," Marco said. Then he kissed her lying lips as if they were the most precious things to him in the world. She wanted to stay here, just like this. His hair in her hands. Her heart slamming in her chest alongside his. She wanted to savor and explore the emotions that swirled within her at the realization that he'd come back for her. That once—just once—a man came back for a nymph.

But as another rocket lit up the night sky, she was reminded that there was no time for that. "Did you pledge yourself to be Ogun's minion?"

"Not yet. The explosions started before I could."

"Then we have to keep walking," Kyra said, scrambling to her feet. "If we can get to the plane, maybe we can get out of the Congo before the fighting stops."

"Kyra, we have to wait until daybreak. It's too dark and I'm not sure where we are. I can't see a thing."

"Maybe I can," Kyra said, tugging at his hand. To summon what power she had left, she'd have to let all her cuts bleed. But perhaps if she focused her strength she could do it. She might not be immortal anymore, but she was still a nymph of the underworld. Darkness posed no barrier. Her inner torch flickered until she glowed in the darkness, but it was a struggle to keep it lit. She took a few steps, squinting, and Marco stumbled behind her, sweeping the air in front of him with his free hand.

"You have to trust me," Kyra whispered, knowing how deeply that ran counter to his nature.

"I do," he said, putting himself in her hands.

Kyra's torchlit eyes burned until tears flowed freely. Until her feet were so sore that she couldn't feel them anymore and her tongue was thick in her mouth with thirst. As she and Marco trudged through the tall grasses, flies bit at the blood she let trickle down her arms. And when Kyra stumbled, Marco caught her around the waist and slung her up into his arms. The sudden weightlessness, the feeling of someone else unburdening her, made her tremble with relief. "It's dawn," Marco said. "I can see, now. In fact, I think I see the plane. Just close your eyes, Kyra. Close your eyes."

Letting her head fall back against his shoulder, Kyra's lids fluttered shut. She'd done it. Just a little farther and they'd be free. And she was in his arms—the only place she wanted to be. He carried her the rest of the way, setting her down in the passenger seat, and never in her life did she think she would be so happy to be inside a plane.

Chapter 22

Kyra woke up in an empty cockpit, sweating profusely in the stifling air. She sat up suddenly, rasping, "Marco?" There was no answer.

Unstrapping herself and standing on shaky legs, Kyra climbed out of the plane, knife in hand. She'd taken only a few steps past the tail before her vision slid, tilted and slammed back into focus. Struggling with her new mortal vulnerability, Kyra needed to sit down. Right where she was. Wherever she was. As it happened, she found herself at the edge of a sparkling blue pond beneath a fat, orange, setting sun. *Gods above and below,* where was she and how long had she been asleep?

"Marco!" she called again, trying to fight the panic in her voice.

"I'm here," he said, emerging from beneath the wing

of the plane. He was red-faced and shirtless, with only a canteen strapped to his shoulder. Sweat glistened on his arms and dripped down his hard stomach, soaking the waistband of his muddy fatigues. He'd been working hard at something—perhaps fixing the plane.

And he smiled at her. It was the first time she'd ever seen a genuine smile on his face, and the beauty of it made everything tighten inside her chest. She'd never seen anyone smile like that, and it made her forget to breathe.

"You're looking a little better," Marco said. "The sleep helped?"

"Yes," Kyra exhaled, relieved to see the aura of his concern. Her powers were returning to her. For how long, though, she didn't know. "I'm thirsty."

He handed her his canteen, hovering while she took deep gulps. "Easy, *Angel*."

For some reason, it no longer bothered her that he called her that. He could call her anything at all in that sexy baritone and it would please her. She took a few more swallows, then squinted. "Where are we?"

"Cameroon. It was as far as I could get from Ogun on the fuel we had. How long do we have before he finds us?"

That was a tricky question. "Ogun doesn't have the gift of sight. He isn't like Hecate. His minions are probably searching for us now, and then he'll catch up."

"How long?" Marco asked, with that infuriating pragmatism of his.

"Just as Ares takes vultures for his minions, Ogun chooses wounded warriors," Kyra said softly, realizing only now that Marco had always been drawn to Ogun for just this reason. In the sunlight, the scar from his gunshot wound on his shoulder was paler than the rest of his skin. He, too, was a wounded warrior. "This place has more than its share of wounded warriors who could report back to Ogun, but as long as no one saw us land here, it could be days before he finds us."

Marco nodded, some of the tension flowing away. She relaxed some, too. Marco took the canteen back, but only sipped from it as if to save the bulk of it for her, as if she were any other mortal woman who could die of thirst. And maybe she could. "Everything really hurts," Kyra admitted. "I don't even remember the plane ride. I don't remember anything after I led you out of the jungle."

"After what you've been through, I'm not surprised."

"This…this exhaustion. This is what it's like for mortals?"

He winced, his eyes traveling over her with guilt.

"Don't look at me that way, Marco. I stabbed you. The poisoning was my fault."

But Marco didn't answer. Instead, he crouched beside her, pouring some of the water from the canteen into his hands and using it to wash her arms. She realized what a mess she must be—her hair matted, her tank top glued to her back with sweat and blood. And it made her defensive. "You're dirtier than I am, you know."

"I don't want your wounds to get infected."

Wounds? Kyra looked down to see marks on her arms—bruises and jaggedly rent skin where Ogun had cut her. Was that a scab on her perfect nymph's skin? It was the way mortal wounds closed, slowly and with a mark to tell the story. It mesmerized Kyra, and when she looked up at the world again, it was with a sense of being alive she hadn't felt before. The world looked new to her eyes, and she wanted to be a part of it.

Kyra peeled her shirt over her head. Marco averted his gaze—apparently trying not to stare at her breasts as she bared them in the glow of the setting sun— but he couldn't hide the naked lust the sight evoked in him. "I'm going to swim," Kyra said. "You should come with me."

Marco's eyes darted toward the gorgeous watering hole, then back at her. "There could be crocodiles. Who knows what's in that water?"

"It's clear to the bottom!" Kyra protested, taking off the rest of her clothes. "Besides, I'm not sure if I've mentioned it before, but I have uncommonly good eyesight."

He smirked. He'd never been a man for whimsy. But something was different about him today. "Okay," he said, his hands unfastening his belt buckle.

Her breath caught at the sight of him. Even after all they'd been through together, her raw need for him was reliable and easily triggered. It was an ache. She stood there watching until he was undressed and splashed into the water up to his knees. Kyra's heart seized with the most overwhelming sensation that she'd somehow seen this before. Seen him walk away from her, into the water. No, it wasn't *her* memory—it was just the story Calypso had told about the day Odysseus left. But as the water embraced Marco, swirling around his hips, Kyra was suddenly and acutely aware that he planned to leave her. Even now as he held his hand out to her. He wouldn't stay. She knew it as she knew herself. Better than she knew her own nymph's nature. And yet, she took his outstretched hand and let him draw her in.

The water was warm as a bath and she tried to shake off her sadness as they washed away the blood and grime and sweat. She told herself to leave it alone, but she had to know. She was already naked. She'd already told him that she loved him, and now they were both clean. She didn't want to dirty whatever it is they had with pretense. "Marco? What aren't you telling me?" His dark hair was wet and slicked back, his shoulders bare and glowing, but his expression was a mask. There was nothing to do but ask. "Are you going back to Ashlynn?"

The mask broke as he looked her dead in the eye. "No."

But there was something he was still hiding. Something dark and looming between them. "But you wish you could be with her?"

"No."

She had trouble believing him. "When I pretended to be Ashlynn, you *wanted* me to be her."

"No," Marco said again, this time shaking his head and sending a spray of water droplets into the air. "I wanted *her* to be *you*."

Kyra didn't dare look at him. If she saw a lie in his eyes it would shatter her into a thousand pieces. Instead, she let him draw her close and kiss her. It was the first time—the only time—they'd been completely naked together. No disguises. Their own faces, their own skin. Nothing between them but the silky water and the heat of their bodies. They matched each other, lip to lip, chest to breast. He was hard against her belly, and it sent a sweet pain right to her core. But some part of her was afraid to be so aroused again, afraid of the wild lust.

No. She knew lust, she knew sex, and she was too primal to fear either. It wouldn't be sex this time, it would be lovemaking. There could be no more pretending, even to herself, that it was only about his hard body or her easy virtue. Marco's teeth captured her lower lip and softly bit down, sending a shiver through her. His hands splayed at the small of her back, clutching her like a drowning man.

"I need you," he whispered.

He *needed* her. How was she to struggle against that and why should she try? Especially when the answering call of her own need echoed through her body. She reached for him below the water and it was like a jolt of electricity arced between them when her fingers wrapped around his erection. He pressed hard into her hand, his mouth suddenly all over her. Her face, her neck, her shoulders. She stroked him, water swirling between them as she did so.

When his lips fastened on the vulnerable hollow of her throat, she smothered a groan and he said, "You don't have to be quiet anymore, Kyra. We're not on a dance floor."

The heat of a blush crept up her skin, but it wasn't shame. His knee shifted between her legs—a vivid reminder of their rooftop dance with all its pleasure and unfulfilled desire. Molten-lava memories flowed beneath her skin—the memory of what he'd done to her and what he could do again if he wanted to. He could drive her right over the edge into orgasm with nothing but his voice, but it was not what she wanted. Not this time. And he seemed to know it. "It's all right," Marco said hoarsely. "When you come this time, I promise I'm going to be inside you."

Now Kyra *did* groan, and it came from the depths of her as his hands slid over her thighs, rough fingers over sore muscles. He hoisted her up out of the water so that she straddled him—and Kyra felt a strange kind of weightlessness. *It's his gift,* she thought. He could lift an earthbound nymph from the world, hold her in the sky and not let her fall. He carried her, his powerful thighs churning through the water until they reached the shore, then he set her down on a bed of tall grasses. The dry weeds must have scratched her naked back. The hard ground must have been unyielding. But all she could feel on her body were the places where he touched her.

He cupped her breasts, kneading them as he settled his weight down on her. She took that weight, loving it. Then her legs splayed in invitation. She wanted him to push inside her. But instead, he lowered his head, kissing a fiery path down her stomach to the downy curls between her legs. Kyra jerked when his tongue found her center.

It was too much. She grabbed his hair, trying to slow him down as he used his teeth to drive her to the edge.

Marco wasn't gentle. He couldn't be. Especially not with her thighs closed around his neck and the taste of her feeding an urgency in him to utterly ravish her. "Please," he heard her muffled whisper, her hips twisting beneath his mouth as if to get away. He thought he might have hurt her until she said, "You promised..."

What the hell had he promised? Marco couldn't remember. He was so far gone he couldn't fasten on anything but the satin of her skin. He looked up to see her hair fanned out on the grass and a flush that stained her bare breasts with pink arousal. Those beautiful lips were parted, her fists clenched at her sides, and that's when he realized how close she'd been to orgasm. "You promised when I came this time, you'd be inside me."

Hearing her say it made him snap. He crawled over her, positioned her hips and, with one thrust, buried himself inside her. She took all of him. Every last inch. And it made him shudder with a satisfaction that throbbed throughout his whole body. He thrust into her. Again. Then again. Until he found a pounding rhythm that made him forget all else. That was vital, because right now, he *needed* to forget everything but her.

Kyra let out a desperate sound, as she rocked her hips forward, but he held her still. If she kept moving like that, making sounds like that, he'd never last. And this *had* to last. This had to last so he could remember it. So he could take this one happiness with him to the grave.

In his rough sexual frenzy, his body made wet slapping noises against her. But he couldn't seem to stop. Then Kyra's eyes fluttered closed. He knew the signs. He'd watched her come before. A ragged breath tore itself from her throat, and he felt her clamp around him. Her body went rigid as her lips parted in a delicious orgasmic cry. He let out a ferocious growl as he emptied himself into her. The pleasure was blinding— white-hot. Wave after wave of intense release, as if he were pouring everything he had, everything he was, into her body.

Afterward, his muscles all gave way. He tried to roll away so as not to crush her beneath him, but Kyra pulled him down onto the pillow of her body. And he lay there, shattered. He'd never felt this way. He must never have been in love before. And this was undoubtedly love. There was no lying to himself about it. It's just that he hadn't known it would feel like this. And it would make everything he had to do so much harder.

Kyra stared up at the night sky. She couldn't remember having ever seen so many stars before. It made her brave. It made her reckless. "Marco, I want you to come back home with me."

His eyes were half-lidded, his breathing even. "I thought you didn't take anybody home with you."

She'd already let him into her heart. Maybe she could let him into her home, too. "That was before."

A sad smile passed his lips and he asked, "What would we do there in your villa?"

She touched his cheek. "Make love. Gather our treasure. Buy a big boat and sail the Mediterranean. Only Poseidon would have to know, and he's not very warlike."

"How long could we live together like that?" Marco asked.

Her newfound mortality didn't frighten her. "Until we die."

He nestled against her, sleepily, and whispered, "I'd like that."

I'd like that, he'd said. And instantly, Kyra knew he was well and truly done with selling weapons. He was done with war. But he hadn't said he loved her, and it was the one thing she wouldn't push him to say. It irritated her, like a prickle on her skin and it wasn't the only one. Kyra touched the scab on her arm and was rewarded with a sharp pain. It was a wound, a real wound. It was somehow more real than anything she'd ever suffered before. She'd have to learn to get used to the kind of injury mortals like Marco endured and risked every day. "You know, you could've been killed," she murmured. "When they bombed Ogun's compound, you could've been blown to bits or riddled with bullets just like any other soldier. How did you know you'd get away?"

"I didn't," Marco said, and his answer chilled Kyra to the bone.

That's when she realized the barrier—the only barrier—that still lay between them. He'd returned to save her, yes, but he hadn't expected to live through any of this. She should've known it by the way he'd been so different today. She should've known it by the way he smiled when she first woke up. Mortals never smiled with quite that much lightness and openness unless they were imbeciles or ready to die. "What were you doing today while I was asleep in the cockpit?"

Marco's voice was flat. Steady. "I was digging a hole."

Kyra hissed like a cat suddenly startled. She knew, though he had not said it, that he was digging a *grave*. She tried to roll away from him but he caught her by the shoulders and made her look at him. "At sunrise, you have to bury me, Kyra."

So she'd been right when she saw him splashing into the water and seen only Odysseus leaving Calypso for the sea. He'd been planning to leave her all along. But he wasn't leaving her for another woman; he was leaving her for the underworld.

"I can't do it," Kyra said fiercely.

"You have to. Even if we escape Ogun, he's not the only war god who will want to use my blood. Until I die, I'm a one-man weapon of mass destruction. You know it."

It was true. It's why she'd tried to kill him in the first place. But that was before she'd fallen so helplessly in love. And now, the thought was too much to bear. Kyra's throat tightened. She shook her head violently. "No."

"You have to do it. Who else will guide my shade after death? You're the only angel I'd ever call for."

"There's another way," Kyra whispered. "Let me stare into your eyes and scourge your wounds with my torchlight. I could try…"

He cupped her chin. "I'd rather be dead than live as a madman, Kyra."

She had no doubt of that. And maybe she'd rather see him dead than ranting and raving as her mother had, locked in his own personal hell. She could kill him if she failed, but would she? "Maybe you wouldn't go mad. Maybe it'd be like…"

"Like what?"

She didn't want to tell him, but he had a right to know. "If I put you to the torch, it would lay you open to me. I'd see everything. Every memory, every pain, every sin you've ever committed and every secret you hold dear. All your weaknesses and fears…"

She swallowed, remembering how *violated* her mother had felt. How her living mother had never been able to distinguish between Kyra and raping, warmongering Ares ever again. She knew before he said it that a man like Marco wouldn't—couldn't—allow her to violate him in this way. Especially since it might not work. He'd hold tight to his mortal dignity even in death.

He had the haunting look of a man who had already made the decision to die. He traced her lower lip where his twilight kisses had burned and asked, "You're a nymph of the underworld. You'll still be able to see my shade when I'm dead, won't you?"

Kyra choked back a sob. "But it won't be like this. I'll be able to see you, but not touch you. It can't ever be like this again."

"Then let's not waste the time we have left," he said, pulling her across him and kissing her with a desperation that cut through her tears.

Chapter 23

A low chug-chug of an aircraft broke through the silent and starry night. "What is that?" Kyra asked.

Marco was on his feet in an instant, grabbing Kyra's hand and yanking her up from the ground. "It's a helicopter. Get dressed. We're going to have to run."

"But it could be friendly—it could be a UN helicopter!"

"It's not," Marco said with the complete surety of an arms dealer who knew every make and model of killing machine on the planet. "It's Russian. Get dressed."

She'd just finished throwing her damp clothes on when the dark sky was broken apart by an intense beam. The chopper's bright lights methodically criss-crossed the field. It was hard to know which way to run. The plane was their only real avenue of escape, but it had no fuel. "Is it Ogun?" Marco asked. "Can you see who it is?"

Kyra looked up, opened her eyes wide and let her torchlight illuminate the sky. She could see right through the chopper. She could see into the cockpit, and what she saw made her gasp. "It's Daddy!"

It was too late to run. Marco knew it, too. He was pressing something into her hand, and she looked down to see it was the handle of her knife. Even so, Kyra searched frantically for an avenue of escape. The grasses were tall. If they kept low, perhaps Ares wouldn't see them. But his vulture would sniff them out. Maybe the water—if they went under the water... but the lights were already on them, blinding and nightmarish, as the chopper buffeted them with bursts of air.

Marco's eyes locked on hers. "Aim right for the heart."

The chopper blades spun closer and closer. Kyra's hair whipped at her face and her hand tightened on the knife. She knew what was at stake. She knew that Marco was willing to sacrifice his life. He was a hydra; until he was dead, his body would be a constant source of the deadliest poison. He was counting on her to be strong. But she wasn't a hardened, tireless immortal anymore. "I can't," she shouted over the noise of the chopper, shuddering with revulsion. "I can't!"

Marco's eyes softened as he put his hand over hers, their fingers wrapping around the handle. "It's all right. I'll do it."

To kill oneself with a knife was harder than most people realized. He was a man trying to cross over the threshold of death and it shamed her that he should have to do it by himself. And yet, Kyra couldn't let go of the knife. The chopper landed and Ares leaped out. He was as tall and terrifying as Kyra remembered him. It didn't matter if he wore the crested helmet and red cape of Spartan warriors or modern combat camouflage, the terror of seeing Ares was always the same.

The Greek god of war came striding toward them as soon as his boots hit the ground, and his vulture chased after him. There was no more time. "Kyra, give me the knife!" Marco shouted, wrestling with her for it. They grappled for the blade, just as they had the first night they met. Her muscles were tight and sore. But not even Marco's arms, those beautiful arms, were as strong as her love for him. It was selfish, it was wrong, but she couldn't let him die.

"No!" Kyra shouted, wrenching the knife from his grip and flinging it away. Time seemed to stand still as she and Marco watched the knife hurtle through the night air, and splash into the dark water. It was over. All for naught. Ares and his sharp-faced minion were upon them and Marco's look of devastation broke her heart.

"I'm sorry, I'm so sorry," Kyra mouthed.

She expected Marco to rail at her, to rage at her for what she'd done. But instead, he pulled her into his arms.

If Ares hadn't been so furious, he wouldn't have been able to bear looking at his daughter. It was bad enough to see a mortal man's hands on Kyra. Nearly intolerable to see how the hydra shielded her with his own body—as if Kyra needed his feeble mortal protection. But worst of all was watching his progeny cast away a perfectly good weapon! Where was Kyra's fierceness now? Where was her once-reliable bloodlust? All subsumed in her tearstained nymph's passion. The time had clearly come for an intervention.

Ares swung his club into the back of the hydra's knees and swept him off his feet. He could have killed him in that moment, cracked his skull open in a fit of unrestrained rage. But the war god knew the prize he'd captured was too valuable for that. Instead, he brought his boot down on Marco's throat.

"Inject him," Ares said to the vulture.

"Leave him alone!" Kyra shrieked, lunging for the vulture.

But for once, his minion was faster than the nymph.

She stabbed the needle into the hydra's arm and pumped the ambrosia into his bloodstream while he struggled. Then Ares brought down his weight on Marco, choking him, cutting off his air, crushing his windpipe. It wouldn't kill him, not with the ambrosia in his system. But it would hurt, and Ares *wanted* him to suffer. He *should* suffer for having made Ares chase him down. He *should* suffer for daring to stand against an Olympian, certainly. But mostly, he should suffer for having made Kyra love him.

If this pathetic mortal died, what would Kyra turn into? Some weeping rock outcropping? Some sad, cooing dove? Ares shuddered to think. Why, was she already changing. Did Ares spy an actual scab on Kyra's arm—a wound that hadn't yet healed?

"Let the vulture give you ambrosia," Ares commanded his daughter.

"I don't want it," Kyra cried. "I'd rather live and die with Marco."

"But your hydra will never die now, Kyra," Ares said as Marco clawed at his leg, struggling for the air that wouldn't come. "He's just going to *suffer*. Do you know how much pain he's in? The way his lungs burn without air?"

"Stop it," Kyra pleaded.

"I'll let him breathe again when you take the ambrosia," Ares said, watching the struggle in his daughter's eyes die away. It confirmed all the worst things Ares suspected about love. He'd told Aphrodite many times that love was a weakness—a chink in the finest, most advanced armor. Now Kyra bore that out. She held out her arm for the injection, wincing as the needle pierced her flesh. All the while, her eyes were on her lover, her mouth open as if she would breathe for him if she could. And then it was done.

"You should be thanking me," Ares said, lifting his foot off the throat of the man who lay choking and gasping at his feet. "I've given your lover an eternity. You'll never have to grieve for him, and chained as my minion, he'll never leave you. You can join with me, too, ride in the tank beside me. The family that fights together…"

Kyra shook her head in denial like a recalcitrant child. Why were his progeny so unreasonable?

"In the meantime," Ares said, taking a gun from his hip, "It's time to gather a little bit of hydra blood." Ares aimed for Marco's leg, at the main vessel—the one that would bleed the most—and fired.

The ambrosia coursing through Marco's veins was like a red-hot burst of adrenaline straight to the brain, but it didn't numb the shattering pain of the bullet as it tore into his leg and passed through the other side. A shout tore itself from his raw throat as the blood bubbled up from his wound, spattering the ground and hissing where it fell. There was blood everywhere and Marco writhed in agony. He'd seen enough combat to know that the bullet had severed his artery. But while the ambrosia did nothing to stop the suffering, it did give Marco a remarkable clarity of mind. As he lay there in the dirt, jamming his fist into the wound in a helpless battle to stop the toxic bleeding, he realized that this was how it was going to be. Ares was going to keep him alive so that he could bleed him like the African Maasai bleed their cows.

And with his ambrosia-colored eyes, Marco saw Kyra clearly for the first time, too. She was the most tenacious woman he'd ever met, and she'd never stop fighting for him. Even now, she was grappling with Ares for the gun, lionhearted as ever, but the war god flicked her away into the mud like she was nothing but a flyspeck of a girl.

Blood pooled under Marco, burning his clothes, burning the grass and poisoning the earth. He'd never been a coward. He'd never been afraid to fight for what he believed in. He hadn't even been afraid to die for what he believed in. But he had feared madness all his life, and now it was his only possible escape.

Kyra had to put him to the torch. "Kyra! Look at me."

Her eyes glittered with confusion. Her lower lip trembled.

"No, *look at me*," Marco said, teeth gnashing. "I love you. I trust you. Do it."

She hesitated, her long eyelashes fluttering as she realized what he meant for her to do. Then her stare went impossibly wide. They turned to liquid light. She burned brighter than any star; he felt the heat of her fiery gaze on his skin and it scorched everything it touched. It was agony. He heard himself howl, clawing at his own eyes, but there was no way to stop it now. The crackling roar of fire drowned out all else.

Kyra was inside him. He could smell and taste her, but there was no pleasure in this. He felt her probing for scars the same way she'd searched out the ones on his body, the unbearable light of her torch exposing every wound. It didn't matter that he loved her. He still felt ripped open, exposed, violated in every way. And it didn't matter that she loved him, either, for Kyra was now a warrior wielding her knife and torch to vanquish a foe.

Like the African women whose deadened eyes told the story of brutal rape, he no longer felt his own flesh. He no longer had a sense of himself in the world. He thought he heard Kyra say his name as she cut him, as she sliced him open, shoving her burning torch into his mind like a hot iron. Then his world went white.

* * *

The serpentine, chthonic beast lurked in the darkest part of Marco's mind. Kyra's torchlight gave it nowhere to hide, and it screeched as if her light were burning it alive. Foaming at the mouth, the monster came for her, fangs bared, trying to lure Kyra into the darkness. But Kyra leaped fearlessly into the breach, shearing off the heads and searing closed each wound. The noise—the shrieking—was unbearable. She imagined the hydra poison on her skin, burning her alive, but she pushed through until she saw the bullet fragment in Marco's shoulder. It lurked like an iron serpent, cold and deadly. She used her powers to burn it, the stink of hatred and Marco's internal rage filling her nostrils but she didn't dare stop. There was no glory in it. She was hurting him and it was grim work—grimmer than any labor of Hercules, for he had not loved the hydra he killed.

She worked as swiftly as she could, but she felt Marco's mind slipping away from her. His blood was bubbling, the poison boiling away. If he couldn't separate his mind from the monster within, she would destroy him, too.

"Marco!" she called as the brightness burned through his eyes, burned through his mind and soul. But where was he? She couldn't see him. She was a *lampade.* She was supposed to guide him back over the threshold of madness. She'd vanquished the monster, but where was the man?

In desperation, Kyra snapped her eyes closed, the sudden darkness enveloping her like a burial shroud. And she wasn't inside Marco's mind anymore, but in the grass.

"You foolish nymph!" Ares roared. "What have you done?"

Kyra was afraid of what she'd see when she opened her eyes again. It was Marco's screaming that finally made her look. She found herself kneeling beside Marco's body, though she couldn't remember having gone to his side. The bullet fragment in his shoulder had pushed through his skin, tearing through the scar, and emerging through his bloody flesh like the malevolent presence that it was. Marco's more recent gunshot wound was healing—the ambrosia doing its work—but he was writhing, his strong face contorted, his lips forming choked words and phrases that she could make no sense of.

It was happening again. Marco was like her mother—lost somewhere within his own depths, somewhere she couldn't reach. And thanks to the ambrosia, he might well be trapped in this madness forever.

"What have you done?" Ares again demanded to know.

Gods above and below, what *had* she done? She tried to rouse Marco—tried to shake him. But he looked through her as if he didn't know her. She called his name and he didn't answer. He was gone. Once again, because of her father, she'd destroyed someone she loved. Turning on the war god in fury, Kyra grated, "What have I done? I've fulfilled my destiny."

"Your destiny is to serve me," Ares said. "To fight beside me."

Kyra laughed, the sound on the edge of hysteria.

"You were born to it," the war god insisted. "You weren't bred for love. You were bred for destruction. Just look around you at everything you've touched."

Kyra looked down at the man she loved, who lay in broken anguish. Even the soil they'd made love upon was now stained with blood. All those dreams she'd allowed herself to reach for in the beauty of an African night were all in shattered pieces. How could she deny the truth of her father's words? But then Ares came up behind her, his golden hand coming to rest on her shoulder, a hollow comfort, insubstantial and unreal. She'd been touched by a man who loved her, and it'd made all the difference.

"Do you know what I was born to?" Kyra raged, her hand still gripping Marco's. "I was born a nymph, and nymphs *change.* Like Echo changed into a voice on the wind. Like Clytie changed into heliotrope. Like Daphne changed into a tree—"

"That's enough, Kyra," Ares warned.

But he would never frighten her again. Never again. "I'm a nymph and I can *change,* and not you or all the ambrosia left in the world can stop me. So leave us alone or I swear on the River Styx that the next time you see me I'll be nothing you recognize. Nothing you know."

Ares snatched his hand away. "You don't mean that."

But she'd sworn upon the River Styx, and they both knew it was the most serious oath she could make. "Do you want to test me? Go away. Just go away!"

"As you wish," Ares growled, stepping over the hollow form of Marco. "He isn't a hydra anymore and his blood is now harmless. He's useless to me."

Ares wasn't a god used to defeat and, deprived of his prize, he turned on his vulture in a vicious fit of anger. "And you've failed me one too many times. You're useless to me, too." He caught the redhead with one hand, his meaty fingers constricting around her throat.

The startled creature gave one squawk before he closed off her airway, and in spite of everything the vulture had done, Kyra shouted, "Stop it! It's me you're mad at, so leave her alone."

But the big god of war had already hoisted his

hapless minion into the air, shaking the vulture like a rag doll as her eyes bulged and she fought for breath. It was only a moment before Ares gave a snort of satisfaction and the vulture's neck cracked in his palm. As she died, the redhead's human form gave way to the scraggly buzzard beneath. Black feathers fell from Ares' hand, then he dropped the dead bird at his feet.

At last, his eyes fastened upon Kyra. She knew he wanted to punish her, to torture her, but nothing he could do to her would hurt more than losing Marco. What she'd told him wasn't a hollow threat. Without Marco, Kyra could already feel her heartbroken self spreading in the night breeze like the seeds of a wildflower. She could already imagine her bones turning to stone. Feathers growing from her skin. Yes, she would have angel wings, after all, she thought to herself with a bitter laugh. She'd turn into a bird—to fly in those skies she had always feared, above a world in which she no longer belonged. She'd fly away high.

She had only to choose the time and the form.

But for now, Kyra saw the vulture's shade rise from the corpse, bewildered and lost—and she knew she had at least one more soul to guide.

Chapter 24

As Marco felt his way through the tangled madness, memories tore into him like the thorns and nettles of a blackened jungle. Vines of nightmare wrapped around his throat, insects stung, and sometimes he felt the eyes of a predator upon him. The whites of Ogun's eyes, the gleam of Ogun's teeth.

He tasted filth and dirt in his mouth as if he'd been buried alive, and maybe he had been. He could no longer remember. Perhaps Kyra had stabbed him in the heart or buried him alive. *Kyra.* He said her name into the darkness. Once, far in the distance, too far to reach, he thought he saw a green spark. But then it winked out like the glow of a lightning bug suddenly smashed between two murderous hands. Still, he went toward it, swimming through the inky misery, knowing he might never see it again.

* * *

Kyra sat perched on the edge of the small bed in the guest room over Hecate's shop. It'd been months since she brought Marco home from Africa, but on the mattress, he continued to writhe, eyes rolling back in his head. If he knew she was there, there was no sign of it but for the occasional thrash of his arms.

"Stand down, soldier!" Marco cried as his clenched fist arced through the air. Kyra ducked out of the way just in time, but it wouldn't have mattered if he struck her. She wasn't sure she'd feel it anymore.

"We should strap him down before he hurts someone," Hecate said.

"Never," Kyra replied. "Never."

"I'll sit with him," the goddess offered. "It's the least I can do after my part in all this."

"Don't feel guilty. I know what Ares must've done to you to make you tell him where to find us."

"Not all the torture in the world would've loosened my lips if I hadn't known you'd escape him. I just didn't foresee the price you'd have to pay. Now, you look so tired, ambrosia notwithstanding. Let me sit with him, and you can get some rest."

It was true that Kyra was tired—not as a mortal woman, but as a brokenhearted nymph. More tired than she could say. "But what if Marco tries to come back and I'm not here to guide him?"

"You can't sit beside him forever," Hecate said.

Kyra rubbed the spot where she'd hoped for a scar and found only smooth immortal skin. "Yes, I can. Forever is the one thing I still have."

For Marco, finding his sanity wasn't like climbing out of the murky deep. It was more like breaking the surface, taking a few gasps of air and sinking down again. The first thing that seemed tangible and real was Kyra was sitting at his bedside.

"Marco?" she whispered. "Do you know me?"

He knew her, but he was raw inside. Shamed. She'd seen everything. She'd seen him steal weapons, kill his enemies and profit from the bloody business. She'd seen his triumphs, his flaws and every failure, great and small. Now they'd both have to live with that knowledge...forever. And he couldn't bear to have her look at him.

When Kyra tried to embrace him, he shied away. A furtive glance showed him her hurt expression. "You hate me," she said, quietly, with a terrible acceptance.

He didn't hate her. He didn't blame her. He just didn't know who he was now, and when he tried to explain, he couldn't. He had it in his head that if he spoke one word, it might shatter the sanity and send him back down into the darkness. And besides, she was so unspeakably beautiful. So perfect. He was unworthy of her in every way. She had to know that. She had to have seen it when she put him to the torch.

It bothered him that she fretted over him. He'd somehow turned a wild creature into something tame. And he himself had become something different, too. His scars were gone. All of them. The bullet wasn't in his shoulder anymore. Even the scar on his hand from where Kyra had slashed him the first night they met was gone.

When Kyra brought a tray with dinner, he took the knife and pressed its edge into his palm. The blade bit down and a line of crimson blood rose to the surface. He watched with astonishment as the flesh wound itself together, mending the gash as if it'd never been there at all. "It will still hurt," Kyra said, as if to reassure him. "But it'll heal."

That's not why he'd done it, though. He'd done it to see if his blood would bubble and burn with poison and was gratified beyond words that it did not. She'd vanquished the hydra inside him. His blood was no longer toxic. Now he was immortal.

But he felt as vulnerable as a newborn babe.

She told herself to be grateful. Even if he never looked at her again, he was regaining his sanity. He was coming back to himself. That alone was a miracle. She'd be a fool to wish for more. Yet a fool she was.

She sat beside him as he obsessively scanned the newspapers.

Marco was presumed dead and Ashlynn's kidnapping had been big news in the West, bringing renewed attention to the problems in Africa. Meanwhile, Benji was cooperating with the international community, but the general had escaped, and this made Marco furious. She didn't have the heart to tell him that Ogun would come again and again. The best he could do, the best anyone could do, was make the world a less hospitable place for war gods. To help deprive them of the forces they fed upon.

"He won't speak," Kyra complained to Hecate.

The goddess nodded. "Maybe he needs to write it down."

So Kyra gave Marco a pen, and watched him write a letter to his mother and one to his sister. Then he filled page after page with all he'd learned about how to stop the genocidaires in the Congo. After that, it was all he wrote about. Maybe all he thought about. Kyra knew he was never going to give up on the people of Rwanda. He was going to spend all his long life trying to make things right.

When Marco was finally well enough to leave the bed, he made his first foray into the streets of the Mediterranean town. Kyra went with him. She watched as he lifted his head to the sunshine, breathed in the salty air and turned down a side street toward a vendor where he bought a pack of cigarettes.

She didn't chastise him—they both knew it wasn't going to kill him.

Marco leaned back against a brick building, lit the cigarette, brought it to his lips and took a deep drag. Then, to Kyra's surprise, he offered it to her. She wasn't a smoker, but she reached for the little cancer stick with trembling hands, letting her lips curl over the end, savoring the lingering taste of his mouth on the wrapper. The familiarity of it made her knees weak, and she had to lean against the wall to keep from making a fool of herself.

He took the cigarette back from her, inhaled sharply, then let it out in a long slow stream of smoke. Whatever weakness had driven him to it seemed to pass. He nodded as if resolving an argument with himself and threw the rest of the pack away.

Then he spoke his first words—his very first words—since returning from madness. "Show me where you live."

She led him a few blocks then opened the wrought-iron gate. They walked into the courtyard together, then down a small flight of stairs to her door, which squeaked on rusty hinges as she opened it. Then he walked in, an expectant look on his face. The silence between them went on and on until finally he asked, "Are you going to turn on the light?"

"Oh!" As a *lampade,* she'd never seen the point of paying an electric bill. She fumbled around in the drawer for some candles and lit them. He picked up one of the candles and held it out in front of him like a torch, navigating the passageways of her small apartment, and nearly tripping over a stone marker in the living room. "You collect gravestones?"

Kyra winced. This was one of the many reasons why she never brought anyone to her home. She felt exposed, but after what she'd done to him, she didn't dare complain. "I don't take the famous tombstones. Just the really old ones from people I once knew that no one remembers anymore."

Friends who were no more. Lovers who had died. Mortals she'd helped over the threshold in a time when they still called for her, instead of angels. It helped her feel connected to the world, but she didn't know how Marco would feel about it, or any of the other ancient oddities in her apartment. "I know it's strange, but—"

"You made your life a memorial to the dead."

Kyra nodded.

"So did I," Marco said, his face illuminated by the flicker of the candle. She saw in it all the grief that still remained, for the people he'd buried. She wanted to take it away. She wanted to use her nymph's wildness like she did the first night they spent together, to bring him pleasure and drive away the hurt. But when she reached out to touch him, he stopped her.

"No," he said, his mouth a grim line. "It's not going to be like that anymore."

She pulled her hand back as if she'd been burned. And she supposed she had been. He didn't want her anymore. And why should it come as a surprise? "I understand," she said, struggling with her pride, and turning abruptly in her haste to get away.

"No, you don't." He grabbed her hand, holding her fast. "You *don't* understand, Kyra. It's not going to be about my being lost and you finding me anymore. It's not going to be about the righteous nymph and the misguided man she's taken up with—the same man she's convinced is going to walk out on her. You know damned well that I'm in love with you. You know damned well that *nothing* is ever going to take me away from you. You *had* to have seen that inside me along with everything else. So if we do this, you need to trust me to stay. You need to trust me to guide *you* when you need it. I don't want you to take away any of my pain unless you're willing to let me do the same for you."

It might've been the longest string of sentences he'd put together since they'd met, and though she treasured every word, there was nothing tender about his tone. He was serious, intense and demanding.

"You think you can be happy with me?" Kyra asked, glancing up at him from beneath her lashes. "I'm complicated, you know."

He drew her closer, eyes heavily lidded. "Thanks to your father, I have a really long time to figure you out. Forever, in fact. So are you going to trust me or not?"

It should've been easy to give this trust that he asked for. But it felt, to her, like asking him to put *her* to the torch. That way might lay the ruin of her, but right here, right now, there was no other path she would take. "I love you...and I trust you."

As soon as she said the words, he blew out the candle and they stood together in the darkness. Then he picked her up into his arms. "What are you doing?" Kyra sputtered as she felt herself, once again, plucked up from the earth and suspended on high.

"I'm carrying you over the threshold," Marco replied, groping his way toward her bedroom. "It's about time someone did that for you for a change."

It seemed odd. Antiquated. Like she was some

damsel in the arms of a knight errant. "I'm not some delicate lady, you know."

"That's okay," Marco smirked. "I don't plan to be a gentleman tonight."

* * * * *

Turn the page for an exciting short story, first published in Nocturne Bites eBooks.
MIDNIGHT MEDUSA is the initial tale in Stephanie Draven's sensual, evocative
MYTHICA *series.*

Chapter 1

Renata forced the cutting edge of her blade against the war criminal's cheek, just below his eye. The man didn't tremble with fear the way she wished he would—not the way she still trembled when she remembered the explosion. Neither did his cruel mouth quiver the way hers did when she remembered being engulfed in flames. No, the war criminal's expression didn't change.

Even though she held his fate in her hands, he wasn't afraid of her. He was cold, stony and remote—even as she brought her hammer down and drove the sharp chisel into his face, for he was made of marble and knew this was as close as the sculptress would ever dare to come.

In the quiet of her studio, Renata slowly came back to herself. She realized that it was dark; she had been carving with nothing to guide her fingers but moon-light and her own depthless rage. And now her dust-covered hands were shaking. Her mind reeled with memories of the war that had killed her father and little brother. Her throat swelled with grief like it had when her mother was abducted by an enemy soldier. Tears burned beneath Renata's lashes and she knew she had to stop working, if only for a moment. She wiped her eyes with the back of an aching forearm, smearing her cheeks with grit and reminding herself that the war was long over.

It was one of those notoriously hot summer nights in New York City, and Renata's unruly tresses were already coiled with perspiration, wet against her neck. Her cotton tank top clung damply to the small of her slender back, perspiration tickling the scars along her spine. It was sweltering.

Renata considered turning on the air conditioner, but she hoped the heat might bring her pet snake from its hiding place. The snake could be anywhere amidst the boxes, stone chips and art magazines that littered Renata's studio, and she sighed, knowing that her foster family would scold her for letting Scylla escape her cage and slither off. Then again, they had never liked her pet snake. True, Scylla wasn't cuddly like a cat or a dog, but Renata knew that just because a snake—or a person—didn't wear her heart on her sleeve didn't mean she didn't have one.

It was already midnight, though; Renata had no time to search for runaway serpents. She had to put her obsessive final touches on The War Criminal in time for the art exhibit tomorrow.

Steeling her courage, Renata took a deep breath and lifted her tools to work again, but as she did so, she heard rustling in the draperies over her window. "Is that where you've been hiding, Scylla?" she asked, and before she could turn around, she felt a cool breeze lift the downy hairs at the nape of her neck.

Was she imagining she heard someone lifting the sash? Had the emotion that always gripped her while working on this sculpture finally driven her mad? Even over the thumping of her heart, she heard a small tearing sound, like fabric being snagged on a latch. Someone was breaking in!

Renata's mind reeled with disbelief and fear. She was alone; she had deliberately rented a studio off the beaten path. It had seemed like a good idea because she prized her solitude, but now she wondered if anyone would even hear her if she called for help.

In the stillness of her studio, Renata gripped her wooden mallet in one hand and the chisel in the other, her knuckles going white. Her instinct was to not make any sudden movements, so she turned slowly, and she glimpsed a dark figure shadowed under the sweep of the drapes. A large lumbering man was silhouetted against the moonlight. Renata forgot to breathe. She saw a gun in his hand. Her heart forgot to beat. She was too afraid even to scream.

The last time someone had pointed a gun at her, she was just a little girl in war-ravaged Bosnia, but the man aiming the cruel barrel of his weapon at her now didn't look like a soldier. "I won't hurt you if you come with me," he said, his voice thick with some accent that Renata didn't immediately recognize.

At his words, Renata went weak all over, terror rushing through her veins like a hot, withering poison. Who was he? What could this hulking stranger possibly want with her? And why should she believe that he wouldn't hurt her when he was pointing a gun at her?

Since she was a little girl, she had been a victim, as her sculptures attested. But Renata wasn't a little girl anymore, and this wasn't Bosnia. Something inside Renata snapped—like the angry strike of a whip— and she decided then and there that unlike her mother, she wouldn't be taken. "I'm not going anywhere with you!"

With nothing but anger to direct her hand, Renata launched her hammer through the air towards her assailant. In slow motion, she watched the tool hurtle towards the intruder, cartwheeling end over end.

The hammer struck him square in the forehead.

It was only a wooden hammer—not one of the metal ones she sometimes used—but it made an audible and satisfying crack against the intruder's skull. Shocked, the man staggered back, his arms tangling with the curtains. Only then did Renata cry out, but it was the intruder who screamed the loudest.

A gyrating tangle of scales and fangs had slipped from the draperies and coiled around the man's shoulders.

Scylla had been hiding there after all, and—as hostile to intruders as its owner—Renata's pet python constricted around the assailant's neck. Perhaps scenting the man's fear, the python pulled into strike position. "Get it off!" the intruder shrieked, fumbling with his gun.

Renata could see that the man was genuinely terrified, but her survival instinct was stronger than her compassion so, seizing the opportunity, she turned for the door and ran.

Only after the detective showed her his NYPD badge for the third time did Renata accompany him inside her studio. Even then, she crossed her arms over herself and tucked her fingers under so that he wouldn't see her tremble.

There was no sign of the intruder or the snake.

Dark, swarthy, and clad in a black leather jacket, the detective took a brief look around the studio. "This is the scene of the crime?"

Renata merely nodded; even under the best of circumstances, she was guarded with strangers, and these were not the best of circumstances.

Still, there was something familiar about the detective's shadowed eyes. He'd introduced himself several times, but she found that she just couldn't remember his name. Maybe it was because she was in shock, or perhaps it was because she couldn't stop staring at his startlingly handsome face.

Renata had nearly been kidnapped, so now was not the time to notice a handsome man, but as a sculptress, she revered chiseled cheekbones and strong jawlines like his.

"Let's go over this one more time," the detective said.

"I've already told you everything," Renata snapped, fixing her cool gray eyes on him. With practice, she had perfected that classic New York City bitchy-but-beautiful stare that drove most men to take a step back, but the detective didn't seem cowed.

"With repetition, sometimes an extra detail or memory comes to mind," the detective insisted. So they sat together on her old beat-up college futon with the denim cover, now as threadbare as her calm.

He wrote Renata Rukavina at the top of a page and took careful notes as she told him all over again what happened.

When she finished telling her story, she noticed that the detective was sitting too close to her, and when he leaned forward she worried for a startled instant that he might try to kiss her. But instead, he exhaled a great breath, and fleetingly, she smelled the aroma of freshly baked bread. It was the middle of the night—no one was baking—but the scent somehow relaxed Renata enough to let the detective take her hand.

There was a strange tugging sensation as her skin came into contact with his. She wondered that she allowed it; with friends and lovers—even with her foster family—there was always a struggle between her need for intimacy and her fear of it. Yet she was letting this stranger hold her hand.

"You just had a scare, but you're okay now," he added.

And somehow, she was.

"You're sure you don't know the guy who tried to break in here?" The detective's mop of dark hair softened the intensity of his gaze. "You've no idea why anyone would break into your studio this hour of night?"

Renata shook her head again. If she'd testified before the war tribunals, someone might have had cause to try to shut her up, but that's why Renata hadn't testified. Why she would never testify.

The detective finally went to the windowsill to dust for fingerprints. Meanwhile, Renata searched for her pet python. As she checked all of Scylla's usual hiding spots, she realized the detective was examining her work. "These are some powerful pieces," he said of the statuary adorning her studio.

"Thank you," Renata said politely. "They're not to everyone's taste. One of my critics said they were nightmares brought to life."

The detective circled a black marble sculpture of a man with a gun strapped over his shoulder, his clenched fist pulled back to brutalize an unseen victim. "Not a nice guy, I'm guessing."

"He was charged with crimes against humanity," Renata said, feeling a well of rage rising as she remembered his deeds. "He died before they could convict him, though." What she did not tell the detective was that the soldier had died the very night Renata finished his sculpture, and thus joined her collection of ghosts.

When she was a fledgling artist, Renata carved the faces of children felled by sniper fire outside Sarajevo. Even now, after years of experience, the only living person in her art collection was The War Criminal, so she watched warily as the detective approached the almost-finished statue and ran his hand over the stone. "This is the guy on trial at The Hague right now, isn't it?"

"Yes," Renata replied, impressed. It seemed unlikely that an ordinary police detective would know anything about it; in Renata's experience, most people chose to forget the war that had destroyed her childhood. That this man seemed to care made Renata willing to talk. "The War Criminal was going to be the centerpiece of my exhibit at the gallery tomorrow to coincide with the expected verdict against him, but now I'm afraid I won't finish in time."

"But you must finish it," he insisted, a ripple of anger passing across his shoulders beneath his leather jacket. His sudden vehemence startled Renata, and seeing this, he measured his tone. "I'm just saying that you can't let anything stand in your way. An art exhibit is a huge deal, isn't it? You've worked hard for it, haven't you? You can't let someone scare you from finishing important work like this."

Renata was flattered that he thought her work was important, but she was terribly unsettled. She wished he would tell her that they had her would-be kidnapper in custody. She just wanted to feel safe—but then, hadn't she always? Renata shrugged apologetically. "I can't do the delicate finishing touches with shaking hands."

"Look," the detective said. "If it'll make you feel

better, I'll keep my squad car parked right outside tonight and make sure nobody bothers you. Meanwhile,
you should just take your fear from tonight, turn it to
anger, and finish your sculpture."

Renata tilted her head at the curious phrasing he
used. "I don't think you should be encouraging that.
My therapist thinks I have anger issues."

He gave a mirthless smile, a gleam of savagery in
his eye. "No doubt. Sounds like you clocked the perp.
Did you throw the hammer because you were scared
or angry?"

"Both," Renata admitted.

"Then it seems to me that your anger is what kept
you from being kidnapped tonight and it'll help with
your art, too."

Renata couldn't help thinking, yet again, that this
was no ordinary police detective. Once again, he took
her hands in his. She felt something tug at her emotions and she realized she was no longer shaking from
fear.

Only rage.

Someone had broken into her apartment. Someone
had pointed a gun at her and tried to take her. Someone
had come into her world, uninvited, and tried to rip
apart her life just like the invading soldiers had done
all those years ago. And someone should have to pay
for that.

Anger roiled and coiled inside her, twisting upon itself with venomous purpose. It was past midnight. Renata picked up her tools and began to sculpt.

Chapter 2

The dark shadows of Renata's studio receded with the sunrise, and she was roused by an early morning phone call. When Renata told her about the break-in, her foster-mother sounded worried. "You should have never taken a studio in that part of town. Why wasn't the boyfriend there with you?"

"Scylla turned out to be much better protection," Renata said, deciding that now was probably not the time to announce that she and the boyfriend had parted ways. It had happened the way it always did: he accused her of keeping secrets from him, and maybe she had been secretive. After all, some pain you just couldn't share except through art. "Anyway," Renata said into the phone. "I just wanted to call and ask you to wish me luck at the exhibit today. I'm a little nervous."

"Oh, Renata, your work is amazing. You're going to be the talk of the town, honey."

Renata would feel better if her foster parents could attend the exhibit, but they were several states away. Besides, they had already done enough for her. They had taken her in as a child-refugee of a foreign war, and stood by her through countless surgeries to repair her scars. The art show was just going to have to be something Renata did on her own.

"Renata, I know the news is unsettling...."

Cold dread pooled in the pit of Renata's stomach. "What news?"

Her foster mother's silence told her all she needed to know. Renata grabbed the remote and turned on the television.

The war criminal was dead.

It was happening again. The International Criminal Tribunal had not even had the chance to pass judgment on him. He had simply died in his cell.

Perversely, the morning's headlines made Renata's exhibit extremely popular. Visitors flocked to see her artwork, all whispering about the mysterious way in which the accused war criminal had died. Renata knew she should be elated by the attention, but she was sad, because no matter how much critical acclaim she received, if not for her foster parents, Renata would be alone in this world.

"Don't stare like that," Marta, the gallery owner, chided. "You look beautiful, but it's very intimidating. Smile, it's your big debut! And here, let me fix your hair."

Renata knew her exotic dark curls were impervious to the taming of a comb or barrette and they'd never submit to the sleek styles that were currently in fashion, so she rolled her eyes and said, "Never mind my hair, Marta! What are they saying about the exhibit? Do they like it?"

"Darling, they love it! And I need to introduce you to a potential buyer with very deep pockets."

For Renata, this was the most discomfiting part about art. She loved creating, she savored the outlet, and she needed to sell her work to pay the rent. But as a sculptress, she felt an intimate relationship to every piece in her collection. It was difficult to let them go. Still, Renata forced a smile and followed Marta through the throngs of well-wishers.

"Renata," Marta began. "Meet Ms. Kokkinos. She's a private collector, and a great admirer of your work."

A private collector? Renata had assumed that any potential buyer with deep pockets would have been here representing a museum. She never expected a private collector would be interested—after all, Renata's art was sad. Who would buy it to adorn a garden or household foyer?

Ms. Kokkinos turned out to be a woman with a perfectly coiffured helmet of silver hair and an unblinking stare. She towered over Renata and her sturdy frame made Renata's own limbs seem willowy. But the older woman's most arresting feature was the disquieting color of her eyes. Renata had never met anyone with eyes as gray as her own.

Before Renata could offer her hand, the tall woman thrust a business card into her palm. "Ms. Rukavina, my nephew sang your praises and I must say, he was not wrong. Your work is devastating."

At a loss, Renata asked, "Your nephew?"

"He's a police officer. I believe he helped you with a break-in at your studio? I hope you weren't hurt."

The detective. Of course. Now that she thought about it, Renata remembered the Greek cast to his features and could almost see them reflected in the severe face of his formidable aunt. "No, no, I wasn't hurt. I'm honored by the detective's interest in my work—and yours, too."

Ms. Kokkinos nodded curtly. "I'm particularly interested in The War Criminal. Would you be willing to make similar sculptures on commission?"

Renata tried not to show her astonishment. No one

had ever commissioned a work from her before. "What do you have in mind?"

"I'd like you to sculpt this man."

Renata already had the woman's business card in one hand, so she had to reach with the other for the sketch. In so doing, she glanced at the drawing and her heart lurched.

She knew the face.

This was the face of the soldier who abducted her mother. And upon seeing him again, Renata's knees threatened to buckle beneath her.

Ms. Kokkinos must have seen the horror writ plain on Renata's face, because she eyed Renata owlishly and said, "You needn't haggle over the price. I'm an heiress to a vast fortune, so you'll be generously compensated."

Renata didn't want to be rude, but she felt bloodless and unsteady. "Would you mind—would you mind terribly if I took a moment to get some air?"

Renata didn't wait for a reply. Clutching the drawing and the business card, she hastily withdrew, navigating her way around the velvet gallery ropes and pushing through the crowd. Renata headed straight for the exit that led to the fire-escape balcony. She just hoped she could get there before her knees gave way.

She found the door and flung it open. Without looking at the sketch again, she folded it into a small square around the business card and tucked both inside her bra, close to her heart. Then Renata took deep, comforting gulps of air. It had always been like this when someone triggered an unexpected memory. Even after her surgeries, when the doctors helped find a way for her to stay in the country, news from Bosnia panicked her. Even when she was safe in an American school, loud noises, such as a bell signaling the end of class, sometimes froze her heart within her chest.

Now as the fresh air calmed her jitters, Renata sighed with relief. The scars on her back were bothering her, but when she reached behind to adjust her dress, she realized that it wasn't the fabric irritating her. Something hard and unyielding dug into her, and as she brushed it with her fingers, she realized it was the barrel of a gun.

"Don't scream," a man said from behind her. His arm wrapped around her, hard as iron, and he clamped a hand over her mouth.

Renata tried to decide if she should kick him or impale his foot with the stiletto heel of her golden sandal. But before she could decide, he hauled her towards the rail. "We're going down the fire-escape stairs."

This was the second time in two days that someone had tried to abduct her at gunpoint, but unlike the lumbering intruder, this man had a graceful strength that prevented her from raking at him with her fingernails when she tried.

"I don't want to hurt you," he said, sighing deeply by her ear. Suddenly, she smelled acrid smoke and charred flesh, the horrible stench of war. The stink of the explosion, the sensation of being on fire, and the sizzle of her own skin as it burned. Then came the blinding pain and the screaming, and remembering, she was overcome.

Paralyzed, she let her attacker pull her down two steps at a time. In Bosnia, when people were kidnapped, they were forced into the woods and shot, so why wasn't she fighting him? Behind her, the gallery was crowded. If only she could scream, surely someone would help her, but his fingers were clamped securely over her mouth!

Her captor pushed her down another stair, and though she fought down her fear long enough to struggle, it only resulted in her shoe falling off and dropping like a golden teardrop to the ground below. Frustrated, the villain hauled her into his arms and dropped to the landing, which groaned under their combined weight.

Thankfully, people on a lower floor of the gallery must have heard the noise or seen Renata's shoe fall because someone called out "Call 911!"

Her kidnapper growled, dragging Renata as she flailed. She was fighting to catch the wrought-iron bars with her hands to stop their descent. Her heart thundered in her ears, louder than the sound of sirens on the streets below. If only she could delay him, the police would rescue her.

Desperate, Renata bit down hard on the fingers over her mouth, and knew she'd drawn blood by the familiar metallic tang on her tongue. Blood was an unmistakable taste, and it sickened her.

Her abductor hissed in pain, but showed no signs of slowing. Together, they dropped the last few feet from the ladder of the fire exit into the alleyway below where a van with darkened windows waited. A side door opened, and Renata was thrown into the vehicle. She landed hard underneath her assailant as two goons slammed the door shut and the van screeched out of the alleyway.

Chapter 3

H er kidnapper used the weight of his body to keep her subdued on the floor of the van while he pushed his bleeding fingers from her mouth and replaced them with a gag. The heart-thumping ride in the darkness gave Renata time to conceive of every possible way he might kill her, and she didn't even realize they had arrived at the airport until they were dragging her onto the charter jet.

It wasn't until after the plane had taken off that her kidnapper finally spoke to her again. "I'm going to take the gag out of your mouth, but you mustn't scream. No one who could help you would hear it anyway, and if you scream you will only frighten the pilot and endanger the mortals."

Renata feared he was a Serbian thug sent to ensure she never testified about the war crimes she had witnessed. But her captor looked Greek and—what had he said? Mortals? What madness was this? Even so, Renata felt safer with this madman than she did with those chillingly sane soldiers in her past, so she nodded her head in agreement.

It was only now that he was so close, that she looked at his face and startled. "Wait, I know you... Detective..."

Why couldn't she remember his name?

"Ah," he said, narrowing his dark, terrifying eyes. "So you've met my brother."

His brother? Yes, Renata could see it now. The chiseled cheekbones and the lines of his jaw were the same, but whereas the detective sported stubble and a messy mane, her captor's dark hair was short and slicked away from his clean-shaven face. They were twins.

"Who are you?" Renata demanded.

"If I told you, you wouldn't remember unless I permitted it, but for now you may call me Damon." He dismissed two of the goons with a single look, as if he were used to being obeyed. His men retreated to the back of the plane and closed the curtains. When they were finally alone, he said, "You're prettier than I thought you'd be, Renata."

So, he knew her name.

Now that her fear was subsiding, anger rose to take

its place. "I don't know why you've taken me, but I want to go home. Right now."

"And where exactly is your home?" Damon asked.

She knew where home was. Home was her studio, with Scylla. So why did she pause in answering the question? "Why do you want to know? Where are you taking me?" she asked, resurgent dread choking her words. She couldn't go back to Bosnia. She wouldn't go back. Not now, not ever.

"I'm taking you somewhere my brother and the war gods can't find you," he said, as if it were the most sensible thing in the world. Then he took a crystal decanter from the nearby minibar, poured two glasses, and handed one of them to her. "I must remember my manners."

Renata reflected that it was exceedingly unmannerly to abduct a woman from an art gallery. But she'd learned from her therapist that deranged men needed to feel validated, so she took the glass warily and tried to earn his trust. "So you think you're a god—a war god—like your brother. And there are others?"

His sensual lips curved into a sardonic smile. "Don't try to manage me, young lady," he said, though he couldn't have been more than a few years older than she was. "I'm not a psychotic or a sociopath and as long as you do everything I tell you, you have nothing to fear."

Renata needed a stiff drink, and since her captor was confidently sipping from his glass, she decided the drink he'd given her from the same decanter probably wasn't poisoned. She took a mouthful, and swirled the unfamiliar spirit over her tongue. It bolstered her. It made her feel warm, all the way to her toes. But she was still angry. "Why have you kidnapped me?"

"Because your art is dangerous," he said. "I can't allow anyone to use you. When I learned that my aunt was seeking you out, I knew I had to take you before she did."

"Your aunt?" Renata asked, remembering the business card and sketch she'd tucked into her bra. The detective had been unusual and his aunt more so, but neither of them had seemed deranged. Did they know about Damon's mental illness?

"Do you mean Ms. Kokkinos? The patroness at the art exhibit? She's your aunt?"

"Ms. Kokkinos? Is that what she's calling herself these days?" The plane was now above the clouds and Damon seemed to relax. "In Greek, Kokkinos means red. Red like blood. Red like battle lust. It's fitting, I suppose, because my aunt is the gray-eyed daughter of Zeus."

Renata tried, in vain, to keep the incredulity off her face. "I'm sorry—she's what?"

He drained his glass and set it aside. "She wants you to sculpt for her, doesn't she?"

Renata didn't have to answer. "Look, I don't want to be involved in your family squabbles. If you don't want me to sculpt for her, just take me home, and I'll refuse her commission."

"As if that were possible," Damon said, straightening the crease of his expensive dress pants with a slow languid motion. "She won't let you refuse her, Renata. You're her aegis."

"What the hell are you talking about?" Renata snapped.

"Don't you know your Greek mythology?" he asked, arching his brows. "Not all of it is myth."

Suddenly, Renata tried to stifle a yawn, without success. He certainly wasn't boring her, so why was she so tired? "Did you put a sleeping pill in my drink?"

He scowled and a little turbulence shook the plane. "No, Renata. You're probably sleepy because you were up long after midnight last night after setting your serpent on one of my men."

So he'd sent the would-be kidnapper to snatch her from her studio. And when the first attempt had failed, he'd returned to do the job himself. "I didn't set Scylla on anyone," she whispered sleepily, "but if I could have, I would have."

"Oh, you would have, certainly," Damon said.

Renata bit her lower lip, wondering what had become of Scylla and her prey, but she wasn't thinking clearly enough to ask. As it was, Renata's eyes were drooping and her limbs felt weak.

"Come," Damon said, reaching across and unbuckling her seat belt. In the sweep of the motion, his fingers brushed the tops of her thighs and Renata felt herself grow warm. "Come lie down on the couch, Renata. You can put your head in my lap and rest. We have a few hours before the pilot will flash the seatbelt light again."

"I'm certainly not putting my head in your lap," Renata snarled.

"Oh, I imagine you'll put your head wherever I tell you to," he said.

As if at his command, she felt inexplicably pliant. "Why? If it wasn't a sleeping potion, what was in that drink?"

"It was laced with ambrosia. It's a…restorative," he said, guiding her to the couch and drawing a blanket around her shoulders as she slipped off to sleep.

Damon stroked her curls as she slept, twining his fingers in her magnificent tangle of dark locks. It'd been a long time since he'd last seen Renata, longer still since he'd touched a mortal woman, even chastely, and now he couldn't resist the silken sensation of her hair.

She was so beautiful, he couldn't help but want her. From the elegant arch of her eyebrows to the Slavic planes of her face, she was perfect in every way. He hadn't expected that. He'd been sure her powers would have made her ugly—at the very least, he'd been sure the explosion would have left her with hideous scars.

After all, he'd been there that day alongside the war gods, goading the warriors to fight. But war had changed greatly since the old days; modern warfare had surprised him. It was just as brutal, but colder, more efficient, and utterly inglorious. There were no more challenges between brave Hector and fierce Achilles. It was all war machines now.

The dishonor of modern warfare changed him— changed his very nature—perhaps even before that fateful chariot ride in Bosnia. He hadn't known the soldiers would launch grenades at civilian homes. He hadn't known that the terror he inspired would give excuse to explode the little girl's house. He hadn't known how these weapons could tear at the flesh and spray body parts across neatly tended gardens.

That day years ago, Renata had been playing in front of the house with a jump rope, and had turned away from the blast just in time. Still, the flames had lashed at her back, throwing her to the ground and melting the dress from her body. A hand landed beside her, severed and slimy with gore. It had been a child's hand—her little brother's hand—and seeing it, she'd screamed that terrible scream. Her scream had been so bottomless, he couldn't have gorged upon it even if he'd wanted to.

He'd known then what she would become.

But Renata wasn't a little girl anymore. She was a woman grown and what was he to do with her? He could secret her away, but she was smarter than he'd hoped. Once he told her what she was, how long would it be until she discovered her power and wanted to use it? When that happened, she would fight him with more than the token resistance. And what then? Would he have to chain her to some faraway mountain and set fearsome monsters to guard her? Would he be forced to hurt her? To kill her?

No. For now, they'd have to keep moving and he'd have to keep her with him always. One moment of in-attention and she'd run; one moment of weakness and the war gods could snatch her away.

They wanted to use Renata to create more conflict—more horror for their appetites. But what Damon feared most was that they wouldn't have to use her—that deep down, Renata was angry enough to wreak destruction on her own.

Chapter 4

Renata woke to the piercing cries of seabirds and the desolate scent of salt water. Opening her eyes, she found herself in a canopied bed, propped up on downy pillows and nestled beneath a cool white comforter. Pulling away the canopy netting, she took in the simple surroundings of a beach house. Shuttered doors were thrown open to allow a breeze and beyond them stretched a stone patio upon which her captor appeared to be taking his morning coffee.

Damon—who was bent over a newspaper—was wearing a linen shirt open at the collar. The stark white fabric set off his tan and made him look like a bronzed god. Of course, she remembered that Damon thought he actually was some kind of god. At least he dressed the part.

"Come have breakfast, Renata," he said before she

could find an avenue of escape. So, in her rumpled green dress, Renata padded towards him on bare feet, squinting in the sunlight. He motioned her towards the bowl of fruit on the table and said, "Make yourself comfortable."

"I'd be more comfortable if you took me home," Renata replied, tucking errant curls behind her ears and folding her arms in front of herself like an armor breastplate. "When the police catch you, you can say goodbye to this cushy lifestyle, you know. They don't have breakfast service in prison."

He seemed amused by her hostility. Then, leaning back into the patio chair, he studied her. "Ah, Renata, that presumes that the police could catch me. It presumes your kidnapping would ever go to trial. It even presumes that you'd want to see me brought to justice, instead of taking revenge yourself."

Something about his words took a vague and disturbing shape, much the same way dark outlines of her sculptures formed in her mind before she had even carved them free of the stone. Something about what he'd said made her bitter, angry…furious. "I know from personal experience that there's no justice in this world."

"Perhaps there would be justice if people were brave enough to tell their stories."

He could only be talking about her unwillingness

to testify before the War Crimes Tribunal. Maybe he was a thug sent to silence her after all, but if so, then why was she still alive? Perhaps it was these thoughts of mortality that made her, quite suddenly, ravenously hungry. "Is it safe to eat these grapes? Or are they also laced with something?"

"Sometimes a grape is just a grape," Damon said, looking out over the cobalt waters.

"Where are we?" Renata asked, taking a seat across from him and popping a few grapes into her mouth.

"I'm not going to tell you where we are, because if you ever managed to escape and get to a phone, you'd be able to tell someone where to find you."

Yes, yes, she would. The first chance she had, she'd call the authorities. Then she'd fish out the business card secreted in her bra and call Ms. Kokkinos and warn her that her nephew was dangerously unhinged.

"You know, I like your brother better," she said, searching the table for utensils. Maybe if she could get a fork or a knife...

Damon looked disappointed. "Are you looking for something with which to stab me?"

Unfortunately, he'd only served fruit and pastries. There wasn't a weapon in sight, so Renata saw no point in denying it. "Yes, and I should warn you, my therapist says I have unresolved anger issues."

"Oh, I know you do."

Absently, Damon put the newspaper down on the table. Renata snatched it up and found an article about her kidnapping on the inside page of the *New York Times*. Renata had to admit that this was higher billing than she'd ever received for her art shows, but she gaped at date on the masthead. "It's been three days! You kidnapped me three days ago? Have I been asleep that long?"

"The precise passage of time isn't my strong suit," Damon admitted, momentarily losing the smugness from his expression as he folded his hands. "But the effects of even a tiny bit of ambrosia can be unpredictable."

Renata stared at his folded hands, the clean fingernails and the unblemished skin. For a moment, a sudden, unbidden thought came to her. She wondered what it would feel like to have those hands seizing her again, and what it would feel like if clutching turned to soft caresses. Then she gasped and covered her mouth.

"Renata, what's wrong?"

"I bit your hand," she rasped. "When you kidnapped me, I bit your hand and broke the skin. I drew blood, I know I did. I tasted it in my mouth. But there's not a mark on you. Not a scratch."

"That was days ago," he said dismissively.

Renata feared she was losing her mind now, but if

there was anything she understood it was wounds. "There should be a scab. A bruise at the least!"

"I heal quickly," he said, finishing his coffee.

Renata breathed slowly, in and out, her eyes widening with apprehension. "What are you?"

"A son of Ares," he said, pausing as if to let it sink in.

Renata tried to match it to the names of any Bosnian separatist groups she'd heard of, but could not. She looked into those dark mesmerizing eyes and realized that he was not toying with her. He believed it.

But did she? "You're really a god?" she asked tentatively.

"Not as you think of them," he said. "But neither am I a mortal man."

"What are you, then?" she asked.

"A son of Ares," he repeated, slightly exasperated, then, perhaps sensing that answer wasn't going to suffice, he attempted an explanation. "A long time ago, my twin brother and I drove my father's chariot whenever and wherever war came to a land and people called upon the ancient gods. My brother instills panic. I inspire terror."

He lifted his chin in defiance, as if to challenge anyone who might doubt him, looking halfway torn between pride and shame; and though she couldn't accept the truth of what he was saying, she knew he wasn't lying. "Terror?"

"Yes. I inspire it and I feed off of it," he said.

Renata wasn't able to hide her distaste, but she had to ask, "You said that was a long time ago. You're not driving your...your father's chariot anymore?"

"My family and I have had a...falling out," he explained. "It's a very complicated matter that has set off a series of struggles around the world, but let it suffice to say that we no longer see eye to eye."

Son of Ares. Could it be true? "So the Olympians are real. When there's thunder, it's Zeus? When there's love, it's Aphrodite?"

As the seafoam inched its way up the sand towards the patio where they shared breakfast, he shook his head. "Certainly not as you've read about them. There are old gods of all kinds. Greek, Norse, Hindu, Meso-American...the list goes on. But most of the old gods no longer hold any power."

Renata was forced to ask, "Why not?"

He folded his napkin and sat back in his chair. "Because the forces that they fed upon and the people that called them are dispersed. But war is powerfully present in every age, and in some places where war comes, the people still call upon the war gods—the oldest immortals—even if they don't always know our names. And when they call, we answer."

Renata knew with sudden certainty that Bosnia was such a place. A meeting of Greeks, Russians and Macedonians, Slavs and Gypsies, Christians and Muslims, Serbs, Bosniaks and Croats. How many old gods had been called upon in the war of her childhood? Lost in thought, Renata watched the ocean waves lap against the shore.

"Are you looking for Poseidon?" Damon asked, pulling her back from the memories that haunted her. "You won't find him today, but this island is lovely and the water is warm, so why don't you take a swim?"

It was an abrupt change of subject, as if he couldn't bear to speak of such things a moment longer. Truthfully, Renata needed a few moments to gather her wits, too. She looked down at the dress she'd been sleeping in for three days and wanted to be rid of it. "As an immortal, can you conjure up a swimsuit for me out of thin air? Do you have that power?"

"No," he said. "But I can make it so that you're not the slightest bit afraid. I can consume your fears—make you so fearless, you'll happily strip naked and step into the sea."

Renata shivered. The sun-warmed patio stones were toasty beneath her feet and the day was warm, but still, Renata shivered. Whether it was the way he spoke to her, the hungry look on his face, or the words he spoke, she couldn't say. But neither could she help wondering what it would be like to swim naked, to no longer be self-conscious about the scars on her back, to be unafraid to let a man see her completely and utterly exposed.

Still, Renata was confused. "You said you and your brother instilled panic and terror..."

Damon leaned forward over the table until his face was inches from hers. Then with great deliberation, he pursed his lips as if he might kiss her. Instead, he blew a soft breath upon her face and it stirred happier memories inside her. She smelled jasmine, the scent of her mother's perfume, and she felt the tension loosen in her shoulders. The thought that she was being held captive against her will seemed far away, unimportant. Instead she felt she was only the guest of an impossibly handsome man at his beach house retreat.

"I can terrify," Damon told her with sad eyes. "But I can also take some of it away."

His face was still inches from hers, and she wondered what he had done to her that she so wanted to kiss him. More than that, she wanted to reach out with the fingers of a sculptress and trace the lines of his mouth. Would his lips feel smooth like marble, rough as granite, or soft like her own? "But why would a Son of Ares want anything to do with me?"

Too late, Renata realized she'd spoken the question aloud. But Damon didn't look surprised by it. "Because, Renata," he said, simply. "You're a gorgon."

Chapter 5

A gorgon? Renata didn't know whether to laugh or be deeply insulted. She'd studied ancient art in school. She knew that gorgons were monstrous harpies with metal claws, snakes for hair, and faces so hideous they turned anyone who looked at them to stone.

Not her disfiguring burns, nor the scars left after plastic surgery, nor even a single bad-hair day had ever made Renata feel so ugly that she'd have called herself a gorgon. Not even in jest.

"What? Literally a gorgon?" Furious, Renata shot up out of her chair and stalked to the edge of the little patio, wondering if she should leap into the sand and just start running away from Damon as far and as fast as she could. But something made her stay. "What are you saying? I remember being a child—I remember my father and my brother and my mother. You're saying I'm Medusa in disguise?"

"Medusa is dead," Damon said, very seriously. "A vigilante named Perseus cut off her head."

A flash of her little brother's severed hand passed through Renata's mind and deep tremors shook her. She was so overcome with revulsion she couldn't speak.

"You see, Renata, not all gorgons are immortal. Some gorgons are not born—they are made."

"How? How are they made?" Renata demanded to know.

"They're forged of righteous rage against a horror they were helpless to stop. That's what happened to Medusa. That's what happened to you."

Renata turned back to him, her hands clenched into fists at her sides. "And so what does it mean? I have no scales, no claws, and my only snake is an escaped pet python."

"Your monstrosity is on the inside," Damon replied.

It was, quite possibly, the most hurtful thing anyone had ever said to her. It wounded her so deeply her muscles all tightened, like she'd been struck, like she'd been shot.

Damon's shoulders sagged as if he realized he was hurting her, but felt he must continue. "Some might say that all the rage you feel, all that ugliness, is coiling around your heart."

Some might say that. Like all the men who had ever tried to love her. Is that why she'd driven them all away with her remoteness and secrecy? Had she been afraid they would see her ugly inner gorgon?

"How am I any different than all the other survivors of war-torn countries? What good is it being a gorgon?"

"Gorgons take revenge," Damon said, coming towards her.

Together they watched two seagulls battle for a scrap of food in the surf, each bird fighting with angry shrieks.

"I don't take revenge," Renata said, bitterly. "I run and hide. I've never gone back to Bosnia and I never will. I can't even face the men responsible for what happened to my family. I can't face them."

"I know you can't," he said, touching her arm lightly, as if to comfort her. "So you turn them to stone. Two of them now have died after you carved them. Did you think it was an accident?"

No. Not in her heart. Somewhere inside her, she had known it was more than coincidence. She had thought it'd happened because she wished them dead, and now Damon was telling her that she had the power to make those wishes come true. She couldn't deny the small thrill of empowerment that flowed through her, alongside the guilt and horror. If she was a gorgon, it meant she never had to see these evil men, never had to face them or relive her story. She only had to put them into her artwork to end their miserable lives.

Being a gorgon meant never being a victim again.

Tears wet her cheeks, but she didn't remember crying. She wanted to say something, but her throat closed shut. Damon tried to make her look at him, but she turned away and her stony gray eyes fixed upon the depthless ocean and all its secrets.

Damon tried again. "I didn't tell you this to hurt you—"

"A boat is coming," she interrupted, forcing herself to speak over the lump in her throat. Her voice sounded foreign and far away.

Damon looked as if he weren't ready to let the matter drop, as if he wanted to encourage her to talk about the confusion swirling inside her, but he seemed to think better of it. "The boat is early," he said, clearly frustrated. "But the boat is for us. It's time to go."

"Where are we going?" she asked, fists clenching at her sides. "I won't go back to Bosnia."

"I won't ever force you to go back there," Damon reassured her. "But we must leave this place now. The cell phone reception is terrible and there's no internet connection. I have work to do in the real world."

The real world? Renata wondered what that even meant anymore. "What kind of work does an immortal do?"

"We do any kind of work we like," Damon said. "My aunt is a professional benefactress. She has always had a special eye for the gifted and a unique way of fostering their talents. She has a stable of favorites. Meanwhile, my brother is in law enforcement—he feeds off the fear of crime victims."

"And you?" Renata asked.

He eyed her with scant amusement. "I'm a security consultant for the global banking industry."

"Security," she sputtered with surprise.

He towered over her with barely constrained menace. "Trust me when I say that I'm an expert at frightening people away from taking things that don't belong to them."

Renata didn't fight against leaving the island with him. She hadn't seen the point. Did she really want her kidnapper leaving her on a secluded island by herself? Moreover, she was still in shock at everything he'd told her. Her hands were cold and she couldn't catch her breath. And as the boat ferried them towards their destination, she almost didn't care where they went. As long as it was somewhere far, far away.

Chapter 6

Ever since Renata sipped the ambrosia, time had passed in fits and starts. She was unable to keep a firm grasp of it. Had it been days or weeks since she'd been kidnapped? Worse, she didn't even know where she was.

Asia. They were somewhere in Asia. That was all Renata was able to surmise from the penthouse window. The billboards that hung over the sprawling streets below were covered with symbols she couldn't read. Chinese? Korean? Japanese? She just didn't know. Renata saw thousands of cars, bicycles, and even the occasional covered rickshaw pass beneath her, but from the isolation of her skyscraper tower, there was no way to call for rescue.

Except for the oriental bathroom with the stylized waterfall tub, Damon's penthouse was thoroughly

Western in its sensibilities. The floor was black marble. The sofas were leather. The accent pieces—mostly Greek amphorae—were genuine antiques. The apartment was spacious, sparse and masculine. Renata might have marveled at the luxury were it not for the advanced security system that had turned this apartment into her prison.

Until they were safely ensconced behind the steel doors and motion sensors, Damon hadn't allowed her any privacy, but inside the penthouse, he gave her his bedroom and contented himself to sleep on one of the sofas.

And as soon as he left her alone, in the darkness that shielded her from the monitors, she slipped the little business card and the sketch wrapped around it out of her bra, and into the pillowcase beneath her head.

In the morning, Renata wandered into the wood-slatted bathroom and saw that a bath had been drawn for her. Fed by an artificial stream trickling over a decorative rock outcropping, the foaming bath beckoned. She peeled off the green dress she hoped never to see again, then climbed into the tub.

"There are new clothes for you on the bed," Damon said, interrupting her tranquility. He was standing in the doorway without a care for her privacy.

Instinctively, Renata sank lower into the water, letting the bubbles cover her nudity.

She knew he wanted her to say something, but she was silent.

"I had to guess at your size," Damon said. "But my people did their best. If you make a list of things you need, I'll make sure that you have garments to wear that are more to your liking."

Again, Renata knew he was looking for a response, but she gave him none. Instead, she reached for a sponge and pulled it under the water, letting the rough texture scrape across her fingertips and awaken her inner sculptress. Or her inner gorgon. Which was which?

Damon crossed his arms. "You're still not speaking to me, then." It was a statement, not a question, but instead of retreating and leaving her alone, he stepped into the bathroom and sat on the edge of the tub.

Renata felt exposed. She wanted to tell him not to sit so close to her, but that admission of discomfort would make her even more vulnerable. A few moments more of awkward silence passed before Damon asked her, "Is there something I can get you, Renata? Is there something you want?"

"I want my mother," Renata said, before the thought had even fully formed in her mind.

He seemed uncomfortable. "Do you really want to involve your foster mother in this?"

"I want my real mother, but not you or anybody else can give her to me, because the soldier took her away."

"Tell me," Damon said.

Renata didn't like talking about it. It was her pain. Her sin. Her secret. She could express herself in sculpture, but it had taken her therapist years to get her to open up. Did he really think he could handle what she had to say? "After the explosion, I was badly burned," Renata said, tentatively. "My mother tried to take me to a refugee camp for help. As we hurried down the scorched side of the road, she kept telling me to be quiet, that the enemy would hear me screaming, but I was in so much pain. I couldn't stop and so the soldier heard us. He pointed a gun at us and took her into the woods. I heard my mother cry out, over and over, but I never saw her again."

The rush of the waterfall over the rock garden filled the room as if to hush her sad tale, and Damon was silent for a long time. "It wasn't your fault."

"Yes, it was my fault. If I had been quiet, they wouldn't have taken her," Renata cried, and her eyes made clear that she would brook no argument.

The tilt of Damon's chin lost its imperious angle. He

stared down at the floor. Finally he asked, "Did you ever look for her?"

"After the war, when I was old enough, I called everyone I knew in Bosnia. My foster parents even hired an investigator. I'd hoped that with the publicity for my art that someone might come forward, but..."

He reached into the tub for her wet hand and clasped it in his own, his fingers twined with hers as if he was tugging something inside her, shaping it, the way she would shape clay. Then he was leaning closer to her. Was he looking at her with pity, or something else? Was it sympathy or desire she saw in his eyes, or both? And why, after having told this stranger her secrets, did she now want him so badly?

Maybe she just wanted to lose herself in a kiss, to forget about wars and gorgons and feel something warm and real. Or maybe it was something more base and raw—she couldn't say. But in that moment, something made her offer her lips to him and something made him take them.

It was, at first, a gentle kiss. But then she reached up and wrapped her dripping arms around his neck. He seemed to tense, then snap.

His hands went to her hair, his lips crushed down upon hers, and he started to pull her against him, heedless of the warm water they were spilling upon the floor.

His grip tightened and he kissed her hungrily, as if he were made of the same fury that was inside her. She parted her lips for him, and his tongue captured hers as if in triumph. Renata's breath quickened as the electricity of their kiss sparked through her, but then he was trying to lift her up out of the water, and she flailed, desperately gripping the edge of the tub to stop him.

His voice was throaty. "I want to see you. I want to touch you."

"I have scars," Renata replied, breaking apart from him and slipping beneath the water, denying the ache of her body for more.

"I don't care," Damon said. "You're beautiful, so beautiful."

Renata knew that the surgeons had repaired the worst of her damaged skin. That in reality, only faint traces of her injuries remained. But in her mind, she always imagined that her scars were deformities so ugly that seeing them would turn a man's desire for her to something brittle that would crumble away. Were her scars her gorgon skin? She couldn't bring herself to ask.

Perhaps sensing that she could be persuaded, Damon offered her a towel, holding it open for her so that all she had to do was step out of the tub to him and come into his arms. She wanted to. Oh, she wanted to, but she said, "I'm not ready yet."

Damon looked as if he might argue, but then slowly nodded. Whatever had been about to happen between them would wait.

He set the towel on the edge of the tub and leaned over to kiss her again. This time, a tender kiss, filled with self-control. "Renata, I know that hearing the truth about what you are has frightened you. I can take that fear away, if you want me to."

"I'm not frightened that I'm a gorgon," she said. "I'm sickened. You tell me that I can kill with my hands, just by forcing stone into the shapes I see in my mind. That I have killed...before."

"It isn't your fault," he said simply. "You can't be blamed. You didn't know what you were doing when you carved those men. Now that you know, it won't happen again."

She eyed him carefully. "How do you know it won't?"

"Because, Renata, I'll never let you sculpt again."

Chapter 7

Later that night, Deimos received the phone call he'd been dreading.

"You had no right to give the gorgon ambrosia," his twin brother snarled into the other end of the phone.

They had not seen one another in years, but Damon could still imagine the way his twin scowled when he said it, black eyes glowing like coal.

"It was only a tiny bit," Damon replied. "But I have enough to make her immortal if I choose, so don't push me."

"It's our crafty aunt who will push you, not me." Static crackled on the line. "How long do you think you can keep the gorgon away from us?"

"I'll keep her as long as I have to," Damon replied.

"We will find you." It was a threat. "You can't hide her forever. I know all your haunts."

"No, you don't. Not all of them," Damon replied much more calmly than he felt, then hung up before the call could be traced.

Just that morning, his men reported seeing an owl perched on the penthouse balcony—probably one of his aunt's many spies. Luckily, this foreign place had many old gods of its own who would not take kindly to her showing too much power here.

Still, it was time to move again.

Renata had been subdued since their kiss in the bathtub and she did not argue when he asked her to pack her things and board the plane again so soon.

This time he took her to his snow-covered chalet in a northern country.

As their entourage marched up the trail, Damon marveled at the way Renata's cheeks turned rosy in the cold, and how the falling flakes settled into her wild black curls. He first thought perhaps she was only a local beauty, that her mortal charm might fade against a different backdrop, but now he saw that she was captivating in any setting. If only he could know what went on behind those stormy gray eyes of hers.

Once they were inside, she stared out the frosted window panes over the pine-dotted hillside and asked, "Where are we?"

He no longer felt the need to keep it from her. "Finland."

Norse territory. An unfriendly place for his aunt, he hoped.

Renata let her breath fog the checkerboard window while her fingers explored the crevices between the rough-hewn logs that made up the cabin walls. It made him sad to see her sculptress fingers still grasping for every sensation, but some things could not be helped.

When he'd planned Renata's abduction, he'd been thinking only of how to keep her powers out of destructive hands. He'd thought he'd have to keep her chained and that she'd fight him every step of the way.

But Renata hadn't triumphed at the knowledge that she had the power to kill. She'd been sickened by it. She'd actually used that word. She wasn't some murderous monster who would take justice into her own hands, renewing the cycle of revenge that turned old grievances into new ones and led to war.

Why hadn't it ever occurred to him that she might not want to use her powers for revenge? Why hadn't he considered that she might simply become his ally instead of his enemy? Maybe he didn't need to keep her as his prisoner. Maybe if he needed to keep her at all, it was only to protect her.

Or to be near her.

Yes, he mustn't lie to himself about that. He remembered the way he'd kissed her in the bath and how she had responded. He remembered the taste of her, like slow-flowing honey. She'd stopped him before he went too far, but left the promise of more. "I'm not ready yet," she'd said.

He could respect that, for now.

The next morning, Damon found her in her room, curled up next to the fire, wearing a bathrobe. "I hope you enjoy crepes," he said, coming into her room bearing a tray.

"You're delivering me breakfast now?" she asked. "Don't you have people for that?"

He was glad to see her in better spirits. It was, he suspected, her fierce resilience that drew him to her, that made him want her so much. "Yes, I have people for this, but I wanted to bring it myself before I went out."

She blinked. "Out? Where are you going?"

He hadn't left her alone before. He'd been too worried that she might run. But he felt he knew her better now. She wouldn't run from him, and if someone tried to take her, they couldn't make her kill.

"I have some work to do, but I won't be long," he said.

"So I have to stay here alone with your goons?"

He arched an eyebrow. "My goons, as you call them, will stay out of your way. If you need me, for any reason, they can reach me on my cell phone."

Renata smiled and waved as he left, as if he were her lover and not her captor. But in her mind, she replayed what he'd said after they kissed.

When he'd told her he'd never let her sculpt again, her heart had hardened against him. Her art was her life. It wasn't just her job; it was her vocation, her identity. She was an artist, and she'd worked hard to become a success in a profession where so few ever made it.

She didn't know precisely how long she'd been away from her studio, but she already missed the feel of her tools in her hands almost as much as she missed her pet python. Poor Scylla. Had anyone found her? Renata had been gone so long she wondered who was feeding her snake. Who was, even now, comforting Renata's foster mom and telling her that Renata would be all right?

Renata had let herself grow complacent. She'd let herself fall under Damon's spell and forget that he was holding her against her will. She resented the security system, the monitors that tracked her every move. And in an act of rebellion, she now climbed beneath the covers and pretended to nap.

Using the coverlet as a shield from the cameras, Renata carefully extracted the paper from her pillow case, and unfolded it from around Ms. Kokkinos' business card. She spread out the sketch of the soldier who had taken her mother and stared at it. She was no longer afraid of him. Tracing the lines of his face with her fingers, she knew she held power over this villain now. She could take his life just by carving his likeness in stone. Why didn't Damon want her to use her powers to give men like this one the ending they so richly deserved?

Perhaps because Damon was some kind of demigod of war, it made sense that he'd want to protect the evil men who helped him instill terror. Perhaps this is why Damon was shielding these wicked criminals from her righteous anger. Somehow, Renata knew she had to escape him.

Just then, she realized that Damon hadn't bothered to unplug the phone by the bedside. He'd trusted his cameras to warn him if she was doing anything he didn't want her to do. But if he was gone for the day, Renata had to wonder if his goons were as diligent at spying on her as he was.

Turning in such a way that the comforter obstructed their view, Renata snaked her hand out and pulled the bedside phone beneath the covers. Then she waited, her heart pounding as she pretended to be asleep.

One. Two. Three. Renata counted the seconds, forcing herself not to move too quickly lest she alert anyone watching.

Renata's first instinct was to dial 911, but then she realized that she was in a foreign country. Did they even have 911 in Finland? Panic frayed her nerves as she realized that she'd never been able to remember country codes. Who would she dial for help?

In her hand, she held the business card. Ms. Athena Kokkinos, it said, and below was printed the number, international country code and all.

She began to dial.

She had only pressed three numbers when the door flew open and Damon burst in, warmth in his tone. "Renata I forgot to tell you—"

Startled, Renata let the comforter slip, and now the telephone was in plain sight. She and Damon stared at one another as her fingers hovered over the buttons, frozen in fear.

"Who are you calling?" Damon demanded, all the warmth gone from his voice in an instant.

When Renata didn't answer, he charged towards her and plucked the business card from her hand. When he read it, a terrible shadow passed over his eyes, and he grabbed the phone. "Did you reach her?"

Renata scrambled back on the bed to escape his wrath. "No, no, I didn't get that far," she babbled, knowing she shouldn't provoke him further, but unable to keep her own temper from rising. "But you can't hold me captive forever. Some day, some way, I'll get free of you. You can't watch me every second."

"And when you do, you'll run to her?" Damon growled. "Even knowing what she wants you to do with your powers?"

"Why shouldn't I run to her?" Renata demanded. "Why shouldn't I save the world the burden of having to hunt these men down? They killed my family. I can return the favor."

"Who killed your family, Renata? Do you even know? Was it the Serbs, the Bosniaks, the Croats, the Montenegrins? Who killed their families before?"

"There's no moral equivalency," she snapped. "Don't equate what happened to them to what happened to us."

"I'm not," he started to say, but she was already clawing at him for the phone. She was on her knees, her legs tangled in the blankets as her nails dug into his black dress shirt.

She got hold of the phone and held on to it with all her strength. "Let me call her, Damon. You can't stop me from sculpting."

The more she wrestled with him the more it seemed to enraged him. "Let go of the phone," Damon snarled.

"You'll have to break my fingers first!" Renata shouted.

His jaw clenched as he brought his face close to hers, warning, "I'll do just that, Renata. I'll break your fingers, one by one, before I let you pick up a chisel again."

The force of his threat carried on his breath as it puffed into her face. It had the scent of gunpowder and the iron tang of blood. It carried the stench of corpses and carrion. It carried the very essence of dread. It was more than just a scent. It was a power that over-whelmed her. It was terror in its most primal form, and Renata could not fight it.

A thousand snakes of terror slithered inside her, coiling and striking her conscious mind. As the memories of her childhood flowed over her, she fell back on the bed and began to scream. Her scream came from such a deep part inside that it exploded out of her and scraped her raw. Her scream was a mixture of keening and rage, of grief and frenzy.

A mirror across the room from the bed shattered, glass shards scattering across the wooden floor like shell fragments.

What had he done to her? He was killing her.

Renata screamed again and the cabin windows rattled ominously. She was hurting her own ears and her skin felt like it was on fire. She was burning, burning. She would make the whole world burn with her.

"Renata, stop!" Damon was shaking her.

She saw him shout the words, reading his lips rather than hearing the sound. All she could hear was her own scream. She felt like her fingernails were fraying, hurt slicing through her, and she couldn't stop screaming.

It was agony.

Damon pushed her down, smothering her body with his own, urgently offering his flesh as the only respite from the pain. "I'm sorry!" he was whispering. "I'm going to take it away."

Desperate, she pressed her cheek to the bare skin of his chest where she'd torn his shirt. Where his skin touched hers, she felt the familiar tingle, the tug at the fear inside her, as if he were drawing it out of her, as if he were devouring it.

His mouth was open in silent feasting, twisted in a grimace. "Give me your terror. I'll take it away."

Renata didn't fight him. She let him have it all. Every nightmare, every secret, every horrible burden she carried. And as he drew the terror from her, Renata's screams turned to whimpers as she shivered against him.

Slowly, he eased her from dread to contentment, and her breathing calmed, easy and languid. In a rush, she scented the woodsy smoke of a warm meal spent in her father's lap, then the cherry Popsicles she used to bring her littler brother, which made him smile and stick out his red-stained tongue.

Damon gave her back these happier memories, eased her down into the bed, and let them flow over her.

She didn't know how long she stayed like that, in his arms, but soon found that she was as calm and relaxed as she'd ever been. She wanted to tell him that he'd taken enough, but he kept holding her, kept pulling from her the fear, the tensions, and more. He lay gasping on top of her, as if he were now the one in terrible pain.

He had taken the poison in her and pulled it into himself. He had saved her. She knew it as sure as she knew her own name. He had saved her, and he was the only one who could.

Beneath him, she felt her body tighten again, but this time with arousal. She wasn't afraid anymore, not of anything. Not of her wants, not of her needs, not of the raw desires that ached in her belly and breasts. Like she had in the bath, Renata wrapped her arms around his neck, but this time without restraint. Writhing beneath him, she kissed his neck, his chin, his mouth.

"Renata—" he began, but she cut him off.

"I want you," she said, and started to unbutton his ruined shirt. "I want you to see me. I'm not afraid."

His expression was pained. "That's because I consumed your fears. I went too far."

Undeterred, she pulled his shirt over his shoulders, and now that she saw the carved lines of his muscled chest, she wanted nothing more than to run her fingers over them. "Even so, I want you," she said again, reaching for his belt with a wanton freedom she'd never felt before.

He growled low in his throat, as if it was taking his every effort to resist her. She felt the hardness between his legs, but still he held back. "Not tonight," he said. "I took your inhibitions from you—this isn't right."

"Inhibitions only stop me from doing what I want to do," Renata said. She was wet, she was wanting, and she could not help but grind her hips. "You gave me terror—you can give me this."

It was too much for him. Using one arm to lift her up, he used the other to untie her robe. They undressed in haste, clothes kicked off and left crumpled wherever they fell. His mouth came down on her nipples and they hardened in reply. His thighs pushed between hers, splaying her beneath him. Then he was pushing inside her, filling her, and she arched up to meet him stroke for stroke.

Her nails dug into the sculpted muscles of his arms as his hips battered her own. Renata had never made love like this before. Never let herself moan aloud, never let herself guide a man's hands to touch her in just the way she wanted to be touched—not that Damon needed guidance. His hands were everywhere, until finally she was shaking at the precipice and with an artful thrust of his pelvis, he pushed her over the edge.

This time, when Renata screamed, it was with pleasure, and the music of it was a delight to her own ears. Damon wasn't far behind her. He let out an animal sound as he flooded her. Then together, they lay tangled and entwined.

Afterwards, Renata let him roll her onto her stomach and plant rows of kisses upon her back. She wasn't afraid. He'd been right. He could make her so unafraid, she'd strip down and swim naked in the sea. He could make her fearless, and it was the greatest gift anyone had ever given her.

As he kissed each tiny scar on her back with reverence, she sighed with contentment. At long last, she turned and rolled into his arms, caressing his face, his chest, and memorizing each line.

Perhaps it was her sculptress's touch that brought regret to his handsome face. "We shouldn't have done that."

"Why not?" Renata asked, quite certain that this was one of the best things she'd ever done.

"I frightened you," he said. "I went too far, always too far."

He looked tortured, so Renata tried to comfort him with a kiss at the corners of his clean-shaven upper lip, and inhaled the soapy scent of his skin. "Those screams had been inside me for a long time. Perhaps they needed to come out."

"Even so, I threatened to break your fingers." He took her hand from where it cupped the curve of his cheek and kissed each fingertip in turn. "It was unforgivable."

"I know you wouldn't really hurt me," she said.

"You don't know that," he said. "You don't know me."

She knew him. She might even be in love with him. He knew what she'd done. He knew what she was—a gorgon. He'd even seen her shatter mirrors, yet his attraction to her had not crumbled away. He knew her secrets, yet still thought she was beautiful. "I feel like I've always known you, Damon. The first time I saw you, your face was familiar, and I don't think it was only because you look like your brother."

It was the wrong thing to say. His eyes clouded over like a storm and he sat up in the bed, pulling the coverlet to his waist. "You don't even know my true name."

Renata was still too free from fear not to ask. "Then what is your true name?"

"Deimos, Son of Ares, and I feed upon fear. Terror sustains me. And I have hurt you, Renata. More than just tonight, more than you know. When I told you that you were a gorgon, you thought I was calling you a monster. But I'm the monster."

"Deimos," Renata repeated with wonder, trying the new name on her tongue and finding it pleasurable to say. She reached for his hand, but he was already up and out of the bed, finding his clothes and dressing.

"Do you know why my brother, Phobos, and I both look familiar to you? Because we were there the day of the explosion. We were both there the day soldiers ripped your life apart."

Renata tilted her head, searching her memories.

"The warriors in Bosnia called on the old immortals and we answered," he said. "My brother and I drove our father's chariot, spreading fear and dread. I saw you burning. I heard you scream that gorgon's scream that shattered windows and stopped soldiers in their tracks."

Renata remembered that now, how the fighting had stopped, how the soldiers had retreated long enough for her mother to scoop up her wounded body and try to get her to safety.

"And when you screamed," he continued, "It froze my blood inside me. I've carried this stone inside my

heart ever since. I swore that I'd never drive my father's war chariot again."

Renata whispered now, "Did you ever drive it
again?"

"No," he spat. "Mortal men create enough fear to
feed me—never again will I help them make more."

Renata wanted to reach out for him, but as he
pushed his dark hair back from his face he warned
her away. "Every bad thing that has ever happened
to you in your life is my fault. So you see, Renata, I
have no right to touch you, no right to love you. And
it won't happen again."

Chapter 8

Since they'd made love, Renata's sense of fearlessness had faded, but she was still left with longing. She needed to talk to him, but he'd stayed away.

Everything had changed.

This time, when the goons came to fetch Renata and whisk her to the airport, Deimos wasn't with them. She was comforted to be back on his private jet, but it alarmed her that he wasn't on board.

When the plane was in the air and the pilot had taken off the seatbelt sign, one of Deimos's men delivered the crystal decanter to Renata. It was accompanied by an envelope with her name written in florid script.

Renata wondered if drinking more of the ambrosia-laced spirits would lift her mood, for she feared what lay coiled and lurking within the envelope. Mustering her courage, Renata tore the envelope open and found that it contained the sketch, the business card and a short, handwritten note.

Renata,
I'm sending you home because I was wrong to have taken you in the first place. You have to make your own choices about how to use your powers, just as I've made my own. If you want to sculpt, then sculpt. I have no right to control, imprison, or decide for you. I can't protect you, but the ambrosia can. The more you drink, the less mortal you'll be. Don't share Medusa's fate.

Renata's studio looked smaller and shabbier than she remembered it, but she was grateful to see that Marta, the gallery owner, had found her python while she was away. Renata pressed her hand against the glass cage and watched Scylla's forked tongue taste the air. Renata lifted her nose to do the same, but didn't smell anything, comforting or otherwise.

She missed Deimos. If she closed her eyes, she could trace the contours of his face with her artist's fingers. She had memorized the smooth planes and the hard edges. But memories were no substitute for the warmth of his skin against hers. She had no way of contacting him, no way of telling him how much she ached for him. He was just gone. Gone from her life as if he'd never been there at all, and she wasn't certain she would ever see him again.

Meanwhile, she wandered around her apartment, aimlessly. Yellow police tape littered her studio like drooping party streamers, and Renata realized that they must have searched the whole place for clues to her whereabouts.

The first call she made was to her foster parents, who were so relieved to hear from her that they insisted on hopping on a plane to come see her. But Renata knew they'd ask questions she didn't want to answer—not yet, anyway—so she told them to give her some time to collect herself.

There were about a hundred calls from her therapist, and Renata deleted them all. It was near midnight. The skyline was as black as her mood, so she tied up her hair, picked up her chisel and began to sculpt.

Renata had been expecting a visit from Ms. Athena Kokkinos and her nephew the police detective a few days after her return, so she didn't startle at the knock. "Good to see you again," the detective said when Renata opened the door.

"I'm glad you think so, Phobos," she said, her heart aching at the familiarity of his face and the sadness of knowing that he only looked like the man she loved.

The detective seemed taken aback by the use of his

true name, but his aunt pushed into the studio and marched over to Renata's workspace. With one good yank, she pulled the canvas off the stone then turned her angry eyes on Renata. "What's this?"

"It's a statue of my father and my brother," Renata said, squaring her shoulders. "I took all the details I remembered, all the sweet little lines of my baby brother's smile, all the rough calluses of my father's hands, and I brought them to life. At least, as much life as a gorgon can give to stone statues."

"I gave you a sketch to carve," the woman barked. "A sketch of a man you should hate. Make an end to him. Avenge your family."

"I should," Renata said. "But not the way you want me to. I won't kill for you."

"It isn't as if he doesn't deserve to die," she said.

"But that isn't why you want me to kill him," Renata said. "He's in jail and you can't reach him, but I can. He's on trial, and for some reason, you don't want him convicted. I only asked you to come here today so I could return your sketch to you. I can't accept your patronage."

The older woman glared at Renata and drew herself up to a towering height. "Do you know who I am?"

"Oh, I know," Renata said to the gray-eyed daughter of Zeus. "And I mean you no disrespect, but you'll have to find yourself another sculptress."

"Do I need to bend you to my will?" Athena asked.

"Only if you want to risk the lives of your other pets," Renata said. "Give me a chisel, and you never know what I might carve. Take my chisel away and I can always make a sculpture with a butter knife and a bar of soap."

Renata had no idea if this was a legitimate threat, but she felt that it was one that she needed to make.

"I'll make you too scared to refuse," Phobos said.

"If you do, I'll scream," Renata warned. "If you come near me, I'll scream my gorgon scream, so terrible that you'll choke on it."

Phobos looked as if he might test Renata's resolve, but his aunt stopped him. "Leave it be, Phobos. She'll change her mind in time, and when she does, she has my card. Let's go."

But Renata didn't think she would change her mind.

Besides, she had a different, more important call to make. This time, she dialed a lawyer in the Netherlands.

Renata stepped out of the International Court of Justice into the afternoon sun. It had been painful to relive those memories, to tell her story to the court, but now she felt as if she were taller, lighter and freer than she had ever been. Underneath the Peace Palace's cathedral-like spires, she felt reverent, and somehow it didn't surprise her to see Deimos waiting for her on the verdant lawn.

It had been more than a year since she'd seen him last, but his face was exactly the same. For he was ageless. As was her love for him. She knew in the moment he folded a newspaper under his arm and smiled at her. Renata wondered if it was the first time she had ever seen him smile.

"How did you find me?" Renata asked.

"Sometimes people call upon the oldest immortals and we answer," Deimos said, and then showed her the newspaper. "The headlines also helped."

"I was afraid to testify," Renata said.

"But you did it anyway," he said, taking her hands. "You helped to convict him, and all his crimes are exposed in the light of day. No one is going to take up his cause as an excuse to make war. I'm so proud of you."

Maybe it was that she was so happy to see Deimos again, or maybe it was that he was proud of her, or maybe it was the worshipful way he held her sculptress's fingers, but somehow she found herself blinking back tears. "I found a way to sculpt without hurting anyone," she said.

He reached up and brushed away her tears. "I'm not accustomed to dealing with people's better instincts, young lady, but I should have realized you'd find a better way. Anyway, I won't keep you. I just wanted to see you one last time."

"Take me with you," Renata said, the words bursting out of her. "Wherever you're going, I want to go with you."

"Renata, I've already told you. Everything bad that ever happened to you is my fault."

"You're wrong," she insisted. "It was mortal men who made war, not you. They called you and if you hadn't come, others would have. What happened to me would have happened with or without you."

"I wouldn't be so sure," Deimos told her.

"Even if I weren't sure, it doesn't matter," she said. "Because I love you and I forgive you."

"No," he said stubbornly. "You can't."

"I can," Renata said, feeling her gorgon's power strongly now. "You changed and that's what matters. You shaped yourself into something else. And that's what we all have to do. We all have to change before things will ever get better in the world."

"I don't know that things will ever get better," he told her sadly. "There will always be other wars—and other gorgons."

"And we'll stop them," she said. "Together."

"Together for how long?" he asked, his eyes off somewhere in the distance. "I left the decanter of ambrosia on the plane for you, but you didn't drink it. I think you mean to leave your options open, to escape my love with old age. You're always trying to run away from me."

"What if I'm done trying to escape you?" Renata wanted to know. "What if I drank the ambrosia now?"

His expression became fiercely possessive. "I'd keep you with me, forever."

"Then take me with you," she said. "We'll toast with ambrosia."

Deimos pulled Renata into his arms and devoured her in a kiss, the lushness of his lips eliciting a whimper from her. He kissed her, right there on the street, where anyone could see them, and Renata wasn't the least bit afraid.

"Let's go then," he said. "The plane is fueled up and ready."

"Where are we going?" Renata asked.

He arched a dark brow. "First? On our honeymoon."

"Then?" she asked, smiling.

He held her close, as if ready to take her fears from her should they ever come again. "Then, we should go back to Bosnia and look for your mother—if you're ready."

To her astonishment, Renata realized that she was.

* * * * *